'A lovely book – sensuous, sad and often extremely
intense, richly-textured narrative. Koning deftly weaves multip
viewpoints … a wonderful portrayal of a girl evolving from hero-
worshipping tomboy to studiedly laconic adolescent' Patrick Gale,
Daily Telegraph

'Koning's narrative captures smartly the brittleness and boredom of
the expat social scene … it is a considerable achievement' Alex Clark,
Guardian

'It is, like L. P. Hartley's *The Go-Between*, an account of an adult love
affair, given added poignancy because viewed with the same
disconcerting clarity of an almost-adult child, who … levels the same
curious, dispassionate, cruelly truthful gaze' Jane Shilling,
The Times

'It whips along … with tremendous gusto … putting the reader under
its elegant spell' Philip Hensher, *Mail on Sunday*

'Koning shows herself to be an expert observer … full of exquisite
writing and considerable charm' Michael Arditti, *Independent*

ABOUT THE AUTHOR

Christina Koning was born in Kuala Belait, British Borneo, and spent her early childhood in Venezuela and Jamaica. She now reviews fiction for *The Times*, for which she also writes on travel. Her first novel, *A Mild Suicide*, was published in 1992.

CHRISTINA KONING

UNDISCOVERED COUNTRY

PENGUIN BOOKS

PENGUIN BOOKS

Published by the Penguin Group
Penguin Books Ltd, 27 Wrights Lane, London W8 5TZ, England
Penguin Putnam Inc., 375 Hudson Street, New York, New York 10014, USA
Penguin Books Australia Ltd, Ringwood, Victoria, Australia
Penguin Books Canada Ltd, 10 Alcorn Avenue, Toronto, Ontario, Canada M4V 3B2
Penguin Books (NZ) Ltd, Private Bag 102902, NSMC, Auckland, New Zealand

Penguin Books Ltd, Registered Offices: Harmondsworth, Middlesex, England

First published by Viking 1997
Published in Penguin Books 1999
1 3 5 7 9 10 8 6 4 2

Set in Monotype Sabon
Printed in England by Clays Ltd, St Ives plc

Grateful acknowledgement is made for permission to quote from the following :
'The Night We Called It A Day', words by Tom Adair, copyright © 1941
renewed by Embassy Music Corp., USA; Dorsey Brothers Music Ltd, 7/8 Frith Street,
London W1V 5TZ; used by permission; all rights reserved;
'Blue Moon' © 1934; EMI Catalogue Partnership; EMI Robbins Catalog Inc. USA;
worldwide print rights controlled by Warner Bros. Publications Inc./IMP Ltd

For Steph and Chas

Acknowledgements

I should like to thank Mariela Briceño of the Venezuelan Embassy in London, Lee George of Thomas Cook Ltd and Brian MacArthur of *The Times* for making it possible for me to revisit Venezuela. I should also like to thank Ana María Rajkay at Universidad Simón Bolívar and María Fernanda Mujica Ricardo at Universidad Católica Andrés Bello, Caracas, for their kind hospitality and Laura Sole at the Shell Centre in London for allowing me to use the company's archives.

I believe this is a very large continent which until now has remained unknown.

Christopher Columbus, Journals, *13 August 1498*

Let's go. Let's go. These people don't want us in this country. Let's go, boys. Take my luggage aboard the ship.

Simón Bolívar, last words, 17 December 1830

The black shadow of the plane moves over the scorched grass of the airfield keeping pace, unwaveringly, with its more solid twin with which it seems to have exchanged elements: air for earth; weightlessness for gravity. From this altitude everything is sharply defined: the sandy outcrops of bare earth, so red it looks as if blood has been spilt there; the bright green trees, distorted into fantastic spreading forms by the wind sweeping off the lake; the runway itself, silver in this light, with its parallel lines of flares, its attendant vultures, which rise as one creature, assuming avian shape as the plane touches down.

As the machine, still juddering with the impact, gradually decelerates, wheeling towards the control tower and its cluster of flat-roofed buildings, it becomes possible to see things in greater detail: the gaping fissures in the asphalt at the runway's edge; tufts of razor-edged grass barely clinging to the eroded soil; blossoms on a thorn bush, red as open wounds. The plan taxis to a halt and a man in the light blue uniform of the airport ground crew walks slowly backwards, waving what look like oversized table-tennis bats above his head.

From here, it's impossible to see whether or not there is anyone waiting in the crowd of onlookers behind the plate-glass windows of the airport building. Only *silhouettes – a woman, a child excitedly waving – can be discerned at this distance. And of course she knows there can be no one waiting. Whatever connections she had with this place have been long since lost. As she waits with her fellow passengers for the steps to be wheeled into place and the doors to open on the white heat of a Maracaibo noon, she can only reflect on what might have been, and remember everything which has led up to this moment.*

1

She's dreaming then she's awake her heart still beating with the aftershock of the vision. Flight. A sensation of falling. Fetching up in a place she has never been yet which she unaccountably recognizes. *Déjà vu.* She knows that's what the feeling is called. You didn't have to be asleep to have it either.

She opens her eyes. Sunlight falls in long stripes across the floor and over the bed. It's quiet: still early she guesses. She lies for a minute or so thinking about the dream her gaze moving around the room noting its familiar objects – the mirror the door the clothes flung across the chair the book open at the page she fell asleep reading. It strikes her that something about the room has changed – although it all looks the same as it did the night before. It is as if while she was asleep everything had been removed and replaced with its exact replica. To the naked eye the difference is imperceptible and yet. You can't prove it isn't so.

She gets out of bed and pads across the room to open the shutters. At once the room is filled with dazzling light. From outside comes the smell of damp earth and flowers. The sound of a sprinkler. For an instant she feels perfectly happy: *to be here and nowhere else.* Then she turns from the window and catches sight of herself.

3

The face in the mirror wears a hangdog look as if it knows it is not the one she would have chosen if she had had a say in it. A long oval with eyes set too high and a long thin nose: the face of a knight in a medieval painting. St Joan her mother said when she'd cut her hair. But her eyes are the wrong colour. Joan's eyes she knows would have been brown not blue. Her eyebrows are too pale – bleached by the sun. In certain lights they look invisible. And her teeth are crooked – she'll probably need a brace. She heard Vivienne talking about it the other day.

The water in the shower is cold its icy droplets sting her into wakefulness. She turns the jet on full and the water batters her face momentarily blinding her filling her open mouth with its rusty taste. Her wet hair lies flat against her scalp – a swimming dog she thinks. She scrubs her teeth so hard flecks of blood appear in the foam. She will not wear a brace. They will have to kill her first.

Getting dressed is a process of compromise as always. Left to her own devices she would wear what she likes – shorts and an Aertex shirt. Her snake belt. Sandals. No socks. But because it is school she has to wear a stupid dress and slides to stop her hair getting in her eyes. It would be simpler just to cut her hair shorter but Vivienne says no. If she'd wanted a boy she would have ordered one she says.

When she has wrestled herself into her dress tied the sash any-old-how and pulled up her socks she goes outside to where her mother is waiting.

Vivienne sits on the veranda holding the letter she has just opened like a picture of a woman reading. The sun falling through the wire-gauze screens which cover the windows at the front of the house throws criss-cross patterns on her face and hair. A faint smile touches her lips as she turns the page.

Vivienne is beautiful Tony knows – she has heard Jack say so. Jack is Tony's stepfather. When he and Vivienne first went to Acapulco he'd be sitting in the hotel bar waiting for Vivienne to join him and he'd know from the way everyone went quiet that she'd walked in.

Tony remembers that time – although she wasn't allowed to go to Acapulco. Instead she stayed with the Rileys. They had barbecues almost every night. Peter Riley taught her how to play mah-jong. It was fun for a while but it got a bit boring after the first week. She missed Vivienne coming in to kiss her goodnight.

Her mother glances up.

'Morning, Antonia. Sleep well?'

'I had a funny dream.'

'Poor darling. You should have called me.'

'It wasn't a bad dream. Just strange. As if . . .' Tony thinks a moment. 'Can you have other people's dreams?'

But Vivienne is no longer listening. 'Mm-hmm,' she murmurs returning to her letter.

'Is that from Granny?' Tony shakes cornflakes into her bowl and pours on milk already souring in the heat.

'Yes. She sends her love.' Vivienne frowns suddenly. 'Have you brushed your hair this morning?'

'Sort of . . .'

'Well, sort of do it again. Guess what?' Vivienne says. 'Your uncle Julian's getting married.'

'Who to?'

'Her name's Phyllis Skeffington. Her people are in Kenya. Granny says she seems very suitable . . .'

'What does that mean?'

Vivienne laughs and shakes her head. 'Ask Granny' is all she will say.

Tony tries without success to summon up an image of her mother's younger brother. She knows what he looks like from photographs of course; but the memories she has of the time before they left England are becoming increasingly vague. Julian exists only as a single memory: a face smiling down at her; a voice saying somewhere above her head, 'What a funny little thing. She doesn't say much, does she?'

'You remember him, don't you?' Vivienne asks. 'He was always so fond of you . . .'

'Was he the one who used to do card tricks?'

She shakes her head. 'You're thinking of Grandpa . . .'

She sounds so disappointed that Tony makes another attempt to salvage the situation. 'Of course. Uncle Julian. He took me to the zoo once, didn't he?'

And Vivienne smiles. 'Fancy your remembering that. You must have been no more than four or five . . .'

In fact she has no memory of the occasion. It's something she's been told about that's all. Now she comes to think of it there's even a photograph somewhere of her and her tall skinny uncle standing in front of the lion's cage. An out-of-focus image – as if the person who took it were standing slightly too close or had moved at the wrong moment. Through the criss-crossed wire of the cage you can just make out the shaggy massive shape of the crouching beast.

Thinking about the lion makes her think about the last time she went to the zoo in Caracas. She'd been looking forward to going but when they got there all the animals were asleep. It was the heat Jack said. She

6

felt sorry for the lions in their tiny cages. Their tails twitched as they slept flicking away flies. There was a bear which walked up and down swinging its head from side to side. The poor thing was crazy from being locked up so long Jack said.

She eats her cornflakes trying not to scrape the bowl too much because it gets on Vivienne's nerves. Vivienne sits silently beside her. Together they gaze out over the garden with its orange trees mangoes and acacias. Things grow like wildfire here. Fan-shaped palms and purple hibiscus; scarlet poinsettias orchids and red-hot pokers. Everything steams with moisture and the smell of decaying vegetation mingles with the sweeter scent of flowers. The January sky is a clear intense blue.

The veranda where they're sitting is the coolest place to be at this time of day: the sun hasn't yet moved round to this side of the house and the wire screens which keep out the mosquitoes make it pleasantly dark. If there's time before school in the morning Tony likes to curl up with a book in one of the bamboo chairs with the rose-patterned chintz covers Vivienne got from Heal's while Consuelo clears the breakfast things and Vivienne does her face.

It's the time of day Tony loves most – with everything cool and peaceful and just the two of them together. Vivienne making that intent slightly frowning face she always makes as she peers in the little round mirror of her compact. Arching her eyebrows as she pats the loose powder over her nose and forehead – 'taking the shine away' is what she calls it. Making a smooth round 'O' of her lips as she puts on her lipstick. Red Velvet by Max Factor.

But today there's no time. As Tony swallows the last

mouthful of cereal the honk of a car horn signals the arrival of Mrs Porter's big green Packard.

'Here's Joan,' says Vivienne starting out of the daydream she's fallen into. 'Better get your skates on . . .'

Tony's satchel is in her room; she runs to fetch it. As she passes the mirror she sees that her hair – now dry – is sticking up on end. She seizes the brush to flatten it down but to little effect. Her face stares mournfully back at her. *I told you so.* She doesn't know what she's done to deserve a face like this. When they're trying to be kind people tell her she's like her mother. She can't see it herself. She supposes she must resemble Ralph – her father. It's hard to tell from the one photograph she's seen: a snapshot of him in uniform taken just before his plane went missing over Germany.

She rushes back through the house towards the veranda. In her haste she's left the buckle on one of her sandals undone. The shoe flies off nearly tripping her up. Muttering under her breath she stoops to fasten it.

In this position half-hidden by the screen door she overhears Mrs Porter talking to Vivienne.

'Ronnie says Jack really tied one on last night . . .'

'It's the same every night,' Vivienne says.

'Of course it's none of my business,' says Mrs Porter, 'but – aren't you just a teensy bit worried about what might happen?'

Vivienne shrugs. 'Oh, Jack's a very good driver. Even when he's half-cut . . .'

'I didn't mean that. I meant, well, *vis-à-vis* the company. These things get about, you know.' Mrs Porter lowers her voice conspiratorially. 'It might affect his chances of promotion. I mean, when Jim Lang retires . . .'

'That's Jack's affair,' Vivienne says sharply. She gives

a little toss of her head. 'Besides, you don't imagine anything I say would have any effect . . .'

'But surely . . .' Mrs Porter starts to reply but then Vivienne catches sight of Tony and makes a warning sign to the other woman.

'*Pas devant l'enfant*,' she murmurs. 'Come on, Antonia, what are you waiting for?' she says.

'Hello, Tony dear,' says Mrs Porter heartily.

'Hello, Mrs Porter.'

As Mrs Porter starts down the steps towards the car, Tony glares at her fat back. Only her friends are allowed to call her Tony. She decides after what she's heard that she doesn't like Mrs Porter any more. She has no right to tell tales about Jack. Mrs Porter is fat and has B O. When she smiles there are flecks of lipstick on her teeth. And she dyes her hair. Vivienne says ladies don't dye their hair. Vivienne wears her hair in smooth blonde waves like Grace Kelly. She wears skirts that almost reach the ground and smells very faintly of eau-de-Cologne.

Tony sits in the back seat of the car which smells of leather and Ronnie's pipe and Mrs Porter's sweat as they bounce over the uneven jungle roads through plantations of banana trees with enormous ragged leaves; beneath tangled creepers which turn the road into a green tunnel.

'How's Ronnie?' Vivienne always asks about Ronnie. Which is strange because Tony doesn't think she likes him very much. 'An awful little man,' she called him once talking to Jack.

'Oh, he's tickety-boo,' says Mrs Porter helping herself to a Player's from the packet on the dashboard. She offers one to Vivienne who shakes her head. 'Looking forward to lovely leave, of course. Just think. Two whole months in GB, away from this hell-hole. Cream teas. The Light Programme. *Hell's teeth!*' The car swerves suddenly to avoid a small black pig which has wandered into the middle of the road. 'Pardon my French,' Mrs Porter says.

Next year there's going to be a new road to join up with the brand-new four-lane highway that goes to Maracaibo; but until then there's no alternative to this winding unreliable track which is bordered on one side by a precipitous drop into a ravine filled with trees; on the other by a wall of soft red rock which turns to mud in the rainy season blocking the road with landslides.

'I had a letter from home today,' Vivienne says. 'My brother's getting married . . .'

'How lovely,' croons Mrs Porter. 'When's the wedding going to be?'

'Oh, not for a while. They'll wait until after the celebrations, I should think . . .'

'Yes, I imagine June will be rather a quiet month for weddings *this* year,' Mrs Porter chuckles. 'Such a pity we couldn't get our leave extended by a couple of weeks, but there you are. Of course,' she sniffs, 'it helps if you've got people in high places to pull strings. Naming no names, but still . . .'

'If you mean the Lumsdens, I gather their leave was booked months ago. It's pure coincidence that they'll be at home in June.'

'It can't hurt that *she's* so thick with the consul,' Mrs Porter retorts. 'Her brother was at school with him, apparently. A word in the right place, don't you know . . .'

Vivienne does not reply. She examines her fingernails as if she has suddenly noticed a chip in the smooth polish. 'Have you got your French grammar with you, Antonia?' she asks without turning round. 'Because I think I've left mine at home.'

'French verbs,' says Mrs Porter cheerily – apparently not at all put out by Vivienne's silence. '*Ooh là là . . .*'

They reach the outskirts of the town passing the wooden shacks where the native workers live and then a row of newly built bungalows for the company employees. All these houses look the same with a sloping roof and a window on either side of the door like a house Tony might have drawn when she was little. They are arranged in neat lines exactly the same distance apart – like Toytown Jack says – but Tony thinks it must be fun to live in a house exactly the same as all her friends' houses. They pass the company store with its Calor Gas canisters and five-gallon containers of water lined up on the porch outside then the still-unfinished hospital and arrive at last in front of the school. This is a white one-storey building with windows on one side. A few trees cast their inky shade over the yard which surrounds it.

Mrs Porter stops the car. 'Well, cheerie-bye,' she says. 'Jack picking you up this afternoon?'

'That's right.' Vivienne lifts the bag containing her schoolwork from the back seat. 'Thanks, Joan.'

Mrs Porter toots the horn cheerfully and the car disappears down the road in a cloud of white dust. Mrs Porter works too – one of the few company wives who does apart from Vivienne. She does the company accounts. 'So she can keep an eye on what everyone else is being paid,' Vivienne says to Jack and then reproaches herself for her unkindness. Joan has a heart of gold she says.

No one else has arrived yet of course. It's one of the

11

disadvantages of being a teacher's child Tony thinks: you're always the first to arrive and the last to leave. Vivienne busies herself setting out the books for the first lesson and then goes to check that the generator for the air-conditioning is working. It's always breaking down. Last month they had a day off school while it was being fixed. No such luck today though. As Vivienne returns a car pulls up outside and the Wilson girls – Jane and Valerie – get out. From where Tony's sitting by the open window she can hear them bickering.

'I didn't,' says Valerie.

'You did,' says Jane.

And then there's a thin scream as one of them – Jane probably – pinches the other. Jane is the elder. She's eleven – the same age as Tony. Tony quite likes Jane but she can be spiteful. Last week she put a stick insect down Mary McBride's back.

'Good morning, girls,' says Vivienne as they come in.

'Good morning, Mrs Lindberg,' they chant in unison.

They sit in their usual place at the back of the class. The desks are arranged in two rows with their seats fixed on metal runners which can be moved forward and back. Museum pieces Vivienne calls them. They came from a prep school in England. Their wooden tops are scarred with the names of boys who have sat there over the years and the holes where their china inkwells sit are black with use.

As Valerie goes to sit down she gives a little gasp. Jane has put something on her seat.

Vivienne glances up. 'What's the matter, Valerie?'

Valerie's cheeks go red. She looks at the floor. Jane is gazing innocently out of the window.

'I . . . I . . . Nothing,' says Valerie.

'Well, just sit quietly until the others get here,' says Vivienne in a tone of mild reproof.

At half-past eight she calls the register. Geoffrey Brown and Michael Brown – present. Belinda Johnson – absent (her parents are only just back from leave). Antonia Lindberg Mary McBride and Jennifer Riley – present. Annetje van Wel – absent. Karel van Wel Jane Wilson and Valerie Wilson – present.

'What's the matter with your sister?' Vivienne asks Karel. 'Not her eyes again, I hope . . .'

He looks uncomfortable. 'Her eyes – bad,' he says painfully. 'Her head too. Very bad . . .'

'Poor child,' Vivienne murmurs. 'Let's hope she feels better soon . . .'

Something about the way she says this makes Tony think that maybe Annetje isn't really ill at all. Last time Annetje was away from school she overheard Vivienne telling Jack about Annetje's mother. 'She keeps that child at home on purpose,' Vivienne said. 'She gets lonely in the house by herself all day. She almost admitted as much, when I spoke to her about it . . .'

'I don't see what's so bad about staying at home,' Jack said.

This is the starting point for another argument about work. Jack wants Vivienne to give up her job. He can't understand why she should want to go on working now she's married to him. She should stay home and take it easy he says. The doctor says so too. Last year Vivienne nearly died. She was going to have a baby but then she lost it. It was working too much in the heat the doctor said.

Vivienne says it's the first time she's had a school of her own. Something she's built up from scratch. If she goes the school goes too. It means too much to her to let that happen she says.

Jack says the company can always get another teacher. It won't be so easy for him to get another wife.

You never had any trouble before Vivienne says.

Jack's been married three times counting Vivienne. Once was to a girl in Texas called Mary-Jean; the second time was to a Venezuelan. Her name was Dolores and she ran away with one of Jack's friends. This is one of the things Tony isn't supposed to know about.

'Antonia –' Her mother's voice breaks into her thoughts. 'Are you paying attention? We're on page fifty-three. Start reading, please.'

Sometimes Tony thinks she's stricter with her than with the others.

She opens her book. 'I wandered lonely as a cloud . . .'

'A little louder, please,' says Vivienne. 'I don't think Michael can hear you . . .'

Michael Brown freezes in the act of flicking an ink pellet at Karel van Wel. The class settles down. Soon the only sounds which can be heard are Tony's voice and the dry whirring of cicadas in the long grass at the edge of the playground.

> 'I wandered lonely as a cloud
> That floats on high o'er vales and hills,
> When all at once I saw a crowd,
> A host, of golden daffodils;
> Beside the lake, beneath the trees,
> Fluttering and dancing in the breeze . . .'

'Go on please, Jennifer,' says Vivienne. She gets up from her chair at the front of the class and begins to

14

pace slowly up and down the room between the desks. As she passes her chair she rests her hand briefly on Tony's shoulder.

'Continuous as the stars that shine
And twinkle on the Milky Way . . .'

Jennifer is stumbling to the end of her stanza when there's a knock on the glass panel of the classroom door. It's Mr van Wel: Karel and Annetje's father. Vivienne goes to speak to him. Tony can't hear what they're saying but through the glass she can see his face as he explains something to Vivienne and the expression on Vivienne's face as she listens to what he's saying. She looks serious – even worried – so Tony guesses the news isn't good.

Karel must be thinking the same thing because when the door opens he gets to his feet almost knocking over his chair in his anxiety.

'It's all right, Karel,' says Vivienne. 'No need to be alarmed. Your sister's got scarlet fever. I've told your father you can stay with us for a bit, to make things easier for your mother.'

Karel's father appears for a moment in the doorway behind Vivienne. He's tall and thin with a bony face and a big nose like a beak. The strangest thing about him is his hair. It's completely grey – although he can't be that old Tony thinks. It's hard to tell with grown-ups. Jack's over forty and his hair's still dark except for a bit at the edges.

Karel's father says something to him in Dutch and after a moment's hesitation Karel goes back to his seat and sits down. Mr van Wel looks at Vivienne.

'Thank you,' he says. It sounds more like *Sank you*. Vivienne smiles slightly – the way she does when she's embarrassed.

'It's no trouble,' she says. 'Really.'

When the door has closed behind Mr van Wel Vivienne picks up *Palgrave's Golden Treasury* from the desk. After looking around to see that everyone is paying attention she begins to read aloud. Her voice is beautiful: low and melodious with the slight huskiness she always gets when she's sad or pleased. It's the way her voice sounds when she talks of home Tony thinks – or about the way things were before the war.

> 'For oft, when on my couch I lie
> In vacant or in pensive mood,
> They flash upon that inward eye
> Which is the bliss of solitude;
> And then my heart with pleasure fills,
> And dances with the daffodils.'

When she stops reading she stands for a minute with the book held open in front of her looking out over their mute upturned faces at the view from the window behind: the cracked earth yard blazing white in the heat; the dead black shadows of the dusty trees.

At midday when school finishes Karel stays behind sitting silently at his desk while Vivienne collects up the books and cleans the blackboard and Tony sharpens pencils. Usually it's a task she enjoys. There's something satisfying about the exactness of the movements necessary to achieve the perfect point: neither too blunt nor too sharp. The clean sharp scent of wood shavings is nice too; and the way they fall in fragile spirals from the revolving tip.

But today her mind's not on it: several times she even ends up breaking the newly sharpened point right off. She's distracted by the presence of a third person – what a nuisance it is having him around. It's not even as if he were one of her friends.

'Would you like a drink, Karel?' Vivienne asks starting to unscrew the top of the Thermos flask of Rose's Lime Juice Cordial she packs every morning for the midday break. Despite the air-conditioning which hums all the time in the background it's already stifling in the class-room and it'll be even hotter outside.

To Tony's surprise Karel shakes his head. No. As if he were angry with her mother for asking such a stupid question.

Holding her breath the curl of shavings trembling on the end of the pencil she's sharpening she watches them both.

'I expect you're worried about your sister, aren't you?' Vivienne goes on calmly as if she hadn't noticed Karel's rudeness. 'But you mustn't worry. Everything will be all right, you'll see . . .'

She pours lime juice into three paper cups and gives one to Tony. Another she sets in front of Karel. 'Drink it,' she tells him. 'It'll make you feel better.'

Then she sits down at her desk and begins to go through a pile of exercise books making small neat marks with a red pencil. After a while Tony sees Karel's hand snake out towards the cup. He picks it up and with another furtive half-angry look at Vivienne he starts to drink.

At quarter-past there's the scrunch of tyres on the dirt

road outside and the honk of a car horn as Jack arrives. Tony waves to him from the window and he raises his hand in mock salute from behind the wheel of the bright red Chevy. It's the latest model. Whitewall tyres and a fold-down top. Vivienne says he cares more for that car than he does for her.

'Jack's here,' Tony tells her – thinking perhaps she hasn't heard the car.

'I know.' She carries on with what she's doing frowning a little as she spots another mistake in Jennifer Riley's French composition. 'Tell him I'll be right out.' As Tony reaches the door of the classroom Vivienne remembers Karel. 'You can go too, dear,' she says to him.

When they step outside it's like opening an oven door. So hot it burns your lungs to take a breath. Midday's the hottest time. It's when everything stops. The company offices close and the factory shuts down. There's a song Vivienne likes to sing when she's in the mood. *Mad dogs and Englishmen go out in the midday sun . . .* It's meant to be funny of course – but Tony knows it's not true. No one goes out in the midday sun. Even the Guajiro Indians stay at home.

They cross the yard where the sun beats down their shoes scuffing up white dust. On the backs of Karel's thin legs are marks like bruises: red fading to purple fading to brownish-yellow. Karel's nine – a lot younger than Tony. His father works for Jack. It's his first contract and Karel and his mother and sister only came out to join him a few months ago. Before they were living somewhere in Holland. Tony can't remember where. Things were very bad for them there Vivienne says.

'Hiya, Sport,' Jack says to Karel as they reach the car.

He leans across to open the rear door. 'Hop in. Where's your mother?' he asks Tony.

'Just coming.'

She climbs in beside Karel who's huddling timidly in the far corner as if he's trying to make himself invisible. The ridged leather seat feels hot against the backs of her legs and a trickle of sweat runs down her back between her shoulder blades as she wriggles around trying to find a cool spot. By the time they reach La Soledad her dress will be sticking to her – even though it's only a short ride.

Jack turns to smile at her. His teeth are very white in his brown face and his hair is combed straight back in crisp waves. A long time ago when he was still a kid in Texas someone broke Jack's nose in a bar-room fight. Over a woman he says when he tells this story. When he was a kid Jack used to box. He was featherweight champion of El Paso when he was sixteen years old. You can still see the scar where he split his upper lip defending the title.

'Hey, Princess,' he says. 'Guess what? The spare parts for your mother's sewing machine arrived today. Wanna come along with me and pick them up from the factory?'

'You bet.'

'That's settled. First thing after lunch.' He winks at Karel. 'Maybe Sport here wants to come along too.'

Karel returns Jack's gaze without smiling. He doesn't say he will come but he doesn't say he won't either. Tony hopes he doesn't. She likes going to the factory with Jack. Having somebody else along would spoil it.

At that moment Vivienne comes out of the building carrying an armful of books. She stands for a minute on the porch shading her eyes with her free hand as she looks around for the car. In her pale blue gingham dress with its wide skirts and narrow waist she looks very cool and remote.

Jack gets out of the car and takes the pile of books from her arms. He opens the passenger door and waits until she's seated before handing them back to her. Then he gets back in and starts the car.

It's true that Jack drives faster than Mrs Porter but somehow when he's driving the journey seems to take no time at all. The Chevy flies over the dirt road scattering rocks and torn pieces of liana and once a flock of parakeets which rise up from the road in a blur of yellow and blue wings.

At intervals along the edge of the road are small structures of brick and whitewashed plaster resembling miniature houses with panes of glass set into the front or an iron grille through which you can see what's inside. Sometimes it's no more than a jar full of withered flowers and a roughly fashioned cross; other shrines are more elaborate – containing statues of the Virgin or even photographs of the dead. When Tony first came here she used to call these makeshift memorials 'chicken chapels'; but even then she knew what they really were. Maracuchos are crazy drivers Jack says. Every so often one of them takes a corner too fast and goes over the edge.

They turn off the road into the drive which runs for perhaps a quarter of a mile through the stretch of cleared jungle which forms the outskirts of their garden. A stream runs through it; most of the year it's just a trickle but it gets quite deep in the rainy season. When they first came to La Soledad two years ago and Tony was only nine she used to try and jump across in one go. She remembers the time she lost her balance and how cross

Consuelo was with her for getting her frock wet. Now she can step across quite easily. It's hard to believe she ever found it difficult.

She gives silent Karel a nudge. 'See that poinsettia bush? I found the most enormous snake there a few days ago. Dead, of course. One of the gardeners had chopped its head off with a machete . . .'

Karel's only response to this friendly overture is a look of horror. He shrinks further back into his corner.

'That's enough, Antonia,' says her mother sharply.

Then the red-tiled roof of La Soledad appears above the screen of bushes. This isn't like the rest of the company houses at all but much larger and built of stone not matchwood – which is what Jack says the company houses are made of. La Soledad has big cool rooms with stone floors and shutters on all the windows to keep out the flies. It has beautiful gardens and stables – a real hacienda Jack says. The man who built it owned all the land for miles around. One of Gomez's boys – reaping the benefits of services rendered. And then they found oil – and old Gomez suddenly wanted his gift back again.

The car pulls up in front. Jack gets out and goes round to open the door for Vivienne but she's already getting out of the car dropping exercise books all over the place in her hurry. As fast as she drops them Jack picks them up and there's an undignified little scuffle as he tries to relieve her of the rest of the pile.

'Give me those.'

'I can manage, thank you.'

Both of them seem for the moment to have forgotten about Tony and Karel. She looks at him and sighs. After the snake episode she doesn't feel much like starting a conversation but she resolves to give him one more chance. She reaches across him and opens the car door taking him by surprise so that he almost tumbles out on to the gravel. She slides across the seat after him.

'Come on,' she says to him. 'I'll show you where you're going to sleep . . .'

But at this reminder of his displaced status his face crumples and his eyes fill with tears. He blinks and looks away. Fortunately at that moment Vivienne remembers him.

'Karel,' she calls from the veranda steps.

Obediently he follows her.

Inside you can feel the coolness rising from the stone floor as your eyes adjust to the darkness. Here the sun penetrates only through the mesh of the mosquito screens: blurred golden circles scatter the worn red tiles as if someone had thrown down a handful of coins.

Through the open double doors is the sitting room which runs the full width of the house and is separated from the rooms beyond by a stone arch. Unlike the Spanish colonial style of the rest of the house the furniture in the sitting room is modern. The chairs are light wood, upholstered in a black and yellow zigzag pattern resembling lightning bolts. The tables are triangular with glass tops. There's a tall black metal lamp with a pleated parchment shade and a set of bookends carved to look like galleons in full sail.

In the corner is a bar with a black and gold speckled top and a ridged front painted to look like bamboo. It's Jack's bar – where he keeps his sets of cocktail glasses and liqueur glasses and highball glasses and the shaker for the cocktails and the chrome ice-bucket you can see your face in. In the evenings when Jack and Tony are waiting for Vivienne to finish dressing he fixes them both a drink and they sit there just the two of them. Jack puts a record on the record player – he likes Frank Sinatra but Tony prefers Harry Belafonte – and lights up his first cigarette of the night and then they talk.

Sometimes Jack tells her about his day at work – about the trouble they've had with the Number Five drilling rig at La Concepción and the fresh seepages they've discovered at Mene Grande and the problems they've got with the union – the CTP – about the increased productivity bonus they're demanding for their workers – although you can't blame them for wanting a piece of the pie Jack says. Production was 2 million barrels a day last year. This year it looks as if it might be even better.

If he's in the mood he might tell her a funny story. The one about the man who was teasing a parrot and the *guacamayo* got hold of his nose with its beak and wouldn't let go. 'When we got that thing off him at last he looked like hell,' Jack says. 'His nose all purple and swelled to three times its size.'

Tony laughs – more on account of the way Jack tells this story than because she finds it funny. She's seen what a parrot's bill can do to a stick. The thought of that pincer grip on flesh and bone is almost more than she can bear.

Jack has other stories like that – which are funny and horrible at the same time. Once he saw a man electrocuted in the factory yard. It was during the rainy season. The man was spot-welding a piece of equipment and stepped back into a puddle with the welding torch in his hand. 'Dead before you could blink,' Jack says. 'And the darnedest thing was, the metal fillings in his

23

teeth had welded themselves together. Like he was laughing all over his face,' Jack says, 'only nobody else could see the funny side.'

Tony prefers the stories about when Jack was a boy. The time he was fooling around in the back yard peeling potatoes for his Mom and picked up an old umbrella spoke that was lying around and fixed a potato to it and bent it back and let it fly. 'The darn thing went over the wall and straight through the storefront window of the Excelsior Carpet Company. The first plate-glass window in town. What a licking I got . . .' The time he played hookey to watch the poker game at the saloon and the preacher caught him. 'I didn't think to ask him what *he* was doing in the saloon . . .' The small town where he grew up – 'Nowheresville, Texas' – with its church its schoolhouse and its drugstore is as familiar to her through Jack's account of it as if she'd grown up there herself.

'You know it's a funny thing,' he says to her one evening. 'But when I look back, it seems like a different world. I guess it *was* a different world . . . but hell, it wasn't that long ago. I'm talking about twenty, maybe thirty years . . .'

'Before the war,' Tony reminds him.

'Sure. Before the war. I guess that about says it all . . .' His voice tails off. It's as if he's forgotten she's there.

'What was it like in the war?' Tony asks him when he has been quiet a while. She doesn't really want to know the answer to this question but it's the only way she can think of to get him to go on talking.

Jack looks at her and laughs. Not the way you laugh when someone says something funny but a different kind of laugh. As if he can't quite believe what he's heard her say.

'What was the war like?' He takes a deep drag on his cigarette. Thinking about it. 'I'll tell you what the war was like. The war was a mess.' He frowns as he says this as if he was angry about something; Tony doesn't think it's her he's angry with but she's not sure about this. 'You're too young to remember,' Jack says with a look that reassures her a little 'but a helluva lot of terrible things happened in those years.' He taps the ash from the end of his cigarette into the Lucky Strike ashtray at the end of the bar. He has a collection of ashtrays with different designs painted on them. Tony's favourite is the one with the Black Cat Girl. 'I lost a lot of friends,' Jack says. 'So did a lot of people. Why, your Mom . . .'

He breaks off what he's about to say as Vivienne appears in the doorway. She's wearing her green silk dress with the pattern of angel fish swimming around the skirt and the gold brooch in the shape of an orchid Jack bought her when they got married.

'My, my,' says Jack softly. 'Do I know this good-looking gal?'

This is the best part of the evening – with Vivienne still in a good mood and Jack still on his first drink and everything the way it ought to be. If they're staying in this is sometimes how things stay. Friendly and relaxed – the way people are in other families. With no one getting upset, no one drinking too much or crying.

Tony can remember an evening like this not long ago.

More often than not Jack and Vivienne are going out – or they're having people in. And then you can be sure something will happen to spoil the mood. It's a feeling in the air like electricity. People are laughing and talking but underneath you can feel the tension. Somebody says something – or thinks somebody else said something –

and the mood changes as suddenly as if somebody flicked a switch.

It was different when Jack and Vivienne first got married Tony thinks. Then they never used to quarrel. Tony'd come in and find them sitting opposite one another at the breakfast table not saying anything just looking at each other. That's what people did when they were in love. One night when she got up to go to the bathroom she'd seen them dancing. There'd been music coming from the lighted room and when she went to investigate she saw them: Vivienne in Jack's arms laughing and protesting as he whirled her around the room to the strains of 'In the Mood'.

Tony goes into the kitchen where Consuelo is making lunch.

'What is it today, Consuelo?'

'Soup,' Consuelo says. It's always soup. 'Quick,' she frowns. 'Your Mama's waiting. And your little fren'.'

'He's not my friend . . .'

'Go wash your hands,' she says before Tony can say anything else. She turns back to her cooking.

When Tony goes into the dining room Vivienne and Karel are already seated. Jack has gone for his shower. He seldom eats with them at lunchtime – preferring to grab a bite to eat on his way out. Sometimes Tony sits with him while he has his meal. Consuelo always puts something by for him: a bowl of the hot spicy soup which is her speciality or a leg of cold chicken which he eats with his fingers – tearing at it with his strong white teeth.

Today it's Tony's favourite – shepherd's pie. When she first came to live with them the only things Consuelo knew how to cook were *arepas* and *chachapas* and *pabellón criollo*. It took Vivienne ages to teach her how to cook English food.

When Consuelo's in a good mood she sometimes lets Tony watch her get the supper. Consuelo sleeps in the room next to the kitchen. Her family lives a few miles away in one of the shacks on the edge of the *pueblo*. One day Consuelo brought her baby with her to work. He's a nice baby Tony thinks. Consuelo's mother looks after him most of the time. He's called Jesús-María. Vivienne says Catholics always have those kinds of names.

Vivienne unfolds her starched napkin with a little shake and spreads it across her lap. This is the signal for them to begin eating. They don't say grace like they do at Mary McBride's. Her father's going to be the vicar when the church is built. At the moment the nearest Protestant church is in Maracaibo, but the main one is in Caracas. Tony went there with Vivienne last Christmas. It was nice; they had a crib with carved wooden figures. And the service was in English; it reminded Vivienne of home.

Last Christmas in Caracas they stayed for a whole week at the Hotel Tamanaco. It's one of Tony's favourite places – all clean and white and modern with terraces like an Aztec ziggurat and waiters who bring you drinks on silver trays. There's a swimming pool with turquoise tiles on the bottom instead of painted concrete and a proper diving board. Round the edge of the pool are little tables with striped umbrellas to keep off the sun. On Christmas Day Jack and Vivienne sat at one of the tables drinking dry Martinis while Tony practised her diving. Later they got dressed up and went out to eat at the Country Club. Its golf course is the best in the city. Jack says he's going to teach Tony how to play.

27

The best part of the whole trip was when Jack took her for a ride on the *Teleférico*. It's scary at first until you get used to it: the way the little car lurches forward and you find yourself suspended with nothing between you and thin air but the flimsy compartment you're in which rocks and sways with every gust of wind. But then you start to move steadily and smoothly along the humming cables with the city spread out beneath you all white and glittering in the sunshine and the distant mountains seeming suddenly close enough to touch.

'When are we going to Caracas again?' Tony asks her mother.

Vivienne looks at her a moment before replying. 'Why?'

'I just wondered, that's all.'

'It depends,' she says vaguely. 'In a few weeks' time, perhaps. Karel, dear, you're not eating. Aren't you feeling well?'

He shakes his head angrily not looking at her.

Vivienne reaches out her hand to touch his forehead. He flinches away. 'You don't feel hot,' she says gently. 'Perhaps you're just tired. Would you like to go and lie down?'

Maybe it's the heat or the fact that he's in a strange place but something seems to have upset Karel. Suddenly without warning he starts to cry. Pushing back his chair he runs out of the room. A moment later they hear the screen door slam.

'Oh, dear,' says Vivienne giving Tony a look that's half-way between a smile and a frown. 'I was afraid something like this might happen. Go after him, will you, sweetie?'

She's about to say that she's probably the last person

Karel wants to see when Jack appears. He's shaved and showered and changed his shirt. He winks at Tony.

'Ready, Princess?'

She pushes back her chair. 'Ready.'

'Are you going somewhere?' Vivienne asks without looking up.

Jack answers for her. 'Tony and I are going to stop by the factory. Don't worry, I'll make sure she's back in time for afternoon school . . .'

'Antonia has something to do first,' Vivienne says. 'Don't you, Antonia?'

Tony gets up and walks reluctantly to the door. 'See you outside,' she says to Jack.

From the raised platform of the veranda she scans the garden – narrowing her eyes against the glare. Karel is nowhere to be seen. Stupid boy. Trust him to spoil things. She goes down the steps to the gravel drive looking around to see if she can spot him.

The trouble is there are so many hiding places in this garden. It depends how far he's run. She checks the shrubbery at the front of the house first then goes round to the back. There's a clump of acacias not far from the house where she goes when she wants to be on her own. But he isn't there either.

Feeling more and more annoyed with each minute that passes she runs to where the garden with its flowering shrubs and carefully tended grass which Juan the gardener waters twice a day becomes the jungle. It's not really a jungle of course – just a thicket of bamboo and razor grass so sharp it can slash your hand if you touch it – but that's what she's always called it. If she wanted to hide this is where she'd come. It doesn't look as if anyone's passed this way recently though. The green shoots of bamboo are unbroken and the grass blades stand stiffly upright like a forest of knives.

A dry rustling sound makes her turn her head – but it's only an iguana startled by her sudden appearance. It looks at her with its golden eye – flicking its long tongue in and out as if tasting the air before darting away into the grass.

She turns back towards the house. If she doesn't find him soon there won't be time to go to the factory with Jack.

Then she sees him skulking by the low stone wall at the edge of the patio. She must have passed him as she came this way – unless he was hiding somewhere else watching her all the time. For some reason the thought of this makes her angry. She rushes up to him and grabs his arm.

'Where've you been?' she hisses giving him a little shake.

He doesn't answer but she can see he's scared of her. His lower lip trembles as if he's going to start crying again. Tony lets go his arm.

'Look,' she says as nicely as she can. 'It's all right. No one's cross with you, or anything . . .'

'I want to go home,' Karel says suddenly.

Tony can't think of anything to say.

At that moment Jack comes round the side of the house. He sees them and waves.

'Let's go,' he says to Tony. 'Your mother wants you back in an hour.'

'OK, but . . .' She looks at Karel. 'What about him?'

'Oh, Sport can sit in the back, can't you, Sport? You never know,' says Jack already walking away, 'I might even buy him a soda pop . . .'

*

In the big factory shed everything's quiet. The men who operate the machine shop are off somewhere having their lunch or resting. It's too far for most of them to go home so mostly they just hang around until it's time for work to resume. There's a group of them playing cards in the open door of the shed. Dark-skinned men with gold teeth. As Jack and Karel and Tony walk past one of them shouts something in Spanish and the others laugh.

Without missing a beat Jack calls something back over his shoulder. There's another burst of laughter.

'What did he say?'

'He said why didn't the boss take a siesta like the rest of them, and I told him I was too busy thinking of ways to work him and his friends into the ground . . .'

They cross the wide empty floor of the vast shed which smells of spilled oil and creosote and something else – a rich smell like rotting fruit or sugar cane – which might just be the smell of the air itself blowing in from outside. It's here that repairs are done and equipment stored – although most of the actual drilling machinery for the site is shipped in from abroad. There's a small airstrip out back where the weekly supplies plane from Maracaibo unloads its crates of whisky and Coca-Cola and bolts of dress material; its spare parts for American cars and English sewing machines.

On the far side of the shed is a door. This is Señor Hernández's office. He's the site manager. Jack doesn't bother to knock but goes straight in. Señor Hernández is leaning back in his swivel chair with his feet on the desk in front of him and a handkerchief over his face. When the door opens he lifts a corner of the handkerchief to see who it is. The minute he sees it's Jack he swings his feet down off the desk and reaches for his jacket.

'Hey,' says Jack parking himself on a corner of the desk. 'No need to get up.'

But Señor Hernández puts his jacket on just the same. He holds out his hand. '*Señor*,' he says clicking his heels together in a way that reminds Tony of Jack when he's being funny. Except that Señor Hernández isn't being funny. Proud as Lucifer Jack says like all his kind.

The two men shake hands.

'So how's it going, Ramón?'

Señor Hernández shrugs and clicks his tongue. 'As you see,' he says.

'And Señora Hernández and the children?'

'All well, praise God. Señora Lindberg too?'

'Never better,' says Jack.

'Ah, *la niña*,' says Señor Hernández noticing Tony for the first time. 'With her little *amigo*.'

'Van Wel's kid,' says Jack.

The other inclines his head. 'Of course.' His dark eyes rest thoughtfully on Karel's thin face anxious beneath its helmet of pale hair. For a second it seems as if he might be about to forget himself – to reach out perhaps and stroke Karel's head the way he would if Karel were one of his own children. But in the end all he does is light a cigarette after first offering one to Jack.

'Any news from La Solita?' Jack wants to know.

Hernández shrugs. 'They let one boat leave the terminal this morning. That's all I know . . .'

'Those bastards in the CTP are pushing their luck,' says Jack.

'*Comunistas*,' says Hernández. '*Hijos de puta*.' He makes a face as if he's about to spit.

'Couldn't agree more,' says Jack. 'The question is – has there been any infiltration at the plant?'

Señor Hernández opens his mouth and then closes it again. His eyes move just a little so that they're no longer looking at Jack.

'Oh sure,' Jack says. He reaches in the pocket of his khaki slacks and pulls out a handful of small change. 'Hey, Princess,' he says to Tony. 'Señor Hernández and I have some business to discuss. Why doncha go get yourself a soda pop? And whatever the kid wants – O K ?'

She doesn't need telling twice. She takes the money from him and walks out of the room. As she crosses the shadowy floor of the factory shed she hears footsteps behind her a ghostly presence and knows Karel must have followed her. She feels a surge of anger – she's not a baby-minder after all – and wonders what he'd do if she yelled at him to get lost. But she decides it's not worth the effort. He's nothing but a kid. Better to act as if he didn't exist.

Walking just a little faster than she suspects he can comfortably manage she reaches the door of the shed where the game of cards is still in progress. She crosses the threshold with Karel at her heels just as one of the players throws down the queen of hearts.

'*Epa, chiquita*,' he says softly whistling between his teeth. The others laugh.

Tony wants to run to get away from that laughter. She turns and says sharply to Karel, 'Come *on*,' and they cross the concrete yard on which the sun beats down so fiercely you can feel the blood sing in your ears.

The doors of the wooden hut which is the site canteen stand open but it's no cooler inside. Flies circle around the broken ceiling fan. At metal tables along the walls groups of men in sweat-stained khaki workclothes sit around eating *empanadas* and drinking *café negro*. There's a strong smell of cigarettes not the filter-tipped kind either – *Cool as a mountain stream* – but the full-strength hand-rolled kind. After a few minutes the smell of them gets in your mouth and nose and stays there.

Tony takes two bottles of 7-Up from the cooler and gives them to the woman behind the counter who smiles at her with her gold-capped teeth. She removes the metal tops with the bottle opener which hangs from a chain on the wall and hands them back.

'*Muchas gracias.*' Tony pushes the handful of *bolívares* across the counter. The woman takes two and pushes the rest back. As Tony starts to walk away she calls after her holding out two paper straws. '*Gracias,*' Tony says again as she takes them from her. The fluted bottles feel nice and cold in her hands. She's so thirsty she could drink them both. Instead she hands one to Karel standing mutely beside her. He mumbles something.

'That's OK,' she tells him shrugging off his thanks. 'Jack gave me the money. Come on. I know a place we can sit and drink these, out of the sun . . .'

On a strip of waste ground by the chain-link fence which surrounds the perimeter of the site is a stack of empty oil drums. Once when Tony was little she crawled inside one that was lying on its side and hid there in the rusty-smelling dark. Now she's too big for such games. She squats down on the grass in the shade of the steel mountain and motions Karel to do the same. It's not exactly cool and the grass feels dry and scratchy against her bare legs but at least they won't get sunstroke.

For a few minutes they sit in silence drinking their

7-Ups. Tony holds on to the last mouthful as long as she can. The ticklish feeling you get at the back of your throat is nice and peculiar at the same time. It's the same kind of feeling you get when you drink beer only the taste is nicer than beer. The time Jack offered Tony a sip of his Solero she pretended to like it so as not to hurt his feelings but really she couldn't understand what the fuss was about. Whisky's worse – the smell of it on Jack's breath when he kisses her goodnight some nights almost knocks her over. Everything about grown-ups is strange Tony thinks – even the things they do for fun.

She sits back on her heels squinting at the scene in front of her through half-closed eyes. The site looks deserted; nothing moves or stirs in the heat. Across the glaring white of the concrete lot which is stained here and there with glistening patches of oil from unloading trucks is a wide expanse of scrubland. Earth baked the colour of an adobe wall when you scrape off the whitewash with your nail. Yellow grass sticking up in tufts. Black thorn trees like crouching witches. Heat haze shimmering above the invisible lake.

'Is your sister very ill?' Tony says to Karel.

He stares at her dumbly.

She tries again. 'I was quite ill once,' she tells him. 'When I had the measles. I had to lie in a darkened room for days and days . . .'

An image of the room floats into her mind. It was in Haslemere – near the school where Vivienne was teaching. Tony was six so she doesn't recall much about it. She remembers the wallpaper though. It had pictures of huntsmen on horseback going up and down in stripes. She used to lie and count them up one side and down the other. One day Vivienne drew a picture of her: a smiling face covered with spots. It made her laugh so much it hurt her throat.

Karel looks as if he might be going to speak. Tony waits for a minute to see if he will. He says nothing.

'You don't die of scarlet fever, you know,' she reassures him. 'At least – not usually. So I really don't think you have much to worry about . . .'

Karel scrambles to his feet. He is making a funny sound – a sort of panting. As if there were not enough air for him to breathe. Before Tony can ask him what the matter is he turns and runs away back towards the factory building where they left Jack talking to Señor Hernández.

'Hey –' She's so surprised she just stands there staring after him. 'What the blazes?' It occurs to her to let him go – serve him right if he gets himself lost – but then she remembers she's supposed to be looking after him. Muttering under her breath she follows him.

At that moment Jack and Señor Hernández emerge from the dark mouth of the factory building and go over to where Jack's car is parked in the shade. They must have finished talking business because as Tony gets nearer she can hear Jack telling Señor Hernández about something someone said to him at the poker game last night. Señor Hernández laughs and claps Jack on the back.

'*Epa, hombre . . .*'

Jack sees her walking towards him and makes hurry-up gestures.

'What's got into the van Wel kid?' he asks her. 'A minute ago he ran by here like a scared jackrabbit . . .'

Tony shrugs. 'All I did was ask him how his sister was . . .'

'Well go find him, will ya? We ought to get going. On second thoughts,' Jack adds, 'maybe I'll go find him. He probably had to run to the can . . .'

He says something in Spanish to Señor Hernández who grins. Then he disappears leaving them together. Señor Hernández is still wearing his jacket although it's hotter than ever out here. Beads of perspiration are standing out on his forehead. He whistles softly between his teeth. Tony wishes he would leave her there to wait by herself but she knows he'd be offended if she suggested it. Once or twice he catches her eye and smiles politely but mostly he just stands there studying his shirt cuffs. They're the whitest shirt cuffs Tony's ever seen.

Luckily it's not very long before Jack returns with Karel tagging along behind him. Something about his face makes Tony think he must have been crying. He doesn't look at her.

Jack claps his hands. 'OK, Tony – let's hit the road. Hop in, Sport. We're gonna have to step on the gas to get you back in time for class . . .'

'What about the spare parts?' Tony reminds him.

He tousles her hair. Mostly she hates it when people do that but with Jack she doesn't mind. 'In the trunk. Any more questions? No? Then let's get outa here. *Adiós*, Ramón.'

'*Adiós, señor.*'

They shake hands again and Señor Hernández clicks his heels. He winks at Tony. Jack says he's got a daughter just her age. She goes to the convent in Maracaibo. Next year Tony's going to boarding school in England.

They drive back along the lake road. Even though she's seen it lots of times before Tony still likes looking at the view across the lake – its mass of offshore drilling

37

rigs with their towering derricks like a forest of metal trees each sprouting a ghostly flame. It's even more beautiful at night. Then the glow of the flames and of the electric lights festooning the wells is reflected in the water a thousand lights shimmering in its pitch-black surface. Thirty years ago there was nothing here Jack says. Fishing villages. A few huts on stilts. Now it's the biggest single oil field in South America. Black gold it's called in Texas. The blood that keeps the world's heart pumping.

As he drives Jack rests one arm out of the open window whistling under his breath. Tony recognizes the tune – it's an old one of Frankie's: 'In the Blue of the Evening'. It makes her think of hotel terraces and men in white tuxedos and ladies in satin gowns with gardenias in their hair.

'When are we going to Caracas?' she asks Jack.

He shrugs. 'Search me. Next time your mother wants some shopping. Why?'

Grown-ups always want to know why. As if you needed a reason for everything.

'No special reason. Can we go on my birthday?'

Jack laughs. 'Maybe. See what your mother says, OK?'

'Will you take me to the racetrack?'

'I said maybe.' He glances over his shoulder. 'Are you a horse-racing fan too, Karel? Or do you prefer baseball?'

Karel does not reply. His eyes are closed and his breathing is deep and regular. His eyelashes are quite dark even though his hair is almost white – bleached by the sun. His face is pale too – with bluish shadows under his eyes and a scattering of tiny freckles like pinpricks across the bridge of his nose. He's still clutching his empty 7-Up bottle.

'He's asleep.' Tony takes the bottle out of Karel's hand and puts it on the floor.

'Poor little guy,' says Jack. 'He must be worn out.'

After a few more miles they turn off the main road and begin the climb towards La Soledad. Some days if there's time they stop at the sugar-cane factory which is on this road a mile or so along. Jack knows the foreman there – he's called Rómulo. Once or twice he's let Tony work the machine that presses the sugar juice out and he always gives her a piece of freshly cut cane to suck on the way home.

The rich dark smell of molasses is one of the best smells in the world Tony thinks. Even the sound of the word is enough to conjure up the smell of it the steam rising from the vats of molten sugar the wooden trays divided into squares where it cools into blocks as moist and crumbly as earth. The men tending the fires which keep the sugar boiling are stripped to the waist their skin shines like gold in the light of the furnace.

Sometimes they get so hot they have to cool themselves down with a swig of moonshine Jack says. They keep the still out of sight because the feds might come calling but when Jack drops in Rómulo always brings out the jug. Jack laughs and tells Rómulo no thanks – that stuff packs a helluva punch. You need to be born and bred to it he says.

When they get back to the house Jack leans across the back seat and scoops the sleeping Karel into his arms. Tony follows him up the steps to the veranda where Consuelo is waiting.

'Ah, *angelito*,' she murmurs looking at Karel. She

sees Tony and frowns. 'Go change your dress,' she says.

Tony's room is at the back of the house. It's quite small – it used to be a maid's room Vivienne says – but it's got everything she needs. There's a table where she does her homework and a round chair like a basket on spindly metal legs where she likes to sit and read. There's a shelf to hold her books and a glass-fronted cabinet for her collection of shells and glass animals. The shells are mostly ones she found on the beach at Chichiriviche. There's a piece of coral which looks like a tiny tree but scratches your fingers if you pick it up the wrong way. It was a beautiful pink when she first got it but the colour's faded and now it's as white as bone.

'Is that you, Antonia?' Vivienne puts her head around the door. Her hair is damp from taking her shower. 'Fifteen minutes on the bed, please. And don't forget to change your dress . . .'

'No, Mummy.'

'Oh – and have you a book I can give to Karel? *Tiger Tim*, perhaps . . .' She reaches up to take it down from the shelf.

'How long is he staying?'

'Who, Karel, you mean? I don't know exactly. A week. Perhaps two. It depends,' she says vaguely. 'They might have to fly the child to Caracas, it seems. Complications. No need to say anything to Karel just yet, though . . .'

Then she's gone. Tony takes off her dress and lies down on top of the bed in just her knickers. It's cool in the room because of the air-conditioning but she can't sleep. She tosses and turns thinking about what she's just learned. A *week*! Or even longer. She doesn't know how she's going to be able to bear it.

When afternoon school is over they go swimming. It's the club pool and everyone who uses it works for the company. There's a wall around it with bougainvillaea growing over and a patio with deck chairs for sunbathing. Some evenings they hold parties here – with all the women in their best dresses and no one under the age of sixteen to spoil the fun. But at this time of day it's just Tony and her friends.

Usually it's a time she looks forward to: the air's cooler but the water's warm. And that first sight of the pool – its oblong of blue like the blue you get in a new paintbox before it gets mixed up and spoilt – is the nicest thing in the world Tony thinks. The moment when you first get into the water and you feel it close around you and you glide with no more effort than breathing through that shimmering glassy coolness – if there's anything which feels better than that she doesn't know what it is.

Some days if Vivienne's finished her marking they go straight from school and arrive at the pool early before anyone else. Then they have the place to themselves and they swim and swim until they're tired. Vivienne's a good swimmer. Her parents used to rent a house in Bexhill every summer so she learned to swim in the sea. The sea in England isn't like the sea here she tells Tony. It's cold all year round and grey not blue.

But today they're the last to arrive because at the last minute Vivienne finds out that Karel's mother forgot to pack him any bathing trunks so they have to stop by the McBrides' house and borrow some old ones of Stuart's that Mrs McBride thinks might fit him.

Jane and Valerie and the others are already in the water when Tony comes out of the changing cubicle. Mary is lying on her stomach on the diving board seeing how far she can lean over before she falls in. It crosses Tony's mind that if someone crept up behind her and gave her a fright she'd lose her balance; then she realizes that's exactly what Jane is about to do. Jane's good at playing tricks. She has a way of looking as if the thing she's planning to do is the last thing on her mind.

Tony watches as Jane edges around the pool towards her quarry. It's a creepy feeling knowing what's going to happen. Half of her wants to laugh and the other half feels almost as if it's going to happen to her – that horrible moment when you feel yourself losing your balance and it's too late to save yourself and you open your mouth to scream but no sound comes out only bubbles as the water rushes in.

But at the last minute Valerie who's floating on her back in the middle of the pool sees what's happening and lets out a yell to warn her friend. Although it's not so much that she and Mary are friends as that she and her sister are enemies. It must be strange to have a sister. Brothers are much better Tony thinks – if you have to have anything that is.

She dives in and swims a few strokes under water slipping for a moment into the old game where she's the Little Mermaid getting back her beautiful fish's tail after walking on knives and red-hot pokers for the sake of her human lover. She hates that story almost as much as the one about the Red Shoes. The dancing feet capering away by themselves along the street with the poor cripple limping after them on her wooden stumps.

When she surfaces again in a shower of bubbles Jane is dancing around the edge of the pool chanting in a low voice meant for Valerie to hear:

'Tell-tale tit, your tongue will split,
And all the doggies in the town will have a little bit . . .'

'Don't care,' says Valerie from the middle of the pool.

'Don't-care was MADE to care,
Don't-care was HUNG,
Don't-care was put in the pot
And boiled till she was DONE . . .'

Tired of her balancing act Mary McBride dives into the pool and surfaces beside Tony. She swims around her in slow circles. 'Want to know a secret?' she says at last.

'Depends what kind of secret.'

Pinching her nostrils between thumb and index finger Tony sits down on the bottom of the pool. Above her in a clear turquoise shot through with flickering golden lights she can see Mary's legs waving up and down like two strange white fish. It's peaceful down here in this underwater world – the only trouble is you run out of air so quickly. She rises to the surface where Mary is waiting.

'My mother's going to have a baby.'

'Oh.' Tony lets herself fall back against the water until she's lying flat. Spread-eagled. The sun makes a rainbow blur through her half-closed lashes. 'Is that the secret?'

Mary swims closer. Her hair fans out in the water in

long pale strands. All the rest of them have short hair but Mary wears hers in two thick plaits. Her mother washes it every night with Johnson's baby soap to stop it going green. All of them have green hair from swimming. It's the chlorine Vivienne says. Mary puts her mouth next to Tony's ear. 'I know how babies come out,' she says.

'Oh *that*.' Tony closes her eyes. 'That's not a secret. I've known for ages. Kate Riley told me.'

'But,' Mary insists, 'do you know how they get *in*?'

'How do what get in?' says Valerie appearing suddenly from under water.

'Never you mind,' says Mary in her most withering voice. She seems annoyed that Tony's not more interested in her stupid secret and after a moment she swims away.

Tony lets herself drift. Weightless. A leaf or a passing water beetle brushes her cheek and slides out of sight before she can turn her head. Sounds reach her as if from very far away. A faint shrieking like a flock of parrots or only the voices of her friends. Above her the sky is as blue as the water; she floats between the two feeling – as she lazily spins – as if she might just as easily swim up into the air to look down on the bobbing heads of her companions.

She amuses herself with this thought for a while imagining how the world would look from very high up with its bright blue swimming pools its red-roofed houses its forests and mountain ranges. She pictures the looks of surprise on her friends' upturned faces as she swoops low enough to brush them with her fingertips then soars out of reach.

She hears her name being called.

Vivienne is standing at the far end of the pool wearing her new black and white Mexican-print swimsuit and her dark glasses. Tony wonders why she hasn't come in for a swim yet and then she sees that Karel is standing beside her. Even with the tape on Stuart McBride's swimming trunks tied as tight as it will go they're still far too big for him. He looks ridiculous.

She swims slowly towards them. She thinks she knows what's coming.

Sure enough when she's almost at the edge of the pool Vivienne says, 'Why don't you and Karel play together for a bit? You can help him with his swimming.'

'Aren't you coming in?'

'In a minute, perhaps,' she says already starting to walk away. 'When I've finished talking to Nancy . . .'

Tony knows this means she will not be coming in at all. Mrs Wilson is one of the mothers who never swim – although she spends every afternoon at the pool as they all do. But she never ventures far out of the shade. The heat doesn't agree with her. Vivienne says it's because she's got red hair; but Tony doesn't see why that stops her from going swimming. Jennifer Riley's got red hair and she swims every day.

She watches as Vivienne joins the group under the awning. Apart from Mrs Wilson who's wearing a white cotton cardigan over her dress and an enormous sun-hat made of pink rafia there's Mrs McBride in the red and white polkadot sunsuit she always wears – because she's too fat for a swimsuit Jane says – and Mrs Riley in a turquoise swimsuit with a pattern of yellow starfish. Mrs Riley paints her toenails and smokes menthol-tipped cigarettes from a tortoiseshell holder. Tony quite likes Mrs Riley. She once gave Tony a pile of *Picture Post*s to keep. And she uses French perfume – Diorissimo – Tony's seen it on her dressing table.

She looks at Karel. He hasn't moved. It's as if he were frozen to the spot staring after her mother with a look of dumb misery. Tony suppresses an urge to grab him by the ankle and pull him into the water. She knows Jane Wilson wouldn't think twice about it.

'Are you going to swim or not?' she says to him – more crossly than she'd intended.

He drags his gaze away from the group of laughing women under the awning. Then he shakes his head. 'I can't swim.'

This is the last straw. Tony glances across to where her mother is sitting but fails to catch her eye.

'Well you might at least get in,' she says to Karel – resigned to having the afternoon spoilt. 'You can stand at this end. It's not deep.' She demonstrates by standing up herself showing him the water level reaching just above her waist. But still he seems reluctant to try.

'What's the matter?' asks Jane swimming up to where they are. Tony explains.

'Come on,' Jane says to Karel. 'It's all right really. You won't drown.'

Karel does not look convinced. They are joined by Mary.

'Those are my brother's swimming trunks,' she says accusingly.

'I suppose that's why they look so peculiar,' says Jane. 'Go on,' she urges Karel. 'I dare you – jump.'

'Jump,' says Mary.

'Jump,' Tony says – adding her voice to this chorus of voices.

Karel jumps. It is so unexpected that none of them

has a chance to stand back. One minute he is standing on the edge the next he has disappeared in a boiling mass of bubbles at the bottom of the pool leaving only the sudden noise of the splash behind him.

Jane cheers and they wait for him to surface. It seems a long time and then Tony remembers: *he can't swim*.

In the time it takes to think this thought Karel's head appears from the water blinded and gasping. His hair is plastered down across his face and there is water running out of his mouth. He starts to choke and in a minute Tony knows he will start to scream.

'Well done,' she shouts in his ear as he stands there choking and shivering.'That was jolly brave.'

'Jolly brave,' echoes Mary patting him on the back.

It's no good though. As soon as he has breath to he starts to cry. It isn't the quiet kind of crying either.

'What on earth is going on?' says Vivienne from some-where above their heads. Tony can't look at her.

'Please, Mrs Lindberg,' Jane says innocently. 'Karel's swimming trunks have come off . . .'

Nothing is said in the car on the way home. Karel sits in the back still wrapped in the towels in which Vivienne has swathed him. From time to time a shuddering sob escapes him. Tony sits in front next to her mother who is driving. Behind the dark glasses her expression is hard to read. But when they reach the house she says in the polite voice she uses when she is angry, 'I'd like a word with you, Antonia. In my room.'

'I don't know how you could be so cruel.'

She doesn't sound angry any more – only disappointed. For some reason this makes Tony feel even worse. She looks at the floor and says nothing. Her mother looks at her.

'I mean – *really*, Antonia . . .'

'I'm sorry,' Tony says flatly.

Vivienne sighs. She sits down on the bed patting the space beside her. Tony sits down fixing her gaze on the zigzag pattern of the Mexican rug as her mother explains why she has to be nice to Karel.

Karel's parents had a very hard time in the war Vivienne tells her. His mother's family were killed by the Germans. She was the only one who escaped. His father was put in prison. 'He's lucky to be alive,' Vivienne says. After the war there wasn't enough to eat. People were starving. 'Don't you think that's terrible?' Her voice sounds as if she's going to cry. 'People dying of cold and hunger. Children, no older than you, scavenging for food . . .'

Tony nods her head but she still doesn't see what Vivienne's getting at. It was all such a long time ago. She was three when the war ended and she can't remember anything about it. She's tried of course – but all she can summon up is a vague memory of holding her grandmother's hand in the air-raid shelter and the sickly taste of concentrated orange juice.

'It's hard for you to understand,' Vivienne says as if she knows what Tony's thinking. 'But when you live through something like that it changes you for ever. It's as if . . . I don't know . . . your life just stops.'

'Was it like that when Daddy was killed?'

Vivienne smiles so sadly that Tony wishes she hadn't asked.

'Yes,' she says. 'Exactly like that.'

'All right,' Tony tells her. 'I'll try and be nice to Karel.'

Although it seems to her it's Karel's parents they've been talking about.

Vivienne seems satisfied with this. She gives Tony's hand an absent-minded pat. 'That's my girl.' She gets up and walks across to the closet where her dresses hang in rows: cotton ones for daytime silk for evening. Frowning she picks out a dress and holds it at arm's length. 'I wonder if I can get away with this old thing one more time,' she says.

'Are you going out tonight?'

'Just for an hour or so. The Johnsons are back from leave.' She yawns and throws the dress on the bed. 'I think perhaps that's one for Consuelo, don't you?'

'Jack likes you in that dress.'

'I know, but the seam's already gone under the arm. Look.' She shows Tony the place. 'They don't make frocks to last here, the way they do at home . . .'

'*Señora* . . .'

'What is it, Consuelo?'

But Consuelo doesn't answer she just turns in the doorway and walks away as if she expects Vivienne to follow. Vivienne raises her eyebrows at Tony. Consuelo's silences can be unnerving until you get used to them.

When they go into the sitting room Mr van Wel is there. He jumps to his feet when he sees Vivienne.

'I'm so sorry,' she starts to say. 'I didn't realize . . .' But he cuts her off.

'Forgive me,' he says. 'It's a bad time . . .'

'Not at all.'

He indicates the battered valise at his feet. 'I bring some more clothes for Karel.'

'Oh, good,' says Vivienne.

49

There is a short silence. Tony wonders what their visitor will say next. He seems very nervous and ill-at-ease. Maybe being in prison does that to you.

Vivienne doesn't seem to find his behaviour at all strange. She smiles at him.

'Would you like a drink?'

'Please,' says Mr van Wel again. 'Thank you,' he adds.

'Sherry, gin, whisky?' says Vivienne. 'I believe there's some vermouth, if you'd like a dry Martini . . .'

'No, please,' says their guest. 'Don't disturb yourself. A small gin,' he murmurs unhappily, 'would be very fine.'

'A small gin it is,' says Vivienne. 'I hope you'll forgive me if I don't join you. It's a little early for me.'

'Of course.' Mr van Wel takes the glass and raises it towards her. '*Proost*,' he says. 'As they say in my country . . .'

Vivienne smiles. She takes a cigarette from the box on the table and looks around for her lighter but Mr van Wel is too quick for her.

'Please,' he says taking his own lighter out of his pocket. He flicks the tiny wheel with the ball of his thumb and a jet of flame shoots up. Vivienne puts the cigarette between her lips and inclines her head to take a light. At that moment Jack walks in.

'Well, well,' he says. 'I guess the party started without me.'

'Hello, Jack,' says Vivienne. 'Mr van Wel stopped by to see Karel . . .'

'Sure,' says Jack pouring himself a drink. 'How's it going, Piet?'

'Very good,' says Mr van Wel. 'Except my wife . . .'

'How is your wife?' says Jack. 'And the little girl?'

'Very sick.' Mr van Wel shrugs. 'Maybe we have to fly her to the hospital, I don't know . . .'

'Well, you know Karel can stay just as long as he needs to,' Jack says.

Mr van Wel bows his head gravely. 'I don't know how to thank you,' he says.

'Don't mention it,' says Jack. 'Sit down, why don't you?'

Karel appears in the doorway.

'*Vader*,' he says.

'Hello, Karel. I hope you are a good boy,' says his father.

Karel says something in Dutch.

'You must speak English, Kareltje.' Mr van Wel smiles apologetically at Vivienne and Jack. 'How will you learn if you don't speak English?'

Later when Tony's in bed Vivienne looks in to say goodnight. The stiff layered skirts of her new black dress rustle excitingly; as she bends to kiss her Tony can smell her faint but unmistakable smell of face powder lipstick and eau-de-Cologne.

'What's that you're reading?' she asks as she straightens up.

'*The Lost World*. Peter Riley lent it to me.'

'Any good?' says Vivienne carelessly glancing at herself in the long mirror on the wardrobe door. She flicks an invisible speck from her skirt and adjusts the silver tissue folds of her evening stole.

'Quite good. It's about explorers. They find a land where there are dinosaurs and things . . .'

'Vivienne,' Jack calls from their bedroom. 'Help me with this damn bow tie, will ya?'

'Don't read too late,' says Vivienne blowing Tony a kiss. 'Sweet dreams.'

She hears their voices in the next room: a murmured protest from Vivienne at something Jack has said; a burst of laughter from Jack.

'C'mon, we'll be late.'

Then the voices recede. She hears the engine start. They drive away leaving her to silence. Almost silence. There's the sound of insects whirring against the screens and the calling of a parakeet in the orange grove. She turns once more to Professor Challenger:

So tomorrow we disappear into the unknown. This account I am transmitting down the river by canoe, and it may be our last word to those who are interested in our fate . . .

She becomes aware of a new sound above the insect whine and the parakeet's harsh shrieking. This is a softer sound than either of these but harder to ignore.

I must hark back, however, and continue my narrative from where I dropped it. We are sending home one of our local Indians who is injured . . .

The sound continues – breaks off – then starts again. It comes from the room on the other side of the passage which is usually empty. It's where Karel is sleeping. Or not sleeping it seems.

I am committing this letter to his charge . . .

Unable to read any further she switches off the lamp and listens eyes wide open in the darkness until the sound of Karel's crying dwindles into silence.

She leans her head back against the uncomfortable head-rest, breathing the stale artificial air she has shared for the past eleven hours with the other occupants of the plane. She closes her eyes, thinking about another journey. Sinamaica. The name alone is enough to conjure everything.

Flying across the lake in an open boat the landscape coming towards you water sky trees the wind in your face is the way dying ought to be. The speed with which they're travelling skimming over the surface of the water is like nothing she's ever felt before: an intimation of paradise. Colours are intense blues greens vivid reds heightened by the swiftness with which they are passing through this strange mirror-world in which everything is seen in duplicate twisted shapes of tree roots arching up out of the water; clouds like fantastic palaces of air and ice reflected in the lake's still surface; a flash of blue and scarlet as a startled bird flies up with a clatter of wings.

She opens her eyes. A voice crackles over the Tannoy: the captain, apologizing for this unfortunate but regrettably unavoidable delay. The stewardess sighs and puffs out her cheeks – signifying, It's hot out there; or merely a humorous exasperation.

2

Karel watches his father leave. Across the shining floor and through the doors and down the steps to where the car is waiting. He turns once, raising his hand in valediction.

The car swallows him up; starts to move away. And Karel sees, through the smeared pane red with the blood of spattered insects, his father's face in profile, already intent on something else.

Vader.

The sound bursts from his throat, emerging as no more than a whisper. Don't leave me, he'd say if he could – but the weight of everything he wants to say lies on his tongue, condemning it to silence.

All Karel can do is watch, as the Land Rover moves off down the drive, disappearing between ranks of trees until nothing is left but the roar of the engine, becoming more distant and then fading away altogether. Then the scene itself – white road, green trees, blue sky – blurs and seems to dissolve. Mocking him with its emptiness.

The woman standing beside Karel reaches down and takes his hand. He knows better than to try and pull away, even though it's the last thing he needs right now. Seeing his father go was bad enough, but having this reminder of everything else he's lost is almost more than he can bear. He bites his lip and concentrates on not crying.

She's talking to him all the time as she holds his hand, saying, Things will be better soon, you'll see. Next week or the week after that you can go home, she says. Just think how happy you'll be.

An image of the low white house with the corrugated-iron roof in the company compound, its windows screened by a wrought-iron grid, rises in his mind's eye. The square of beaten earth with the tree and the home-made swing. The place where he tore his knee jumping off the wall.

Inside, it's a square divided into five: living room, kitchen, bathroom and two bedrooms; each room (a smaller square) with its complement of furniture. Every-thing – beds, chairs, table – new and unused-looking, even after five, nearly six months' use.

Karel remembers the way it looked that first time. Arriving late at night, after the jolting ride in the back of the Jeep. Stepping out into the hot night, half-blind with sleep, to find himself home, apparently. He sees his mother walk from room to room, opening all the doors. His father trying the windows, which have rusted shut, then turning to her with a shrug.

Wat denk je ervan?

Wat moet ik ervan denken?

It's the noises which keep him awake, that first night. Shrill screams of laughter and sounds like gurgling water. Flutings and rustlings and the minute whine of mos-quitoes. Transfixed by terror, he lies breathless and sweating, until the sky starts to grow light and he falls at last into a dead sleep.

Five months on, he's grown used to the noises; now,

other things disturb his sleep. Dreams of a cold, dark country, where men in black coats wait for him in the street; and his mother looks out at him from the window of a moving train.

Karel knows the stories, of course. The trains taking people away to an unknown destination. The cellars where the others hide. The men waiting outside in the streets. The snowbound city. He has no memory of these things, and yet they haunt his nights – so that it's a relief, each morning, to wake to the glaring sky of a landscape without snow, without memories.

There are daytime terrors too. The sly look on the faces of his classmates, when he opens his mouth to speak. The way the words tangle themselves around his tongue, so that the clearest thought comes out clotted and difficult: foreign-sounding. The barely stifled laughter when, choked into silence, he stands there, waiting for it to be over.

Thank you, Karel. You may sit down now.

And here she stands, his kind tormentor, pointing out flowers in her garden:

Do you see? We have some English marigolds. Dear little things, aren't they? I brought the seeds from home myself . . .

He knows those flowers – they have them where he comes from too. A word pops up, unbidden:

Goudsbloem.

That's right, Karel. But we must try and remember what your father said, mustn't we? Now tell me the English name.

Ma . . . ma . . .

Marigold. Well done, Karel. Let's see if we can teach you the names of some other things . . .

Still talking, she turns and draws him in, towards the room where the man is waiting. He sees Karel and grins.

Hey, Sport. Do you like the funny papers?

He throws Karel a printed sheet which on inspection turns out to be covered with drawings. Men with balloons coming out of their mouths and light bulbs over their heads. Women with big eyes and tight dresses. One strip has an oddly familiar look. *Donner und Blitzen. Der Katzenjammer Kids.* A fat man in baggy pants and a peaked cap chases two boys with a hammer. They hide from him under the table where he sits eating his dinner. The pepper makes one of them sneeze. The fat man chases them again, waving his arms like windmills.

Karel looks up and sees that the girl is watching him. She doesn't smile, but goes on staring with those wide blue eyes, as if he were something unfamiliar to her; a creature from another world. After what happened today at the pool he doesn't trust her; in fact, he suspects she means him no good. And yet she's polite enough – has even offered him the loan of her bicycle. Would an enemy do as much, he wonders.

Karel knows about enemies: they come in a variety of guises. Thin Jopi with the mad eyes, who held his hands against the hot pipe until he said his mother was a whore; pale fat Klaas, who stole his lunch and made him swear he wouldn't tell; Maartje, who kissed him for a dare and ran away shrieking. These, on occasion, haunt his dreams, displacing the men in black and the moving train. But he doesn't fear them the way he used to. They are phantasms, merely. It's the real world and all its terrible surprises he's come to dread.

Days when he crawls from sleep as out of a black pit, to find himself in treacherous sunlight. Such a beautiful world, a picturebook paradise, with such greens and reds. Flowers which lean their faces down to him, as he passes, each calyx like a throat. Small jewelled birds, which hover for an instant on blurred rainbow wings. The sky so blue it burns his eyes to look at it.

In the kitchen, something waits: a shadow, with a woman's shape. Paler and more silent with each day that passes, she sits at the table, clenching her fists. Some days she hardly seems to see him, waiting passively, silently, as Karel bolts his bread and milk, her gaze fixed somewhere above his head. Other days, he's barely able to take his seat before she starts, her voice never rising above a whisper, telling him what she thinks of him, and all the harm he's done. These are the worst days. He almost prefers the blows, which are bound to follow. Stinging the backs of his legs and buffeting his shoulders. *Dwaas. Domkop. Idioot.*

His sister plays on the periphery of this violence. Short-sighted, delicate; a child as fair and slender as the princess in a fairy tale. *My mother killed me, my father ate me; my little sister buried my bones under the juniper tree.* Sometimes, when the beating's over, she brings Karel something she's found: a flower, perhaps. A dead dragonfly. He doesn't hate her, even though her skin (so fine it looks transparent) will never be marked with bruises like his own. She smiles at him shyly, her weak eyes watering, and kisses him better.

There are days when their mother doesn't get up at all.

Then it's up to Karel to get the breakfast: a dry *broodje* for him and one for Annetje. Milk, if he can find some that hasn't gone sour. There's no one to tell him not to open the door, so he does so, sitting on the step overlooking the patio and the dry grass beyond it. In the flowerbeds by the wall are the gladioli his mother planted. She wanted something to remind her of home, she said.

He chews the stale crust slowly, feeling the heat of the stones through his thin sandals, smelling the warm dry air. His sister squats in the dust, trapping ants with a stick. As each one rises from the dark crevice, she separates it from its fellows, fencing it in until, by judicious manoeuvring, she has collected a small colony. Her sash trails in the dirt; he notices her hair needs brushing.

Niet doen!

She looks up, blind and innocent. He says it again and her face crumples, but she throws down the stick at once. He knows he can make her do whatever he likes.

He tells her it's time for school.

At once she rises, obedient to his wish. She waits for him at the gate as he fetches the bags. Now all they have to do is stand in the road, until someone – a colleague of their father's maybe – stops to offer them a lift. If they're quiet, they can get out before anyone knows they're gone.

Kom hier.

He knows better than to pretend he hasn't heard. He stands in the doorway of the darkened room, opening the door no more than a crack because the light hurts his mother's eyes. She asks for a drink and he brings her a glass of water from the five-gallon jar. He fetches a cold cloth for her head. He thinks now she might let him go, but she calls him back.

Waar is je zuster?

This is what Karel's been afraid she would ask. He

tells her Annetje's gone to school. Fetch her back, she tells him.

It's no good arguing. He goes to the open door and calls. At once the child appears, slips past him into the dark, stale-smelling room.

Mijn engel. Kom bij Mammie . . .

He leaves them together, remembering to close the door quietly. If he runs, he might still make it to school on time . . .

Are you coming or not?

The girl is speaking to him. The impatient note in her voice suggests that she has had to repeat her question. He starts to mumble an apology, but before the words are out of his mouth she has turned and is walking away. She glances back over her shoulder as if she expects him to follow.

Come on.

He has no choice but to do what she requires. She leads him through the house – past the dining room with the big mahogany table like the one he used to hide under in Oma's house; past the room where she sleeps and the room where he is going to sleep and the bathroom where, that afternoon, he saw the lizard – to the kitchen at the back of the house. Here, the dark woman with the gold earrings speaks to Karel in Spanish, ruffling his hair with thin dark hands that smell of the fish she has been cleaning.

Pobrecito . . .

He slips past her to the back door, where his new friend is waiting. Impatiently, she grabs his hand, dragging him after her across the beaten-dirt yard to a low stone building, once a stable block. From an iron ring attached to the rafter hangs the shrouded cage.

Look.

She whisks the cloth away like a conjuror to reveal the drowsing bird. Scarlet breast, blue wings and powerful curved beak. A strange wise eye that looks at him sideways before the shutter comes down. The bird moves swiftly along its perch, a bobbing, crabwise motion. Snatches the offered fruit and ducks away. Its voice, when it speaks, is shocking: clear, inhuman.

Diablo!

Electrified by the sound, Karel stands motionless. The round bright eye observes him for an instant, vanishes, then reappears. It's so exactly like a human wink that he catches his breath. He waits for it to speak. But the creature remains obstinately silent. Nothing more escapes it but a few whistles and clicks, followed by a burst of rude laughter.

His companion, reaching through the bars to stroke the soft plumage with the tip of her finger, makes kissing noises, murmurs, *Pretty boy.*

Even before Karel opens his eyes he knows he's in a strange place. It's the smell of the room which is different, maybe, or the sounds he can hear floating in from outside. The sound of a spoon being scraped against a pan and of a woman's voice, softly humming words in a foreign tongue. He opens his eyes. The sun through the ornamental wrought-iron bars on the window throws a pattern of interlocking 'S' shapes across the bed. On the end of the bed are his clothes, neatly folded. His shoes have been placed side by side, waiting for him to step into them.

The walls of the room are a pale pink. There are pink and grey striped curtains at the window and a pink rug on the floor. The bedspread, which is also pink, has a fluffy, raised design he can trace with his fingertips. If he pulls a little bit too hard, small pieces of the fluff come away, leaving a pattern of holes. Karel notices this only when he has been doing it for a while.

On the wall in front of him is a picture of a house surrounded by trees. The house is brown with a white roof studded with coloured lozenges like sweets. The windows have shutters with heart-shaped holes cut out of them. Two figures stand in front: a boy and girl, holding hands. The girl has fair plaits and a white apron over her dress. The boy, who has blond hair like his sister's, wears shorts with a bib at the front and braces.

Karel looks at the picture a long time, drawing his knees up close against his chest. His fingers pluck the bedspread.

The sound of scraping has stopped and with it the singing. It's very quiet. Karel slides his legs out from beneath the covers, until his toes are touching the floor. As he makes a move towards his clothes, he sees there's another presence in the room. It's a boy in striped pyjamas, his fair hair sticking out in tufts around his shocked white face. He stares at Karel, and Karel stares at him. In his hand are the grey woollen socks Karel has just picked up from the bed.

There's a sound of footsteps outside the door and a moment later the girl, Antonia, appears in the mirror behind him. She's already dressed, in bright red shorts and a blue and white striped top. Her long legs are bare and she is wearing red sandals with a pattern of hearts cut out around the toes.

'Aren't you dressed yet?' she demands. 'I've been dressed for ages.'

She stands in the doorway, swinging herself to and fro against the frame.

'Come on,' she says, pivoting so that her back is towards him. 'Jack's already loading the car . . .'

With one final swing, she propels herself out of the room. He hears her feet in their red shoes clattering away down the hall.

Karel dresses as quickly as he can, but somehow his fingers won't do what he wants them to. He buttons up his shirt all wrong and has to do it again and the laces of his heavy black shoes tie themselves in knots which won't come undone. The boy in the mirror – now also dressed – tries to smooth down his sticking-up hair with the palms of his hands.

'Ah, there you are, Karel dear . . .' It's his teacher, kind Mrs Lindberg, smiling down at him from the doorway. She looks different from the way he's seen her look before. For one thing, she's wearing slacks, which are cut very tight and short. Her white blouse shows her slim brown arms. In her hand she carries a large straw hat.

She, in her turn, seems struck by Karel's appearance. She looks at him, her head on one side. 'Oh, dear,' she murmurs. 'Those *clothes* . . .'

Karel was feeling hot before, but now he feels even hotter. In his grey flannel shorts and long-sleeved shirt, the boy in the mirror looks hot too.

'We'll have to see what else we can find you,' Mrs Lindberg says, taking Karel's hot hand between her cool fingers. 'Come along. Consuelo will be wanting to clear away the breakfast dishes . . .'

She leads him out to the covered porch at the front of the house, where a place has been laid for him at the round table. She sits down opposite Karel and passes him things to eat. The food isn't the same as he has at home and at first he isn't sure if he likes it. Instead of bread, there's toast and dark, bitter-tasting jam. There are dry flakes in a bowl. There's juice to drink instead of milk, and a round yellow fruit, whose cut surface is covered with a brittle crust of sugar.

From where Karel sits, he can see through the thick mesh screen into the yard beyond, where the big red car he came in is parked, its trunk standing open. Into this the others – his new-found friend and her father – are loading quantities of stuff: folding chairs, straw mats, a large striped umbrella and what looks like a smaller version of the metal chest in which Karel's parents brought their household goods from Holland.

'We're going to the beach,' Mrs Lindberg tells him, following the direction of his gaze. 'You'll like that, won't you?'

Karel looks at her. His mouth is full but he nods, to be polite, even though he isn't sure what the right answer to this question is.

'Poor lamb,' she says, as if she guesses this. 'I don't suppose you've ever been, have you?'

When everything is in the car, Mr Lindberg slams the trunk of the car shut and says something to Antonia. She turns and comes running across the yard towards the house. She takes the steps two at a time.

'Jack says to tell you we're all set,' she says.

'Karel's just finishing his cereal, aren't you, dear?'

Antonia makes a face. 'If we leave any later, there won't be time for a swim before lunch,' she says crossly.

'There'll be plenty of time,' says Mrs Lindberg. 'Tell Jack we'll be five minutes. I have to powder my nose . . .'

She gets up and goes back into the house, leaving Karel with Antonia.

'If you don't want that grapefruit,' the girl says, after a minute or two, 'I'll have it.'

She reaches across him and takes the yellow fruit, scooping up the cut segments with a teaspoon. Then she eats the toast he has barely touched. 'Drink your juice,' she tells him. 'Or we'll be here all day.'

When Mrs Lindberg returns, all the plates are empty. She smiles at Karel. 'You must have been hungry,' she says. She holds out her hand to him. 'Shall we go?'

The beach is a wide white space, with blue at the end of it. A strip of darker blue, which is the sea, and the paler, shimmering blue which lies above it. In the shade of the coconut palms, Karel stands and stares.

The others are taking the things from the car. Deck chairs, a folding table, an ice-box loaded with bottles of beer and Coca-Cola are set out, one by one, beneath the trees. With magical swiftness, a small encampment takes shape. Further along the beach, similar camps are being set up, with beach umbrellas and canvas windbreaks. Fires are being built, with the aid of a few bricks and sheets of chickenwire. Bottles are being opened.

'The Rileys are here,' Antonia says. She is already in her swimsuit, her hair pushed up under her straw hat, which shades her face as far as the tip of her nose.

Mrs Lindberg spreads a plaid rug on the sand. She lifts the lid of a rectangular basket and unfolds a checked tablecloth. She spreads this out too and weighs down the corners with stones. Then she opens the basket once more and takes out knives and forks, cups and plates. Karel waits to see what else will appear. Thermos flasks.

A whole chicken. Hard-boiled eggs. Sandwiches. Fruit. He wonders if all this food can be for one family.

'Mummy . . .' Antonia sighs.

Mrs Lindberg looks up. 'Run along, then,' she says. 'If you're going to swim, you'd better be quick. Lunch is in fifteen minutes. Oh, and Antonia . . .' Antonia stops in her tracks. 'You might take Karel with you . . .'

'But, *Mummy* . . .'

'Don't be silly, Antonia.'

'But he can't even swim . . .'

'He can paddle.' She turns to Karel and smiles. 'You like paddling, don't you, Karel? Of course you do. All children like paddling. Take your shoes and socks off, there's a good boy. And while you're about it, you'd better get out of those hot clothes. Your swimming trunks are in the car . . .'

Antonia waits, scuffing her sandalled feet in the sand, while Karel changes. Then, walking very fast, she sets off down the beach. He follows, at a distance.

The dark-haired woman is lying in a deck chair, smoking a cigarette. Her long legs, revealed by the daringly brief swimsuit she is wearing, are as brown and smooth as polished wood.

'Hello, you,' she says to Antonia.

'Hello, Mrs Riley.'

'If you're looking for Jennifer, she's gone in already,' the woman says, waving scarlet-tipped fingers in the direction of the sea. She fans herself with the book she is reading. On the cover, Karel sees, is a picture of a man with a smoking gun. A woman in a red dress lies at his feet. She may be dead or just asleep – he has no way of telling.

'Oh,' says Antonia. She traces a pattern of circles in

the sand with her toes. 'When does Kate break up?' she asks, after a minute or two.

Mrs Riley yawns and fans herself some more. 'End of June sometime. My husband will know. Frank,' she calls.

Mr Riley is on his hands and knees in the sand, digging a hole for the ice-box. 'Yes?' he says, without looking round.

'When are we expecting Peter and Katie?'

'June the 21st,' Mr Riley tells her.

'June it is,' says Mrs Riley. She yawns, again. 'God, it's hot,' she says. 'I hope Jennifer isn't getting too burnt in this heat. She always peels so disgustingly, poor child. It's the red hair, I suppose.' She stretches out her own brown arm and examines it with satisfaction. 'Of course she gets that from Frank's side of the family,' she murmurs.

On the sand at the edge of the shore is a ragged edge of foam, left behind by the receding breakers. The sea is warm and very clear. Karel's toes dig into the smooth wet sand, making tiny earthquakes.

The sun's hot on the back of his neck and on the white cage of his hunched body. He feels he could sit here for ever, doing nothing, and wanting no more than for things to continue.

The waves make a soft sound, like voices murmuring in another language. However hard he tries, he can't make out what they are saying.

Other sounds drift towards him: cries of seabirds; shrieks of girls, surfacing like mermaids from the deep; laughter and shouting from the people gathered around the barbecues and beer coolers.

Beside him on the glittering sand is the pile of shells he

has collected. These are of various colours – pink, translucent purple, palest yellow – but their shape is unvarying. Each is a convex triangle, with rounded corners – resembling nothing so much as one of his own toenails. He grades the shells according to size and places them, beginning with the largest, on the ends of each toe.

A shadow falls across him and when he looks up, the dark woman is there.

She stands against the light, framed by its brightness. Her face in shadow, under the black cloud of hair. He can't look at her. He looks instead at her feet, in the water beside him. Their brilliant nails like the darting fish he has watched all afternoon. She sees him looking and smiles.

'Paddling's such *fun*, isn't it?'

He smells the smoke on her breath, as she crouches down beside him. There's another smell too, which it takes him a moment longer to identify. It's the way his father smells when he comes in late from work. Leaning over Karel's bed to kiss him goodnight.

'I thought I'd escape for a while,' Karel's companion tells him. She jerks her head towards the crowd on the beach. 'Nice people, but they can be such frightful *bores*.' Red lips curving slyly, she taps his knee with one red-painted fingernail. 'I'll tell you a secret. Not that it's really a secret. The biggest bore of the lot is my darling husband . . .'

Laughing softly, she scoops up the shells he's been collecting and begins to throw them, one by one, into the water.

'How's your mother?' she asks suddenly. 'Or is that the sort of question one shouldn't ask?'

*

Sofie van Wel sits beside her sleeping child, in the darkened hospital room. She sits very still – so still in fact that it seems as if she too might have fallen asleep, except that her eyes are open, their gaze never moving from the child's face.

At intervals during the day a nurse pads silently into the room, to take the patient's temperature and to give her some water to drink on a spoon.

Throughout these ministrations, Sofie's jealous gaze never wavers; when the nurse has gone, she leans across to straighten the rumpled sheet, a look of faint scorn on her thin dark features.

Annetje stirs and mutters something incoherent. The fierce expression on her mother's face softens momentarily. She sponges the child's flushed face with a damp cloth, smooths back the sweat-soaked hair.

'Rest now,' she murmurs.

She stands, nervously twisting the wet cloth between her fingers until the child is asleep once more. Resuming her seat, she notices that one of the curtains isn't quite closed. A line of sharp white light falls across the floor, almost touching the bed. She goes to shut it out.

For an instant, her gaze takes in the view outside the window: the white city, sweltering in the noonday heat; the green slopes of the mountains beyond; the cloudless sky. How she hates the sight of it all. Hates the city, with its dazzling new apartment blocks and its broad avenues, filled with monotonous sunlight. Hates the people, with their smiles and their soft language, so different from her own harsh tongue.

The air-conditioning unit by the window blows a jet of stale cold air into her face. It has no smell, this air, and no taste; it is artificial as the city. What she wouldn't give for a breath of real cold – the raw, icy wind that sweeps in across the polders from the North Sea; or the cold you get before the first snowfall of winter, freezing the breath in your lungs and the tears in your eyes.

Her fingers twitch the curtain across, restoring perfect darkness.

She sits and broods, as the feverish child tosses and turns on the bed beside her, her thoughts returning, as they always do, to that other city on the far side of the world. This – the city of her imagination – is a dark city, of narrow streets and tall houses built of blackened brick and grey stone. Its centre is a maze of waterways, connecting five concentric rings of canals. A spider's web, she used to think. Once you were caught it never let you go.

Her first memories were of this place: of the cramped flat above the clockmaker's shop where she was born, and of the view from the window into the street below. There was the baker's shop, with its smells of new bread and its pans of dough set to rise on the great black oven. There was the fishmonger's and the ironmonger's, and old Mijnheer Bloem at the corner, who mended chairs. If you leaned out far enough over the sill, you could glimpse the stepped gables of the fine houses on Prinsengracht and, in the summer, the leafy tops of trees along the canal.

Once her brothers had improvised a cannon out of an old stovepipe, directing it out of this same window to rain coals down on the passers-by. It was worth the beating, Sam said, just to see the looks on their faces. He and Jacob were always in trouble for one thing or another. Fighting with the boys from the Catholic

73

seminary. Breaking windows. Throwing firecrackers in the street.

Of the two, Sam was the ringleader, the fearless one; Jacob the more reserved. It was understood in the family that Sam, as the elder, would eventually take over their father's business – a prospect he regarded with disdain. He had plans to travel, he said – join the navy – anything to get away from this backwater. He wasn't going to end his days as a fucking clockmaker, that was for sure.

Jacob's aspirations, if less caustically expressed, were no less ambitious. Sofie thinks of the day she came home from school to find him at home – perhaps he had been ill, she can't remember now. He was lying curled up in the windowseat, a blanket over his knees. Resting on the blanket was a wooden board, covered with sheets of foolscap. 'Sofie, come here.' Obediently, she had gone to stand beside him. She had tried to see what it was he was doing, but he had covered the flimsy sheets with both his hands.

'Look out there,' he had commanded.

She had looked. Nothing much to see except the familiar street, and Mevrouw Weissmann coming out of the baker's shop.

'Now look at this.'

He had taken his hands away from the paper. And there was Mevrouw Weissmann once more, in her black shawl, with a loaf of bread under her arm – captured for ever by a few strokes of a pencil.

There were other drawings too. Sara Bronsveld, arm in arm with her best friend, Etty Bloem. Hendrik van Rijn, slouching along with his hands in his pockets. Juffrouw Abraham, the schoolteacher, pedalling furiously by on her bicycle.

She had clapped her hands with pleasure at the precision with which he had caught them, these inhabitants of her world: it was magic – no less.

'I'll tell you a secret,' he had told her, growing more expansive in response to her praise. 'I'm going to be an artist. A proper one. At the Academy. Only don't say anything to Father. He'd say it was a waste of time.'

She remembers the way it started. Whispers in the street as you walked home from school. Girls who were once your friends who wouldn't speak any more.

She remembers the day a brick was thrown through the window of her father's shop; boys running away, laughing; her father, muttering to himself, shaking his head, as he stooped to sweep up the glass. She was furious – as much with his acceptance of the crime as with the perpetrators of it. 'Why don't you *do* something?' she'd screamed at his bowed head. 'Go after them . . .'

He'd lifted his eyes from his task. Among the glittering shards at his feet lay the scattered letters of a name, written in faded gold script: she made out 'S', 'i', and 'l' before her vision clouded.

Her father smiled at her. 'Go after them? What for?'

That was it. The sum total of his resistance: *what for?* How she'd despised him for it.

Her mother had been as bad. When their neighbour, Mevrouw de Wit, started throwing her dirty slops over the front stoop and affected deafness when spoken to, her mother had merely sighed. 'Poor woman. She's afraid.'

She would have left it at that, Sofie saw, incensed by such a refusal to be provoked. 'Afraid? Afraid of what? Of *us*?'

Her mother had shrugged and said nothing, her lips compressed, her brows drawn together in a look which had become habitual.

It was the look she was wearing the last time Sofie saw her: a gentle look, of resignation and sadness.

Sofie had been angry with her about something – she can't remember what, she only knows she left home in a rage, almost falling over herself in her fury to be gone, to put as much distance between that house and herself as possible.

She had turned, however. She thanks the God in whom she does not believe that she had turned.

Her mother had been standing there, at the corner, where Weteringstraat ran into Prinsengracht: not making any further move towards her, just looking at her from across the street. Her face so sad, so pale, it seems to Sofie – looking back across the years – as if she must already have known her fate.

Although how could she have known – how could either of them have known what was to follow? I should have known, Sofie thinks now, clenching her fists. I should have stepped back across that gulf and saved her.

All she did, though, was to raise her hand. A slight gesture of valediction; of remorse, perhaps – but one which (she hopes and prays) her mother saw, and understood.

Later that day, when class had been dismissed (the last class; the last day – although she had not known that either), she had been walking home, her usual route along Herengracht towards the Leidsestraat, when she felt someone take her arm. Lena van Wel. Tall, blonde Lena, two years older than her and in her last year at school. They'd played together as kids, of course (Lena's mother and hers had been friends since childhood), but the two girls weren't particularly close. So she'd been all the more puzzled by Lena's sudden friendliness, especially since so many of her other friends had lately been giving her the cold shoulder.

'Don't look surprised or anything,' Lena had said. 'But you can't go home any more. I've come to take you home with me. It's all right. Your mother knows all about it. She arranged it with my mother last time they met . . .'

That was the way it started, her new life. After that day, it was as if the old life had never been. She became Lena's cousin from Dordrecht (an orphan, poor thing), who had come to live with them until things were better. Lena's home became her home; Lena's parents, kind Tante Mieke and Oom Hans, became her parents.

Her own mother and father she never saw again; her brothers – well, maybe she saw them and maybe not. After all these years even Sofie isn't sure.

All she knows is that Sofie Silberman became Sofie van Wel; in fact as well as in deed. Marriage to 'cousin' Piet seemed only another way of securing the connection between the two families – the living and the dead. 'You were meant for each other,' her adopted mother – soon to become her mother-in-law – had told her. 'She would have wanted it so.' 'She' being Sofie's mother – the true, not the fictional one – whose face, after all these years, still reproaches her with its sadness, its forbearance, as she sits in the half-dark of a hospital room in a foreign land with her sleeping child beside her.

At the back of the drawer is a box; it once held Christmas cards. 'Wondrous Night'. 25 cards $1.00. When you care enough to send the very best.

Inside the box are the slides he took that day on the beach. More than forty years ago. It could be yesterday.

She takes them out of the box one by one and holds them up to the light.

A view of the beach: coconut palms, a swathe of blue water, white surf. She doesn't recognize the figure standing with her back to the camera.

A picnic table set up in the shade. Still life with beer bottles, Planter's Peanuts and Lucky Strikes. An orange and white Penguin paperback, its title indecipherable, face down on the table. The open trunk of a red '53 model Chevrolet in the background. Beyond this, a desert landscape.

Two children, a boy and a girl – aged about ten and twelve respectively – staring straight at the camera. Neither is smiling. Their hair is bleached almost white above their sunburnt faces and the eyes of both are a deep blue which looks almost black in the bright sunlight. They might almost be brother and sister, she thinks.

A close-up of a woman sitting in a deck chair. She's wearing a blue swimsuit with an abstract floral pattern, and dark glasses with tortoiseshell frames. She's smiling, but there is tension in her pose. She sits as upright as it is possible to sit, holding her head away from the back of the chair. The arm nearest the camera is pressed against the tubular steel armrest so hard that it leaves a mark on the smooth flesh.

In some of the slides, the colours have faded, leaving only sepia tones and an occasional touch of red (less fugitive than the greens and blues) so that certain things – a woman's lipstick, the metal cap on a Coca-Cola bottle – have acquired a distinctness they did not have at the time.

3

It's half-past five and Jack's on his way to work. He loves this time of day: the sun coming up and the sensation of being the only one around to see it. Watching the sky change from deepest black to purplish-grey growing gradually lighter and lighter until the clouds are as pink as a woman's cheek. The empty red dirt road stretching ahead as far as the eye can see – no one else on the road but himself; the harsh cry of a *cara-cara* intensifying the quiet.

In this country, you were never far from the wilderness – even here, in the heart of the biggest oil operation in the world. You'd be driving along and suddenly it would hit you: you were alone. Nothing but emptiness around you.

He remembers a trip he took into the interior – more than ten years back, it must have been. They'd had reports sent back from El Dorado indicating the presence of mineral deposits and the possibility of oil. People were already saying that if drilling went on the way it was they'd drain Lake Maracaibo dry in twenty years. That, and the rumours that were always flying around about the fabulous seams of bauxite, iron ore – even gold – to be found upcountry, meant that expeditions like this were happening all the time – the company saw to that.

They'd fly you down to Ciudad Bolívar – stopping at Maracay because those little aircraft they had in those days couldn't fly for more than a few hours without refuelling – and then you'd hop another plane to some airstrip in the jungle and then as often as not you'd finish the journey by boat. In those days the only roads were the ones along the coast that went up into the mountains – and even those were often little more than beaten tracks. Jiménez and his programme of public works had made a hell of a difference of course, but there was still a long way to go before this country found its way out of the Dark Ages.

Flying over the jungle was an experience, he had to admit. Looking down from the cockpit of the biplane (Jesus, those things seemed antiquated even then) to see the forest spread out beneath you, an immense living tapestry of every shade of green imaginable, was something he'd never forget. Here and there you'd see mountains breaking the surface, their bare rock summits glowing rose-pink in the early morning light; white ribbons of waterfalls, motionless from this distance; the flash of silver as the light caught the surface of the vast river. It was the landscape Jimmy Angel had seen when he'd found the Falls. The Land That Time Forgot.

If flying in one of those old-fashioned crates was like going back in time, the river journey was even more so. You travelled by dug-out canoe – like something out of the Stone Age. Heading downstream – the river stretching before you like a broad mirror, dense tangled vegetation on either side, the enormous sky. The sound of the oars dipping in and out of the water hypnotic in the stillness. Intense silence – like nothing he'd known before or since. As if the earth held its breath. And that unvarying landscape – water and sky, sky and water. Hours passed. You'd lose track of time. Water and sky. Unchanging, interchangeable elements.

If he's ever been tempted to go back – and there've certainly been offers, over the years – it's memories like this which give him pause. Texas is a desert; there's nothing left for him there. The only people who still remember his name probably think he's dead – or wish him dead, one of the two. Taking one hand off the wheel, Jack takes a cigarette from the pack on the dashboard and lights it. The first smoke of the day is always the best.

It's been light for an hour and the sky is now a pale clear blue above the distant mountains. Last night's rain has flattened the dust on the road and the temperature is still pleasant. Sun warms the back of his neck as he drives with the Chevy's canvas top pushed down to get the air on his face. Flicking ash out of the window, he whistles a snatch of 'Smoke Gets in Your Eyes'.

He's driving along a dirt road with a stretch of cleared jungle to one side – bare rocks and torn-up trees and the criss-crossed tracks left by earth-moving equipment – and a mangrove swamp on the other. Above the tangle of vegetation the silver skeletons of offshore drilling rigs flash in the early morning light. A chainlink fence marks the perimeter of the site, with a sign on it which says NO UNAUTHORIZED PERSONNEL. He honks the Chevy's horn and Pepe comes out to open the gates, a cigarette hanging from his lower lip as if stuck there with glue.

Jack thanks him with a wave of his hand and drives on, along a road whose surface is made of crude oil poured on sand and gravel – a rudimentary asphalt. He drives past the cluster of corrugated-iron sheds and wooden huts which house the electrical generators and compressors, and the sheds for the winching machinery and pumping equipment, until he reaches the lines of eighty-four-foot steel towers, cylindrical storage tanks and sprawling pipelines which make up Campo La Rosa.

This isn't the largest camp in the Maracaibo basin – that distinction belongs to Lagunillas, on the eastern side of the lake – but it has been one of the most productive, in its time. The famous blow-out of '22, when 100,000 barrels of crude oil spurted out of the earth with the force of a geyser, is still talked about. Of late, output has fallen off a lot – of La Rosa's 800 wells, only a handful are still in use. They'll close it down in a year or two, Jack thinks – unless the prospecting boys strike lucky.

He parks the car in the only spot of shade available and walks across the wide stretch of asphalt which already shimmers with heat haze to the office building. As he draws nearer he sees that someone is waiting for him, leaning against the wall with his hands in his pockets as if the bastard hadn't a care in the world. Luis Saez, of course – who else?

'*Buenos días*, Luis. *Cómo estás?*'

'*Muy bien, señor.*'

Luis is short and heavy-set – a typical Maracucho – with the broad features and jet-black hair of the *mestizo*. His family, Jack recalls, are from one of the villages on the far side of the lake. Sinamaica lagoon. He'd been there a couple of times – the last was a year ago. He'd taken the kid along for the ride. Vivienne had been worried it might be too much for her, but she'd loved every minute of it.

An hour's boat ride through the mangrove swamps, where tangled roots reared up from the water taller than a man and sunlight fell through the interlaced branches of trees so tall you couldn't see the tops, was to find yourself in another world, another time almost. People living the way they had before the Spanish conquest: in flimsy huts made from papyrus mats sewn together and thatched with palm leaves, perched out over the water on stilts. Duckboards ran between those of the houses which were built close enough together, but some of them could be reached only by boat. As they steered their way between the boardwalks, the sound of their outboard motor loud in the intense quiet, naked kids in fishing boats gazed at them with big dark eyes. A woman, very young and very pregnant, turned from hanging out her washing to watch them go by.

Sure, these people knew about progress, said their guide. Look – they even had a petrol station. And sure enough, there was the familiar sign – yellow shell on scarlet ground – above the tin shack with the twin petrol pumps perched on a jetty built out over the water, as if any other form of architecture were unthinkable in such a place.

Luis had left all that behind him now. He had a brand-new bungalow in the workers' quarters. Drove a brand-new pick-up truck. All of it courtesy of the company. Perhaps he needs reminding of that, Jack thinks.

'So what's new?' he asks with studied unconcern. Luis's visits to his office generally mean trouble, in his experience. As well as being the site foreman, Luis is also the local union representative. What'll it be today, Jack wonders – complaints about the food in the staff canteen; or demands for an increased productivity bonus?

In fact, it's worse than he'd anticipated. The men are refusing to work at all, Luis tells him. Half of them haven't even showed up this morning.

'What the hell's it all about?' Jack tries unsuccessfully to suppress his impatience at the leisurely way Luis is getting around to tell him all this, as if they had all the time in the world. Whereas the truth is – Goddammit – they're losing money with every second.

Luis gives a pained shrug. 'A man calls another man by his name, *señor*. He – the second man – becomes very sick. He has fever. He thinks he will die. And now the men refuse to work with the other man.'

Jack holds up his hands. 'OK, OK. This first guy called the other guy a bad name . . .'

'His real name, *señor* . . .'

'I don't get it.'

'All the Guajiro are the same,' Luis says indifferently. 'They have a real name and another one – a Spanish name. That's the name you use . . .'

'Like Luis, for example . . .'

'*Sí, señor* – like Luis. You don't tell a man your Guajiro name, because then he has power over you. Very bad luck to call a man by his real name . . .'

'You mean like the evil eye?'

'*Sí, señor.*'

Jack groans aloud. 'So because some crazy Indian thinks some other crazy Indian put the evil eye on him I've got a fuckin' strike on my hands. Jesus H. Christ.'

Luis stands with his hat in his hands, placidly awaiting orders. Jack flings himself into his chair and rips the seal off a new pack of Luckies. He offers one to Luis. The two men gravely consider the situation. Nothing stirs in the little office except the blades of the ceiling fan, endlessly stirring the air into sluggish currents.

From the window opposite his desk Jack can see out over the site, with its converging parallel lines of towers, its unwavering light. Men in hard hats and coveralls – fewer of them, he observes with hindsight, than he might otherwise expect to see at this hour in the morning – stand around in uneasy groups. As if nothing could be further from their thoughts than the business of getting oil out of the ground.

'So whaddya think it'll take?' he says at last.

Luis is all polite incomprehension. '*Señor?*'

'Health insurance? Free glasses? A subscription to *Reader's Digest* ? Find out what they want and let's get them back to work . . .'

'*Sí, señor.*'

'I don't have to tell you,' Jack goes on, 'what losing even half a day's production could end up costing the company . . .'

Luis says nothing, but his face shows he is paying attention.

'That means you and me, pal. Because that's what we are,' Jack says, exhaling a mouthful of smoke. 'Company men, through and through. Ain't that the truth?'

Luis's shrug is almost imperceptible – no more than a slight spreading of the hands, a hitching of the shoulders. The gesture is not lost on Jack, however.

'You know what that means, don't you, Luis, ol' buddy? It means the company owns us, body and soul. It means everything we do, we do because of the company. And for the company, you might as well say, oil. The roads we drive on are made of oil. The gasoline we use to drive. The electric light we use – and that includes the electric light in that fancy new place of yours – is powered by oil. The food we eat is cooked on gas from the wells . . .' He pauses, takes another drag. 'I could say more, but I don't have to, do I?'

'No, *señor*.' There is a submissiveness in the man's demeanour now; his gaze is fixed on the floor.

'Good.' Jack smiles. 'I'm gonna walk over to the canteen in fifteen minutes for a cup of coffee. When I get out there, I don't wanna see anyone standing around lookin' as if they got nuthin' to do – *comprendes?*'

He's walking without haste across the yard to the site canteen, secure in the knowledge that everything is now running according to schedule, when he sees Piet van Wel heading towards him, his hat down low over his eyes to shield them from the glare of the sun.

'Hey,' says Jack. 'How's it goin', fella?'

Piet smiles. 'Very good,' he says. 'The men went back to work, no trouble.'

'Glad to hear it,' says Jack. 'Keep an eye on the situation, will ya? Easy for this kind of thing to get out of hand if you don't stamp on it fast.'

'Sure thing,' says Piet.

He makes a move to go, but Jack detains him. He likes this serious young Dutchman, with his angular face and his no-colour hair. He's watched him at work a couple of times and liked what he saw. The man has the makings of a good engineer – and in Jack's book, that means a lot. They are of much the same height – Piet is taller, if anything – but Jack is the heavier build, his broad shoulders and muscular torso giving him the physical edge over the younger man.

'And how's the family?' Jack asks. 'Everything OK?'

Piet smiles. 'Everything's fine,' he says. 'The little one is much better. The doctor says in a week, maybe two, she can go back to school.'

'Terrific,' says Jack. 'And your wife – how's she settling in?'

The other looks startled. A flicker of something like alarm crosses his face. 'She's OK,' he replies guardedly.

'That's good,' says Jack. 'Because I know it takes some people a while to adjust. Coming from Europe an' all. It's a shock to the system . . .'

Piet says nothing, his gaze shifting away as if he would rather be somewhere else. But Jack, it seems, is in no particular hurry.

'Take me, for example,' he says. 'First few months out here I got drunk just about every night. Nothin' else *to* do. Somethin' about this place drives people a little bit crazy. It's the heat, I guess . . .'

'I guess,' echoes Piet.

'Well,' says Jack. 'Nice talkin' to ya. Drop by for a drink sometime, why doncha? Vivienne'd like that . . .'

'OK.' A brief smile flashes across Piet's face. 'Sure thing.'

Nice guy, Jack thinks, watching him walk away, his shadow bobbing and weaving beside him. If you could only get him to loosen up a little. Some could make the transition, some couldn't. This country took people in all kinds of different ways.

Arriving in '38, Jack thought it the most beautiful place he'd ever seen. That first sight of the coastline, blue in the distance, then – as the ship drew nearer – the shore, with its white sand, its windswept palms. Beyond it, the green sweep of hills, rising towards the thunderheads. After the arid border town where he was raised, it seemed a vision of paradise. He hadn't known green could be that green. And mountains. Jesus Christ. He'd seen mountains – Mexico was full of damn volcanoes – but these . . . these were something else. Out of this world.

Joining the boat at Puerto Rico was a group of Dutch brides, on the last stage of their journey to Curaçao, where they were to meet the men they had married by proxy before leaving their native country. He remembered their cries of amazement, as they crowded on deck for a first sight of land. Most of them were city girls, whose idea of untamed wilderness had been limited, until that moment, to the flat fields of north Holland; confronted with such a landscape, most of them could only stare, and wonder what kind of place their brave presumption had brought them to.

He'd been here fifteen years – not counting those few months cooling his heels in Texas in '42, when he was trying to enlist, and they told him at pushing thirty he'd be of more use doing essential war work back in the oil fields – but he'd never forgotten that moment. As he'd stood there on deck looking out at the world he had come so far to find, his eyes had filled with tears, so that he'd had to pretend he'd gotten a speck in one. Stupid, really – but what he'd felt that day was exactly like falling in love. People said that, didn't they, talking about places? And he for one could understand how it could happen – becoming as obsessed with a country as you did about a woman. The difference was you never lost your feeling for a place.

*

Waiting for Manuela to bring his coffee he lights up a cigarette. His thoughts turn – as they can't help turning – to the reproachful, unhappy figure of his wife. His sweet Vivienne. What was it she wanted from him, exactly? What did any of them want? If you made it a lifetime's study – and God knows, he'd tried harder than some – you'd never find out the answer to *that* one. Women. Love 'em or leave 'em alone – and one thing was for sure, he wasn't about to do that.

Sure, he'd done some bad things in his time – things he'd have to answer for on Judgement Day – if there was any truth in all that, which personally he doubted – but hell, he'd had a lot of fun. And if he found himself headed for a hotter place than this, while the rest of them were joining the queue for the pearly gates, he'd say it had all been worth it. At least he'd had his taste of heaven on earth. That was the thing they didn't understand, the women – all the ones he'd ever come across anyhow. You only came this way once. The least you could do was to have a good time. It was a sin not to.

He sees himself as he was a few months ago, sitting in a bar in downtown Caracas, raising a glass to his lips. Ahhh. Liquid fire, so cool it made your eyes burn; then the raw heat as it hit your stomach. Hot music playing – the kind he likes. A woman singing, and that sweet sad sound of muted trumpets. Saxophone. Jazz piano.

Around him, waiters are running from table to table with orders – *Señor! Señor!* – the bartender in his scarlet jacket is polishing up the glasses. Behind him, the big gilt mirror over the bar reflects the up-ended bottles of Bell's and Gordon's and Cacique, and the men laying bets on the big fight tonight, and the pretty women in ridiculous little hats glancing sideways at their reflected selves.

Life's not so bad, all things considered, he remembers thinking. To be here, in this place, his favourite spot in all the city, with money in his pocket and the night ahead. What more could any man ask?

That woman's voice. So harsh and pure it could break your heart.

It stirs a memory – the way only music can – of a place and a time. A girl he'd known in one of the bush camps – San Cristóbal was it, or La Dorada? – the back of beyond, that much was for sure. A dirt road slashed through the jungle and when you got there nothing but a few huts. The bunkhouse where the men lived. Jesus what a dump. Nothing to do on a Saturday night except hitch a ride to the *bodega*. That was where he saw her first. What was her name again? La Paloma. Skinny little thing, not much to look at – but a voice like an angel's. Clear as a bell, but with a kind of catch in it as if she were about to cry.

Those nights in the *bodega* – what a time they'd had. It wasn't much of a place – just a shack with a tin roof on which the rain rattled like hailstones, a bunch of broken-down tables and chairs and a bar selling cheap beer and the worst rum you've ever tasted – but it felt like home. He and the boys – Red McIntyre, Hank Green, Babe Zelinski and Paddy O'Dare – sitting at their favourite corner table, playing blackjack and drinking rye. *I drink to the health of Colonel Puff, Puff, Puff* . . . Ceiling fans whirring, cigarette smoke spiralling into a blue haze and the night sounds of the jungle drifting in through the open door. And then one of the Maracuchos would pick up a guitar and start picking out a tune, and somebody else would join in on the maracas and then that little girl would get up and start to sing.

What was that song she liked so much? Something about love. All those songs were about love. 'Nuestro Amor Fue Una Guerra'. How did it go again?

> Tu me humillaste
> Me provocaste hasta que me reventara
> Fuiste tan cruel
> Lo que hizo el otro
> En mí la tomaste cara
> No olvides hombre
> Que lo que se hace se paga . . .

One day you'll have to pay for everything . . . He can see her now, standing there in that old red dress, with her black hair hanging down her back and her arms spread wide as if to embrace a lover. Sobbing out words of pain and despair and passionate reproach, so that you'd almost believe she meant them. Then when the song was over, she'd waltz over to your table and bum a cigarette.

One night in '40 – no, it must have been '41, because they'd just heard the US was getting into the war and he'd been celebrating – he and the girl had ended up in bed together. He'd had a fight with his regular girl, Elvira, and La Paloma had offered him a shoulder to cry on. She wasn't a looker, Paloma, but she could sing all right, and she was a great dancer. She wasn't so bad between the sheets, either, even though she was so skinny it hurt to look at her – no tits at all and legs like Bambi. She must have been no more than sixteen. Funny little kid. He wonders briefly what happened to her.

And now the thunder, murmuring all day at the periphery, moves in closer. The humidity is intense. On the sidewalk in front of where he sits, overlooking the square with its dusty palms and its statue of El Libertador, the women stroll up and down, swaying their hips in lazy rhythm; passing the time of day. One peels off her white cotton gloves to fan herself, casting dark glances all around as she does so. Beads of sweat on her short upper lip; a smell of warm flesh and stale perfume rising from the front of her dress. Another offers him the ghost of a smile from under her broad-brimmed straw hat.

Overhead the ceiling fan barely stirs the warm air. Thunder. A flicker of lightning along the distant ridge. The city lies in a ring of mountains, like a pearl in a cupped hand. Everything good that's ever happened to him and a lot that was bad has happened to him here.

His glass is empty. He clicks his fingers, but already the attentive boy is at his side.

Por favor.

Whisky splashes like molten gold into the glass. A tiny sea, encircling an island of ice. He lifts the glass, and in the same moment a thunderclap rattles the rooftiles overhead. Women shriek and run for cover. At once the room is full of people.

The dark girl with the Panama hat and her plump little sidekick hesitate in the doorway. The dark girl fingers the string of cheap pearls at her throat, her eyes searching the crowded bar as if for a friend.

He stands up, indicating the vacant seats at his table.

Won't you join me, ladies?

The answering look in the dark eyes. The red curve of a smile. She looks away, then returns his gaze. Her friend still isn't sure. A murmured consultation ensues.

94

Panama frowns, then laughs, her mind apparently made up. She sits down at the table, languidly crossing her long slim legs. Miss Prim follows suit, with a bad grace.

You are too kind.

A low voice, only slightly accented. A secretary, perhaps? Or somebody's mistress. Small pretty hands, with painted nails. Beautiful eyes. Spanish blood, he thinks, with maybe a touch of Indian in the narrow slant of the eyelids, the high cheekbones.

How about a drink?

He summons the waiter, who stands, notepad at the ready, head sardonically cocked, while the girls make up their minds. Panama, at least, knows what she wants.

Whisky-soda, por favor.

He orders another for himself and, after a moment's further prevarication, a sarsaparilla for her friend. Then, choosing his moment (the crackle of electricity already in the air between them), he leans across the table towards his guests.

What brings you two ladies out on a night like this?

They've just knocked off work, they tell him. They're sisters, it seems. And now he comes to look at it, the resemblance is there, if only in the narrowness of eyes, the breadth of forehead beneath the low fringe of coarse black hair. But whereas in one sister the configuration spells beauty, in the other, the effect is merely of a certain pugnacity, which manifests itself also in the heaviness around her jaw, the faint shadow of a moustache on her upper lip.

Beauty's name (elicited after a show of bashfulness) is Angelina. A good name for her, with her air of slightly bruised innocence. The lazy way she glances at him, sidelong through her lashes, as if the effort of opening her eyes any wider is just too much. Sister, less fortuitously, is called Rosalita. She works as a clerk in a government office, filing letters all day for one of Jiménez's boys; perhaps, unwillingly, going to bed with the boss when one of the prettier secretaries can't be had. She says this – *I work for the government* – with a little toss of the head, as if to establish once and for all her right to a certain respect – even from one of his kind.

Angelina's a mannequin, for one of the big department stores downtown. All day she models the latest styles in cocktail dresses and afternoon frocks for the benefit of rich Americanos and their women. Demure in her neat black work dress, her eyes downcast, taking the proffered gowns; vanishing behind the velvet curtain, to emerge, after an interval, transformed. Society hostess in rustling taffeta, or a vamp in oyster satin. The client (some big shot from Standard Oil, wanting something cute to take home to his wife) sits up with a bang on his flimsy gilt chair, eyes popping at the sight of all that pearly flesh on view in the low-cut gown. That swaying walk. *I'll take it. Wrap it up.*

Jack can just see it. He grins to himself. Glancing up, he meets the cold eye of Big Sister. Politely, he offers her another drink – something stronger, perhaps? She declines.

We have to go, she says abruptly. The bus leaves in ten minutes.

Angelina shrugs. She's in no hurry, she says. If they miss one bus, they can get another. Over her sister's shoulder, she catches Jack's eye and smiles. When he escorts her to the bus stop later that night, he has her telephone number in his pocket, scrawled on the back of an empty pack of Luckies.

That was six months ago. Jack stubs out his cigarette in the saucer of his empty coffee cup and slips a *bolívar* under the rim for Manuela. Six months of meetings, which take place in Angelina's apartment in Caracas and occur as often as he can contrive a reason to visit the city. Six months of partings – which are frequently stormy and accompanied by tears on Angelina's part and promises he has no intention of keeping on his. The funny thing is, when he's with her, he almost believes the lies. I'll always love you. I'll never leave you. I'll never love anyone but you.

Vivienne and Jack are the perfect couple: everybody says so. 'Oh *you*,' Sylvia Riley is given to saying, 'you two are just too perfect for words. You with your perfect looks. And Jack . . . so perfectly *Jack*. You're probably still in love. It's almost indecent in a married couple . . .'

Vivienne knows she is lucky. Jack is all she could want in a man. Strong, successful, unassailable: a protector. She smiles at the old-fashioned word, with its overtones of Victorian liaisons, but it sums up how she feels. With Jack she feels safe; provided for. Protected.

She thinks of the first time they met. It was at the club, her first week out. New Year's Eve. He'd been leaning on the bar, a drink in his hand, saying something to Frank Riley and she'd walked in and he'd turned and their eyes had met, like that moment in *Casablanca* . . . No, it hadn't been like that at all. What had happened was that Frank had seen her and waved her over to join them, and it was while they were talking that she'd realized Jack was watching her, and Frank must have picked up that he was interested too, because he'd said, 'Do you two know each other?'

And then he had introduced them, and she had smiled at Jack and said she was pleased to meet him.

'My pleasure,' Jack said, with a warmth in his voice that awakened a response – a visceral shiver – she had thought dead and buried.

Every time she'd looked at him she'd found he was looking at her. So she stopped looking at him, contenting herself with the information gained in those first few seconds: that he was tall, dark, sunburnt (as everyone here was, except herself), and that he was attractive without being, strictly speaking, handsome. Not that she minded – she liked a face with character; a face which said its owner had lived a bit. Jack struck her as the sort of man who knew his way around. A man of the world, her mother would have said. He was certainly charming. Americans were like that. Direct – in a way that would have seemed familiar if not actually rude coming from anyone else, but which somehow they got away with.

They had spoken of this and that – she can't, now, remember exactly what; her plans for the school, perhaps – and then Jack had glanced at his watch. 'Hell's bells, is that the time? I'm late for the poker game. Nice to meet you, Mrs Thompson. I'll see *you* later –' this was to Frank – 'you old son-of-a-gun.' And then, turning, as if the thought had just occurred to him, 'You'll be at the party tonight, won't you, Mrs Thompson?' And when she'd said no, she had no one to go with, he'd said that was lucky, because he didn't have a date either. 'Tell you what – why don't I pick you up at eight? That is, if there's nothing you'd rather do . . .'

And she'd said no, she had no other plans, and yes,

she'd like that very much, and he'd nodded and said, 'Fine.'

'He's a fast worker, I'll give him that,' Frank had said, as they watched Jack make his way towards the door. 'Are you sure you'll be all right?'

And she had laughed and said, 'Don't worry. I'm a big girl now. I can take care of myself . . .'

At the time she had believed it, thinking herself very much the sophisticate – a widow of thirty, with a child to care for – although beside some of them, Sylvia Riley for instance, she must have seemed hopelessly naïve. As, indeed, she was. The few brief weeks of her marriage to Ralph, followed by the long blank of her widowhood, hardly constituted much of an amorous career.

She remembers those months in the summer of 1940, during which she and Ralph had been stationed together at Grantham. Then their honeymoon, and the few times he'd been home on leave after that. Amounting to no more than a handful of days. No time at all, if you thought about it.

Ralph had been little more than a boy himself when they had married – two years older than she was; and she, at twenty, was as innocent about sex as – well, as someone of Antonia's age. More so, probably; children nowadays knew everything – whereas she, growing up in the years between the wars, had enjoyed what her own mother would have described as a 'sheltered' childhood.

Sheltered. The word conjures up an image of the suburban haven in which she had grown up, with its spacious mock-Tudor houses – the height of modernity in 1926, the year her parents moved from London – 'to be nearer the country', her mother said. The large square gardens of the houses in Sandymount Road were planted with lilac and laburnum, their lawns crisply rolled into stripes, their flowerbeds filled with those orderly blooms beloved of the middle classes: lobelia, hollyhocks, dahlias and antirrhinums.

If she closes her eyes she can see it all, just as it was.

Her mother standing in the open French windows, in what now seems an improbably short skirt, her hand shielding her eyes. *Girls! Where are you? It's time for tea* . . . She and Sylvia-next-door hiding in the rhododendrons, stifling their laughter, trying not to make a sound. And then – a later memory – cycling to the tennis club, past woods full of bluebells, and Sylvia stopping out of sight of the house to rub Sno-Fire on her cheeks, in case Madge Baker's brother was on the courts that day.

Summer's evenings in Carshalton Beeches (in her memories, it is always summer): shadows lengthening, swifts skimming low over the grass, the soft *plunk* of tennis balls against racquets and the sickly sweet smell of hawthorn blossom hanging over the gardens. Perfect summers. People said, didn't they, that the summer before the war was the best of all? She was just nineteen. Too young to know much about life. She'd had to learn soon enough, though. She sees herself in memory leaving the house. Turning along the unadopted road which led to the coppice (ditches filled with cow parsley; midges dancing in the air) to where someone was waiting for her in the gathering dusk . . .

I've got my call-up papers.

When do you leave?

Next week.

Oh, my God . . .

We could get married. That is, if you wanted to . . .

Had that been Ralph? No, they hadn't met until

Grantham, a year later. Perhaps, after all, her memory was playing her false. Writing scenes which had never happened – at least, not to her; borrowing characters and situations from books she'd read, or films she'd seen.

Must you go? We've had so little time . . .

That had been real enough – the situation, if not the words. There had been so little time. You could hardly call it a marriage, more a series of brief encounters. Sad farewells on station platforms. A walk along a winter beach. Boarding houses and hotel rooms.

On her wedding night she had learned what being 'sheltered' meant. It was simply another way of describing ignorance. She lay there, rigid with shock, as he wept and begged her to forgive him. He was a brute, he said. How she must despise him. On the wall at the foot of the bed was a framed text, worked in cross-stitch. *Thy Will Be Done*. From downstairs came the sound of crashing crockery and a smell of burning.

All that night she had been unable to close her eyes. Ralph was a restless sleeper; each time he stirred, she felt her whole body stiffen with remembered outrage. It amazed her that she, who had never shared a room, much less a bed, with anyone, should have so casually contracted to spend the rest of her nights beside this relative stranger. What did she know of him, after all? That he was tall and slim, with brown hair and blue eyes. That he preferred his tea black – an astonishing aberration, in her mother's view – and that he had a scar on his chin where a cricket ball had struck him.

Towards morning, he had cried out in his sleep. Muffled, incoherent words whose sense she could not decipher. She had stretched out her hand to break his dream; touching him, she had felt the stirrings of tenderness. He had turned to her, still half-asleep, and taken her in his arms. After that it had been all right.

Ralph called her his angel, his dearest girl. He carried her picture next to his heart, a talisman.

For a time, at least, the talisman seemed to have worked. Over the next year he'd flown more than thirty missions, from which his plane had sometimes been the only one to return. Once he'd lost his entire crew and had landed the crate single-handed, blacking out from sheer exhaustion at the controls. Another time he'd brought her down with the wings on fire. He'd been lucky to get out of that scrape alive.

The luck of the devil, his chums in the squadron called it; Ralph knew better. It was his guardian angel, he said, who kept him from harm. When he was up there in the sky with the bullets whistling all around him, he had only to think of his angel and he'd feel safe as houses.

With the average life expectancy for pilots of Lancasters being what it was, it was hardly surprising one became superstitious, Vivienne thinks, entrusting one's safety to a good-luck charm or a photograph.

So that when the telegram came, informing her of Ralph's presumed death, a part of her felt that she was responsible; that she had, in fact, caused it – not deliberately, of course, but through some fatal inattention. All those nights she had prayed for him, holding the image of him in her mind as if by sheer force of will she could keep his plane airborne, could shield him from destruction. Now she wondered – she knew it was nonsense, but still – whether anything she had said or done might have made a difference.

She remembers as if it were yesterday the night it happened. She was pregnant then, of course; although she hadn't known it. She'd been at the theatre with Sylvia – they'd had tickets for *Dangerous Corner*. An incendiary had fallen in the street outside – she remembers the juddering shock of its impact; the sensation that time had momentarily stopped. All around her in the crowded auditorium people were screaming and fighting their way to the exits. She'd stayed where she was, too numb with surprise to move; her terror translated into a strange calm – as if a wall of glass lay between her and the others.

It was only later, when the all-clear had sounded, that she gave in to her fear. So white and trembling at the thought of what has passed that Sylvia was quite concerned for her – asking her if anything was the matter, and if perhaps she'd missed her period that month. She remembers the relief she felt as the truth of Sylvia's observation hit her. That had to be it. All the signs had been there all along; she had simply failed to interpret them correctly. She wondered what Ralph would say when she told him the news.

Crossing Waterloo Bridge to get the last train home, she'd felt as if she were walking on air. The worst that could have happened had happened – and had left her unscathed, it seemed. Above the burning city the sky was flooded orange and rose: a false dawn. Flames from blazing warehouses along Bankside were reflected in the water, so that the river itself seemed on fire. She had never seen it look so beautiful.

How happy she'd been that night – how little intimation she had had of what was to follow. At the same time – perhaps the very moment – she had been celebrating her good fortune, Ralph had been about to die, or was already dead. She wonders now if it had been simply this – the shifting of her attention from her husband's safety to that of her unborn child – which had made his plane falter in the air for just that split second which would bring it within range of enemy fire.

Those long drab years of the war during which, after her marriage, she had moved back to Carshalton – the sheltered world grown suddenly threadbare, its lawns and flowerbeds turned over to vegetable production, its once well-stocked larders now empty of all but the most basic fare. Lying once more in her old bedroom, the child asleep in the cot beside her, she had watched the early light come filtering through the curtains with their familiar pattern of roses, and wondered where her life had gone.

The meagreness, the dullness of those years seem beyond belief to her now. Interminable evenings in the vast, dark sitting room (made darker still by black-out curtains), while her mother darned socks or turned sheets in a never-ending demonstration of make-do and mend, dropping remarks into the silence about what the vicar's wife had said at the WVS meeting, and the possibility that Mrs Carmichael's Freddy (home on leave; a squadron leader) might like to make up a foursome at bridge.

Leaden hours after supper, when there was nothing her mother thought worth listening to on the wireless, and Vivienne sat swallowing one yawn after another, looking forward to the moment when she could escape to bed. Above them in the night sky men were fighting and dying; they might as well have been dead themselves she thought. In the shadowy room with its once stylish furniture grown imperceptibly out of date, the clock ticked on the mantelpiece and the gas flickered in the grate, and her father read out extracts from the *Telegraph* about Mr Churchill's latest speech or the army's latest victory in the desert.

The most excitement she could hope for was the chance to go up to town to meet Sylvia – now married and settled in Surrey, with a baby a few months older than Antonia. Tea at Lyons Corner House, followed by a visit to the flicks, to see *Gone With the Wind* (Sylvia's favourite) or *Dangerous Moonlight* (hers). Once she had spent the evening with Sylvia and Sylvia's husband, Frank, who was home on leave, and a man from Frank's battalion whose name she now forgets. A Welsh name, she thinks. Hughes or Pugh. She remembers his thick black hair, glossy with Brylcreem, and the bluish look of his close-shaven jaw.

They had gone to Rules, because Frank said he must have some decent beef, after the muck they put up with in the officers' mess, and had managed to get a table in one of the booths. Hughes had been sitting beside her – too close, she remembers thinking – and every time she moved away a little, he shifted closer. Half-way through the soup course, she'd felt his hand on her knee; she'd pushed it away but after a minute or two it returned, like a persistent animal.

As a single woman who had once been married, Vivienne found she had acquired an ambiguous status. Modesty and shyness – qualities desirable in a virgin – were deemed inappropriate in a matron. There was even a suggestion, from one or two of the men whose advances she rejected, that there was something unpatriotic about such prudishness. Vivienne took to dressing in sombre colours and cut her long blonde pageboy short. She had already decided she would not marry again.

A year or so after the war ended, Vivienne took her daughter to visit the war memorial at Runnymede. It was a beautiful autumn day; the sun was shining, and the leaves on the aspens lining the perimeter flashed gold and silver against the intense blue. Starting at the beginning of the alphabet, they walked the length of the great marble wall on which the names of the dead were inscribed, until, nearing the end, they reached the place. Here she found the name she had come to find and, with the fingers of her ungloved hand, traced the letters one by one.

It was while she was doing her teaching practice – she had qualified the previous year – that she received a letter from Sylvia. After the war, Frank Riley had gone back to his old job at Shell; he and Sylvia had been posted to Venezuela in '47. 'It's a wonderful country, darling – you really should come out,' Sylvia wrote. 'The climate's marvellous, and there are heaps of lovely bachelors just waiting to be snapped up. I've even found you a job (details enclosed) . . .'

The headmaster of the school where Vivienne had been doing her teaching practice was a widower with three boys. He had made it clear to her that a permanent position was available, if she wanted it. Vivienne, think-ing of the boys, was aware that she might be required to fill a more than professional role. But good jobs were not easy to come by, and there was Antonia's future to consider . . .

She had the letter of acceptance already written out; all she had to do was address the envelope. As she reached for her pen, her hands shaking a little with the enormity of what she was about to do, she knocked the bottle of ink across the table, and a great tear-shaped swathe of blue spread over the surface, like the map of an unfamiliar country.

When she had cleared up the mess and thrown the spoiled pages in the wastepaper bin, she took a fresh sheet, picked up her pen and began a letter to Sylvia.

They'd sailed from Plymouth on a bitter cold day in December, with everything shrouded in fog. She remembers the wet green fields rushing past the train window; her mother fretting about the luggage. *Where's that porter? Drat the man! I suppose he'll want a shilling for his trouble* ... Her father had seen them on board. Looking around dubiously at the tiny cabin. *You'll be all right, old thing?* And then, embarrassed, handing her an envelope. *Just a little something for expenses. Only wish it were more. Little secret between ourselves. No need to mention it to your mother* ...

She remembers the faces – her parents' among them – of the people standing on the dock: white shapes above a sombre mass of coats. The long, mournful wail of the ship's siren, as the boat began to move away from shore. A flurry of handkerchiefs from the watching crowd. Faces gradually blurring, slipping into obscurity. Antonia clutching her hand. *Goodbye, goodbye* ...

The crossing had taken two weeks. Cabin class on the *Santa María*, calling at Lisbon and Puerto Rico. The ship was a pre-war liner, requisitioned as a troop carrier at the start of hostilities, which still betrayed signs of this previous function. For while the upper decks and lounges had been repainted in peacetime shades of eau-de-Nil and cream, the lower decks where the third-class cabins were – all she could afford on her widow's pension

– remained a utilitarian battleship grey. Lying awake at night in the narrow bunk, with Antonia asleep in the one below, she sometimes thought she could hear, beneath the crashing waves, the hurrying tread of soldiers' feet in the corridors.

They had been at sea three days when the heavy Atlantic swell which had laid them both low with seasickness gave way to calmer seas. One day they had gone to bed in foul weather, the next they'd risen to blue skies, a warm breeze smelling of orange blossom, fishing boats casting their nets off the coast of Spain.

As they neared the tropics the mood of their fellow passengers, like the climate, took a turn for the better. Those who'd stared coldly through one at dinner or nodded a curt 'Good morning' as they passed by on deck now displayed a less daunting exterior. Smiles and small civilities were exchanged over the breakfast kippers. *Fine day, isn't it? Oh yes, rather* . . . Brief romances flared and died under the wheeling stars.

A red-haired accountant from Basildon asked Vivienne to dance three times in a row at the Captain's Ball and then told her to call him Raymond. A clergyman named Woods introduced her to his mother over tea in the second-class lounge. And at the party held to celebrate Crossing the Line, as people in funny hats waltzed on deck and a group of pie-eyed marine engineers jumped fully clothed in the swimming pool, a man whose name she never got around to asking told her the story of his life.

Those first weeks in Venezuela were heaven – there was no other word for it, Vivienne felt. It seemed as if all her prayers had been answered at once.

For the first time in her life, she felt truly grown up: a woman of independent means, she said, describing this feeling to Sylvia. *I suppose it beats being a kept woman, darling*, Sylvia had replied. But even her married friend's cynicism couldn't spoil Vivienne's pleasure in her new life.

She loved the neat little bungalow that went with the job and she loved the job itself. The newly built school building, with its smells of raw plaster and fresh paint and its incongruously old-fashioned desks. The piles of unused exercise books in their buff-paper covers. The children's faces turning towards her as she walked into the room.

'Oh, you must meet Mrs Thompson. She's doing such wonders with the school,' people said, introducing her at parties. In a community whose population was evenly divided between married couples with school-age children and unmarried men, her new-found status was a passport to social success, it seemed.

'You know what?' Jack said that first evening when he came to collect her. 'You remind me of a teacher I once had. Miss Feeney. In seventh grade. Boy, did I have a crush on that woman. I guess she just about broke my heart . . .'

And Vivienne, recognizing a line when she heard it, replied that he must have been forward for his age.

'Why, not at all,' he'd told her, settling her wrap around her shoulders so deftly that his touch barely grazed the skin. 'I just knew a good thing when I saw it. Still do, as a matter of fact . . .'

Whether it was the effect of the champagne she'd been drinking, or the excitement of being in a strange place, or the fact that a new decade was starting – or a combination of all these things – but that night she'd felt almost delirious with happiness. As if nothing and nobody could hurt her. What was that song the band had been playing? They'd danced to it over and over again. 'My Blue Heaven'. A silly thing really; but for days afterwards, she hadn't been able to get it out of her mind.

She remembers those first few weeks of their marriage. The summer of 1950. How happy they'd been. Making love in the long, drowsy afternoons, the warm breeze blowing the long gauze curtains back into the room and that golden light. Lying there with Jack, her legs curled around his, her face resting against his shoulder breathing in his smell; too lazy and drunk with pleasure to move.

She'd lie beside him on the white bed stripped of all but its sheet in the white room beneath the revolving ceiling fan, her fingers idly playing with the dark hairs on his chest as she gazed into his face, trying to read what was written there. If she'd had enough time, she might have been able to work it out; but there never was enough time.

Sooner or later, she'd feel him stir, and know his mind was elsewhere. Already preoccupied with the demands of the outside world. His world, not hers – she couldn't help resenting it. After a while, she'd feel him shift position. Disturbing their perfect equilibrium.

Baby, I gotta go.

And she'd wind her arms around his neck saying, *Don't go yet. Stay a little while longer. We've all the time in the world . . .*

He'd sigh and shake his head, but his hands would already be exploring her body. *You know my trouble,* he'd murmur, *I can never say no to a lady* . . . Kissing her closed eyes, her mouth, her throat, her breasts. Moving inside her: she knew then what people meant when they called it being possessed.

Her mother had been horrified when she heard her new son-in-law was an American – a fact her letter did not attempt to conceal. *I must say I was surprised at your news. Are you sure you know what you're doing?*

Vivienne's mother had a low opinion of foreigners. *I hope he won't expect you to go back with him to Texas. It doesn't sound at all a suitable life* . . .

Vivienne had found these remarks amusing enough at the time. *Jack's quite civilized, you know*, she had written back. *He's even been known to dress for dinner* . . .

Now she wonders if her mother might have known something she didn't.

Oh, it had been fun at first: the drinking and the partygoing. Jack's amusing friends, with their refreshing American ways. *Hey, who's the cute dame? Don't keep her all to yourself, Jack, will ya?* And Jack: *Ain't she something? A real English lady* . . .

The trouble was, Vivienne thinks, there was nothing beyond the drinking and the parties. Little by little, she began to realize that she had married a man with whom she had nothing in common – or only one thing. And even that – their mutual desire – was not enough, in the end, to bridge the gulf between them.

They were from different worlds, she and Jack, with no shared interests. Jack didn't even like her friends. Those stuffed shirts, he called them. Has-beens, clinging to the worn-out dreams of Empire.

She'd found his friends no less impossible. Loud Texans, for the most part, with wives so determinedly vivacious they made her feel gauche and shy. Women who swapped recipes for popovers and angel-food cake; who said *Gee* and *Swell* and *Pardon me?* Babs Johnson was all right – but then she was from Connecticut. People there were practically English – they understood about social nuance. With most Americans, it was first names straight off and no standing on ceremony. But did one end up knowing any more about them?

After three years, she sometimes wonders if she really knows Jack at all. *What you see is what you get*, he'd told her. She suspects this apparent candour was only another of his evasions.

She and Jack had been married a year when Vivienne found she was pregnant. It was sooner than she'd antici-pated of course – but Jack was overjoyed. He'd been married twice before, but there'd been no children. Now he was going to be a father. He couldn't get over how good it made him feel.

And Vivienne – once she'd got over the initial shock – was happier than she could remember having been in a long time. The baby was a new beginning – in every sense. She could make her life over again, discarding everything she wanted to forget. Ralph's death and the years of poverty and loneliness which followed it could be consigned to obscurity, like the drab austerity suits she no longer wore but preserved at the back of the wardrobe against some unlooked-for emergency.

The pregnancy had been an easy one; she had never felt so well, so full of energy. When she had been expecting Antonia, she had suffered terribly from morning sickness; even the thought of food made her sick – and yet food was all she or anyone else in those famished times could think of. She wonders now if her sickness hadn't been made worse by her resistance to the whole idea of becoming a mother. She was twenty-two and a widow; the last thing she wanted was a child. And so she was sick and lost weight when she should have been gaining it, so that a week before the baby was due she was obliged to stand the whole way from Edgware Road to Embankment because no one on the crowded underground train could tell from looking at her that she was pregnant.

But this time it was different. People kept telling her how well she looked. It was true, she could see it herself: her skin glowed, her hair shone, she put on weight. That in itself was hardly surprising, with the wonderful food they had out here. Fresh fish and prime steak. Vegetables and fruit of all kinds – most of which she'd never tasted before – mangoes, guava, avocados. She couldn't get enough of them – gorging herself on the soft sweet flesh as if to make up for all the years of privation.

A latent sensuality betrayed itself in other ways. She felt alive: charged with erotic promise. When she moved she could feel the swaying of her newly rounded hips, the aching fullness in her breasts. She yearned for Jack's touch with insatiable hunger. Sometimes, going about her work during the day, she would be assailed by a memory of the night before – an image of their entwined bodies, glistening with sweat; the sound of her own voice crying out – and would feel a flush of shame steal across her face.

In retrospect they should have known that something was wrong. The heightened colour that everyone took for health was in fact indicative of something else. The weight gain people told her was normal – *you're eating for two* – was another danger sign. And certainly she recalls near the end of her time feeling unaccountably tired: dull and heavy, as if the blood had turned to sand in her veins. Her ankles swelled – this too was normal, people said. The doctor told her to rest and to avoid salty foods.

It wasn't far into the labour that she realized the baby had stopped moving. When she looked for reassurance on the doctor's face, as he moved the bell-shaped brass stethoscope around on her stomach – trying to find a heartbeat – she found none. Through the haze of 'twilight sleep' she caught snatches of the hurried consultation he was having with the midwife – a Scottish girl who'd only arrived that week, she recalls; poor girl, what an awful start, she remembers thinking. There was a bit of scurrying around while they found Jack. He wasn't at the hospital at all as it turned out, but celebrating in advance with a few of his cronies at the club. They needed his permission as next of kin to perform the operation – an emergency Caesarean.

She wonders now if the delay might have made a difference; although in her heart of hearts she knows it was already too late. Her blood pressure was dangerously high – in the end, they went ahead without Jack's say-so. Not that it mattered either way – all their efforts weren't enough to save the child. It was a boy: perfectly formed – in fact, perfect in every respect – except that he'd never had the chance to draw his first breath.

When they told him the news, Jack's reaction was to go out and get drunk. He stayed drunk for three days and at the end of that time he came back to her. That was his way of dealing with it – a better way than her own, she sometimes thinks. Her response was to withdraw, as far as she could, from living. If she could simply have ceased to exist she would have done so. Since that was not possible – there being others to consider – she contented herself with subtler forms of self-abnegation.

She had cried so much when Ralph died that she now found it difficult to cry; besides, what would have been the sense in mourning someone who had never been truly alive? It had been a mistake, she decided, to have invested so much hope in something so fragile. It wasn't Jack's fault, of course; but Vivienne found, as her milk dried up and her body resumed its normal shape, that she couldn't help blaming him a little. After the baby died, a coolness persisted between them.

Oh, they'd patched things up since then; but it had never been the same. In the months since it happened – over a year, now, she realizes – Jack had thrown himself into his work with a vengeance. Just lately, he'd been away an awful lot. And even when he was at home, he seemed preoccupied.

That's a man for you, Sylvia had said with a shrug, when Vivienne had hinted that things might be less perfect than they seemed. Marry the man, and you end up married to the job. Take my advice, Sylvia had added, and get yourself a hobby – or a lover, darling. Anything to pass the time.

Vivienne wanders from room to room of the empty house, unable to settle to anything. In a state of extreme nervous irritability, she picks up objects and puts them down again, straightens cushions and flicks specks of dust off polished surfaces. She sits down, only to get up again a minute later; walks from one end of the house to the other, her footsteps echoing on the tiled floor.

'Consuelo,' she calls, before remembering that Consuelo is out, visiting her sister who has just had a baby. Another baby. Poor little blighter, Vivienne thinks, with a mixture of scorn and envy. The fourth – or was it the fifth? Extraordinary how easy these women found the whole thing. Giving birth just like shelling peas – a baby a year. Whereas she . . . Sighing, she pushes the thought away.

Catching sight of herself in the bedroom mirror, she pushes her hair back behind her ears, frowns at her reflection. Am I losing my looks? she wonders, smoothing away the frown with the tips of her fingers. I look strained. Worn out. Old. Thirty-three isn't old. It's the climate here – it does terrible things to one's skin. What I wouldn't give to have skin like Sylvia Riley. Dark women had all the luck. And Sylvia was certainly dark – one could almost have mistaken her for a Venezuelan. 'A touch of the tar-brush,' she'd heard Betty Brown say once. Jealous little cat.

Vivienne runs her fingers along the row of dresses hanging in her wardrobe, looking for something to wear to Sylvia's tonight. The navy and white spotted organdie was nice – but she'd worn that to Babs and Ted's last week. The pink silk had a tear in the hem – she must get Consuelo to look at it. She was tired of the blue chiffon. That left the black georgette. It would do, she supposed. She could wear her pearls. That would please Jack – he always complained she never wore the things he gave her.

She returns to the sitting room and sits down at her

desk. Yawning, she opens the first of the exercise books on the pile which lies there. Michael Brown's history composition. *Things I Know About Sir Walter Raleigh*, she reads. *Sir Walter Raleigh discovered the potato and tobacco. He wanted to discover Eldorado the Land of Gold. He led his men along the Orinoco to discover it but before they could discover it his men died of fever or were eaten by crocodiles so he went home. When he got home he was sent to the Tower where they cut off his head. This is all I know about Sir Walter Raleigh.*

A fair try, she writes. She picks up the next book. This is Karel van Wel's. Misspelled and badly written, as usual. Poor child. He's finding it hard to keep up, although heaven knows she's tried to help him as much as possible. During the two weeks he was staying with them his English came on a bit, but since he returned home he's seemed a lot more withdrawn. She suspects the other children tease him. *The Land of Gold*, she makes out, between the ink blots and the crossings-out. *There is no Land of Gold. There is a swamp full of flies and snakes. There is Death and there is no gold . . .*

'Excuse me . . .'

She looks up. It is Karel's father. How long he has been standing there in the open doorway she has no way of telling, but the hairs on the back of her neck prickle with the consciousness of being watched.

'You startled me,' she says.

'Forgive me. I . . .' He looks abashed. 'The door was open.'

Vivienne smiles, to make up for her momentary loss of composure. 'Well, now you're here, won't you come in?'

'I don't want to disturb,' he says. 'I only come to say

thanks. For looking after Kareltje. And to give you this . . .' He takes an envelope from the breast pocket of his jacket and holds it out to her.

She looks at him.

'It is money,' he explains, with an earnestness she finds more painful than the gesture itself. 'For Karel's food. You must take it, please . . .'

'Oh no,' cries Vivienne, dismayed. 'It really isn't necessary. Karel was here as our guest. I mean, I hope you didn't think . . .' She pushes away the envelope, which he has placed on the table in front of her. 'Oh, this is too awful.'

'Please,' Piet van Wel insists. 'My wife wishes it,' he adds gravely.

'Even so,' Vivienne murmurs. 'I really can't accept it. It isn't as if,' she adds, trying to dispel the embarrassment of the moment with a joke, 'Karel ate very much while he was here. I mean, the maid throws away more than that every day of the week . . .'

Piet merely shrugs. The envelope lies untouched on the table between them.

'Won't you have some coffee?' Vivienne says, desperate to salvage the situation. 'I was just about to make some.'

'Thank you, but . . .'

'It's really no trouble,' she insists. Although it is rather a bore having to make conversation with someone she hardly knows, she permits herself to reflect, as she stands in the kitchen waiting for the coffee to percolate. He seems pleasant enough, though – if a bit reserved and prickly. People often were, when they first arrived. She wonders idly how old he is – not more than thirty, she guesses. And yet he looks older – with a seriousness in his face that has nothing to do with youth. Terribly proud, of course. She wonders if she has offended him by refusing the money. The whole thing is too absurd.

Vivienne picks up the tray, with its silver coffee pot and bone china cups – adding, as an afterthought, a plate of ginger biscuits – and carries it through to the veranda.

Piet van Wel is standing by the desk, reading what lies there. When he sees her, he gives a guilty start. 'I'm sorry,' he says. 'But I saw Kareltje's name and I wondered . . .'

'Do read it if you like,' Vivienne says. 'Karel's coming along very well,' she adds – which isn't strictly true, but the poor man surely has enough on his plate, without worrying about his son's lack of progress at school.

'I read it already.' He frowns, perplexed. 'You think he's doing OK?'

'As well as can be expected,' she says. 'Under the circumstances. I mean, having to adapt to a different language and so on. Cream and sugar?'

'Thank you.' He takes the cup from her. His cuffs are frayed, she notices – hating herself for noticing. And the sleeves of what must be his best jacket are shiny and thin with wear.

'I want him to do OK,' he tells her earnestly. 'Very important that he works hard at school. Working hard is the way to a better life, I tell him . . .'

'I'm sure he understands that,' said Vivienne. 'Do help yourself to biscuits.'

'Thanks. Trouble is, I don't speak so good myself. My wife neither. It's hard for us to help Karel. You know?'

'Of course,' she reassures him. 'But you really mustn't

worry. If you like,' she adds, thinking as she says it, I must be mad, 'I can give Karel a bit of extra help with his English. Just to set him on the right track, as it were . . .'

'You are very kind. But . . .' He seems agitated. 'You see, we can't pay . . . Unless maybe next month, when I get my salary . . .'

'Don't worry about that,' she says hastily. Thinking, Oh God, what am I letting myself in for? 'Karel's a bright boy. I'm sure he'll make excellent progress. More coffee?'

'No thanks. I must go now.' Awkwardly he gets to his feet.

'How's your little girl getting on?' Vivienne asks, accompanying him to the door. Now that he is on the point of leaving, she finds to her surprise that she is in no particular hurry for him to go.

'Very good. Still a little weak, you know? She is sleeping a lot. But much better than before . . .'

'It must have been a worrying time for your wife.'

A shadow crosses his features. 'Yes. My wife, she . . .' He struggles with what he is trying to say. 'It is not easy for her here.'

'I suppose it must all seem very different.'

'Yes.'

'You must bring her over one evening. It might do her good to meet some new people. I mean, after being cooped up for so long at home . . .'

'Thank you,' he says, acknowledging the invitation without actually accepting it.

It is only after he has gone that she sees he has left the envelope behind.

*

'Vivienne, darling. Jack. How lovely to see you . . .'

Svelte in pearl-grey satin, Sylvia Riley approaches her guests, her arms extended as if for an embrace. She kisses Vivienne; throws Jack an ironic smile. 'Darling,' she murmurs holding Vivienne at arm's length, the better to admire her. 'What a lovely frock. Is it new?'

'No. It's just that you haven't seen it for a while . . .'

'Well, I think it's lovely,' Sylvia declares, releasing her hold on Vivienne's shoulders. 'But you always look lovely. I hope you realize,' she adds, with a sly glance at Jack, 'what a lovely wife you've got.'

'Gee, Sylvia,' he says. 'Thanks for bringing it to my attention . . .'

Sylvia raises her eyebrows at Vivienne. 'Aren't men awful?' her look seems to say. 'Frank,' she calls over her shoulder to her husband. 'Get these people a drink, will you? They must be dying of thirst . . .'

'Coming up,' says Frank Riley.

Frank is as large and stolid as his wife is small and vivacious. His wife makes no secret of the fact that she considers him dull. At parties he is generally to be found in a corner with a drink in his hand, while Sylvia holds court in the centre of the room; unless the party is one he is giving, in which case he is happiest tending the bar. 'Frank likes making himself useful,' says his wife, in a tone of voice which implies this is all that can be expected of him.

Tonight he wears an apron which reads Chief Cook and Bottlewasher. He picks up two glasses. 'What'll you have?'

'Oh, I don't know,' Vivienne says. 'A dry Martini, I suppose . . .'

'Why not try something different?' Frank says.

'You name it, I can make it. Manhattan? Singapore Sling?'

'Well, actually . . .'

'Old Fashioned? Tom Collins? White Lady?'

'You can keep the fancy stuff,' Jack says. 'I'll have a bourbon on the rocks. And a dry Martini for my wife. If you can remember how to make one, that is . . .'

'Remember?' Frank says. 'Why, I'll have you know I patented the original recipe.'

'Frank,' calls his wife from across the room. 'The Johnsons can't make it. One of their children is ill, or something. Such a bore. Now we'll be two down for Canasta . . .'

'Thank Christ for that,' mutters Frank. He gives Vivienne a sheepish look. 'Sorry.'

Vivienne smiles at him. 'That's quite all right. You should hear Jack sometimes. He turns the air quite blue . . .'

'Leave me outa this,' growls Jack. 'And hurry up with that drink, will ya? Three fingers. Plenty of ice . . .'

Frank complies with these instructions. 'Pretty bad business in Kenya, what?' he remarks, handing Vivienne her drink. 'Heard it on the World Service. Shocking thing.'

'Terrible,' Vivienne agrees.

'Got a cousin out there. District Commissioner. Retired now, of course. Bought a farm near Nairobi. Life savings, you know. Talking about selling up and coming home, if this business gets any worse . . .'

'What a shame,' says Vivienne.

'When you think,' says Frank, sounding more impassioned than either of his listeners have ever heard him, 'of all we've *done* for those people. Roads. Schools.

Proper sanitation. It makes my blood boil, it really does . . .'

'Never trust the natives,' Jack drawls.

'Jack, *really* . . .' Vivienne protests.

'Of course, we can't expect you Yanks to know what running an empire's like,' Frank says to Jack. 'You've never had any colonies to speak of. Unless you count Hawaii. And even then, you couldn't keep the bloody Japs out . . .'

'Talking politics already?' Sylvia shakes an admonitory finger at her husband. 'Vivie dear, you mustn't let these men bore you to death. Come and meet some people . . .'

'Colonies,' Jack says. There is a dangerous edge to his smile. 'I learned about colonies in high school. The Boston Tea Party – that was something to do with a colony, wasn't it?'

'Oh, ha *ha*,' says Frank. 'Vivie, how can you stand being married to this man?'

'I sometimes wonder,' says Vivienne.

This is the way it looks that night in the living room of the Rileys' bungalow, with its fashionably modern furniture – all triangular shapes and splayed metal legs – its throw-rugs on shiny parquet floors, its black wrought-iron lampstands and vases filled with scarlet gladioli. Music – Sinatra or Duke Ellington – issues from the Philips record-player, a vast mahogany box with the company logo picked out in fretwork over the speaker. Light spills through French doors on to the white concrete patio, where a few couples, attracted by the night air and the big pale moon hanging over the Rileys' swimming pool, stand overlooking the dark garden, their presence marked by the glowing coals of cigarettes.

> There was a moon out in space
> But a cloud drifted over its face;
> You kissed me, and went on your way,
> The night we called it a day . . .

Inside the room, conversation grows animated, as drinks are consumed and canapés (offered round by the silent maid in the black and white uniform) left untasted. These are people who have met before, on many such occasions, and know all there is to know about each other. In such a community, the most jealously guarded secrets become common knowledge within days: whose marriage is going through a bad patch; whose husband chases other women; whose wife has a drink problem. These matters are not openly discussed. Instead, the talk is of inconsequential things. The men talk about work and last night's poker game; their wives discuss the servant problem, boarding schools, dressmakers' bills and the new people from Europe.

'So what's she like? The wife, I mean . . .' This is Jean McBride, already bursting out of her vast maternity smock – although she can't be more than three or four months gone, Vivienne thinks. She likes Jean; it's Duncan she can't stand. A humourless man. Something of a bigot – with a bee in his bonnet about Catholics. He had once announced, in the middle of a dinner party, that the Anglican Church was merely the English wing of the Church of Rome.

'No one's met her. Has anyone met her?' Nancy Wilson, her red hair and freckles not effaced by turquoise crêpe de Chine, looks around for confirmation or denial. Not for the first time Vivienne thinks how extraordinarily plain Nancy is. Really quite strikingly plain. And yet Roy Wilson is one of the best-looking men in the camp. Although admittedly rather dull – as handsome men so often are.

'I took one of my coconut sponges round. But no one was in.' This is Betty Brown, a small, soft-featured blonde in pink rayon – pretty enough, thinks Vivienne, albeit in a rather vulgar way. The kind of looks Vivienne's mother, never at a loss for a caustic phrase, would have called 'chocolate box'. 'No, I tell a lie,' Betty corrects herself fussily. 'No one came to the door. Although I could have *sworn* I saw someone looking out of one of the windows . . .'

'I think I'd lie low if Betty came to call,' murmurs Sylvia Riley to Vivienne. 'Maybe she doesn't eat cake,' she says, loud enough to be heard by everyone.

'Very funny, Sylvia,' says Betty with a sour little smile.

'*He* seems quite nice,' good-natured Nancy puts in quickly. 'Not that I've actually spoken to him, of course, but Roy says . . .'

'Vivienne's spoken to him, haven't you, Vivienne?' Sylvia smiles at her friend with malicious sweetness.

'Oh, you know me,' Vivienne says lightly. 'I have all the luck with the men . . .'

'Is this a private party or can anybody join?'

It's Jack, a drink in his hand, come to see what the girls are talking about. Sooner or later, Vivienne thinks, you can trust Jack to end up with the women. Women talk about more interesting things, is what he says. And they're easier on the eye. Jack's necktie is undone and his eyes are unnaturally bright – both danger signs. He had a couple of highballs before they came, and the drink in his hand isn't his first – or his second either, Vivienne thinks.

'Vivienne was just telling us about Piet van Wel,' says Sylvia naughtily.

'I was not. I hardly know the man . . .'

'Piet's a nice guy,' says Jack. 'Smart too. He'll do well out here – if he decides to stay . . .'

'You mean if his wife decides to stay,' says Sylvia.

'Sure she'll stay,' Jack says. 'What choice does she have? Nothing left for them back home, is there?'

She dreams she is back in Maracaibo. Driving along the dusty road towards the lake, past rows of flat-roofed concrete houses painted ice-cream colours: pale pink, lemon, pistachio, mauve. The gardens of the houses are beaten earth, with apamate trees casting an inky shade. Each house has exactly the same layout: three steps up to a veranda; a glass-panelled door, protected by a wrought-iron screen; a window on either side, like the eyes in a face.

In the intense heat of noon the streets are deserted, as if abandoned at the rumour of invasion. The light wind flutters the pages of a newspaper left on a veranda chair and stirs the coloured bead curtain over a door. Ahead stretches the empty road, with the hot blue sky above it: cloudless, infinite.

When she wakes she has the taste of cigarette smoke in her mouth, although she gave up more than a year ago.

4

Jack's going to Caracas – even though it's barely a month since he was there the last time. But there's a problem at Divisional HQ which requires his immediate attention. Tony heard him telling Vivienne about it last night when she was supposed to be in bed. She'd got up to get a drink of water and when she was carrying it back along the passage walking slowly so as not to spill any she heard her mother's voice.

'You might take Antonia with you . . .'

The sound of her own name stops her in her tracks. She knows she ought to let them know she's there but she wants to hear what Jack is going to say.

'It's strictly business.' He doesn't sound very pleased. 'Hell, I'd like to take the kid along but I don't know what I'm gonna do with her. There are things I have to do. People I have to meet . . .'

'You can leave her with the maid at the hotel. She's old enough to amuse herself for an hour or so . . .'

'Suppose I get delayed? I can't just leave her all by herself. Kids need to eat and sleep and all that stuff . . .'

'I don't know why you're raising so many objections,' Vivienne says calmly. 'It's not as if you haven't taken her with you before . . .'

'That was when she was little,' says Jack. 'If I had to

meet somebody I could take her along. Leave her with the bartender or something . . .'

'I don't see why you can't do the same now.'

'Vivienne . . .'

'Please, Jack. She's been pestering me for ages about going . . .'

'Oh hell,' says Jack. 'I'll think about it, OK?'

'Thank you.'

'I said I'll think about it,' Jack mutters. Holding her breath Tony watches him cross the lighted oblong which is all she can see of the room. 'See you later,' he says.

'Are you going out?' Tony hears her mother say.

'For an hour or two. Don't wait up.'

'Oh I won't,' she says already speaking to the empty room.

Flying in over the mountains they run into some cloud. Turbulence Jack calls it. He holds her hand.

'Not scared, are ya, Tony?'

'Nope.' The little plane – a Lockheed Electra which Jack says must be twenty years old if she's a day – jolts and shudders under the buffeting wind. 'Not really.'

'Attagirl.' He gives her hand a squeeze and at once she feels better. She's never sick on planes or in cars but when it's bumpy like this she sometimes feels a bit giddy.

'We'll be landing soon,' Jack tells her and sure enough at that moment the cloud parts and she catches her first glimpse of the city spread out like a map beneath them. Forgetting her giddiness Tony cranes her neck trying to pick out landmarks – but they're still too high. Down there the sun is shining. Up here they've got different weather.

The plane isn't very full: apart from her and Jack there are half a dozen roughnecks from the oilfields – Texans mostly – playing cards and drinking Red Eye at the back of the aircraft and Mrs Wilson who's going to visit her dentist in Las Mercedes. They have the same dentist – he's called Mr Phelps. He wears a light on his forehead which shines in your eyes when he looks in your mouth. Sometimes he gives Tony miniature tubes of toothpaste. To stop her dolls getting cavities he says. Tony doesn't play with dolls any more of course but she doesn't tell him that.

Just before take-off when the Lockheed is taxiing along the runway at Maracaibo she leans over and offers Mrs Wilson one of her sweets. It helps to stop the buzzing you get in your ears – which is caused by the change in pressure Jack says.

But Mrs Wilson smiles and shakes her head. 'Oh no, dear, I couldn't possibly. Mr Phelps would have fifty fits.'

Then she asks about school and Tony tells her about her trip to Caracas. They're going for the whole weekend – just her and Jack. They're supposed to buy her some sandals and a new dress and pick up some curtain material for Vivienne. Jack has somebody he has to meet he says. It's strictly business so she'll have to amuse herself for a little while. But they're going to do lots of other things too. Tony's hoping Jack will take her to the racetrack. All he says when she asks him is maybe. That's all they ever say.

When the plane lifts off Mrs Wilson leans her head back against the seat and closes her eyes for a minute. She opens them again and sees Tony looking at her. 'Thank goodness *that's* over,' she says with a forced kind of smile. Sometimes Tony doesn't understand grown-ups at all. Taking off's the best part she always thinks.

They chat for a few minutes more and then Mrs Wilson takes out her *petit point* and Tony reads her comic. Jack disappears to the back of the plane for a while. From time to time as she turns the pages of *School Friend* Tony can hear him swapping funny stories with the roughnecks. Because of the turbulence they've left their safety-belts fastened. Tony can feel the metal clasp of hers against her stomach – a reassuring weight anchoring her to the seat. A moment later they hit another bank of cloud and the plane gives a lurch as if it might be about to fall out of the sky.

'Hells bells!' shouts one of the Texans. There's a whoop of drunken laughter from the back of the plane.

Mrs Wilson gives a little scream – then pretends it's because she's just pricked her finger.

'Don't worry,' Tony tells her. 'Cristóbal's flown this crate a hundred times, through worse storms than this. He'll bring us down safely, you'll see.'

She's only trying to make her feel better but Mrs Wilson gives her a strange look. 'You *are* a funny child,' she says closing her eyes again. She looks as if she's going to be sick.

The round window films with frost. There's nothing to be seen but cloud and more cloud. On the highest peaks here you get snow Jack says. You get all kinds of weather in this Goddamn country.

Suddenly they're out of it – into clear skies. The city lies below them glittering in sunlight. The white blocks of offices and hotels on Avenida Libertador. The red-tiled roofs of the Spanish quarter. The swimming pools and gardens of La Florida. The Ford building and the Chrysler building and the Hotel Tamanaco.

The plane casts its moving shadow over it all.

The hotel is as nice as Tony remembers. Everything clean and shiny and modern as can be. Elevators which rise so swiftly and silently you don't even know you've left the ground. Soft carpeted corridors which muffle your footsteps. Chrome fittings in the bathroom which throw back your reflection like a funfair mirror.

Tony's bathroom has a set of fluffy white towels with a big 'T' in the middle which stands for Tamanaco, although Jack says it's 'T' for Tony. It's the first time she's had her own bathroom – in fact it's the first time she's had her own room. Last time they stayed here at Christmas she slept on a little pull-out bed in Jack and Vivienne's room. Jack says she's older now and has to be treated like a young lady. Young ladies need their own rooms.

Tony's window has a view of Mount Avila and the new hotel – the Hotel Humboldt – they're building at the top of it. When it's finished a cable car will carry people up there. The view from the top is going to be something else Jack says. The party they're going to throw for the Grand Opening will be the biggest thing the city's ever seen. There'll be champagne and beautiful women in Paris gowns. El Presidente will be there – if they don't shoot him first Jack says – and he'll cut the tape and all the fireworks will go off and everyone will dance till dawn.

When they've showered and changed they go down to the bar and Jack orders a cold beer for himself and a Coke for Tony and they sit out on the terrace and drink their drinks. Tony looks out over the bright blue swimming pool and the row of palm trees behind it and the mountains rising up between them and the sky and thinks she'd like to sit here for ever. Jack catches her eye across the table and says, *Hey, girl*. And she knows he's thinking the same thing: that he's happy to be there drinking his Polar beer and lighting up his first Lucky of the night in the place they both love best in all the world.

For breakfast next morning in the hotel dining room Tony has *tostadas* with scrambled eggs – the way Consuelo makes them at home. Thinking about home makes her think about Vivienne and she feels a pang of guilt because she's forgotten all about her until this moment.

'Can we buy Mother a present?' she asks Jack.

From his startled look Tony can tell he must have been miles away; he recovers himself then shrugs.

'Sure thing. If you like. Why not?'

'We could get her those handkerchiefs – the ones she liked in Sears Roebuck . . .'

'Whatever you say, Princess . . .'

When she's eaten all she wants and Jack's finished his coffee they get a cab downtown. The doorman clicks his fingers and a big white Cadillac glides up. The seats have fluffy leopard-skin-patterned covers and there's a little plaster figure of the Virgin Mary on the dashboard. When the driver goes to turn the radio down Jack tells him to let it play. The song's one of his favourites: 'I'm a Fool to Want You'. He drums his fingers in time to the music as they turn down Avenida Rio de Janeiro.

It's still early but already you can feel the heat. The sky is a pure deep blue above the green mountain slopes.

Big white clouds roll down from the peaks to the flimsy shacks where the poor people live high up on the mountainside. Tony thinks how strange it must be living up in the clouds – like the way she used to imagine heaven when she was small.

When she says this to Jack he laughs and says, Funny kind of heaven. A heaven for bad angels if you ask me. Just last week they shot the Chief of Police right between the eyes. He went in there after some gangster and never came out alive. That's the kind of thing your angels get up to he says.

At night the *barrios* look quite beautiful Tony thinks – a vision of fairyland with lights scattered over the mountainside like twinkling stars. In daylight they look different of course. Then you can see that the fairy-tale palaces are built out of garbage: flattened oil drums rough bricks rusty corrugated iron and a whole lot of other things no one else wants any more.

Each house is a flat-roofed box with holes for windows and a door on to the patio in front which is also the roof of the house below. On top of every house is another with another one stacked on top of that all the way up the mountain – like an ant hill Jack says. Tangles of electric cables feed off the powerlines which is how the *rancheros* get the power to work their electric lights – those same lights that look so pretty at night.

Sometimes when the rainy season is particularly bad whole sections of the mountain crumble away bringing the houses down too and all the people in them. Jack says it doesn't happen very often. It helps keep the numbers down he says.

The cab drops them off in Sabana Grande and they go first to Sears Roebuck for Tony's dress and Vivienne's curtain material. Tony likes this shop with its smells of perfume and new leather and its haughty salesgirls in elegant black dresses. Near the door there's a display of handkerchiefs stiff folds spread out like fans to show the fancy embroidery; she looks for the ones Vivienne liked with the drawn-thread border, but they seem to have gone. Jack buys a *Herald Tribune* from a sidewalk vendor and glances at the headlines while he's having his shoes shined by the shoeshine boy.

'Well, whaddya know?' Jack lifts the foot wearing the shiny shoe off the little wooden ramp and puts the foot with the not-so-shiny shoe in its place for the boy to work on with his cloths and brushes. 'Old Uncle Joe's dead.'

Tony doesn't know who Uncle Joe is but she tries to look sympathetic.

'Not that I ever trusted the bastard,' Jack says.

He stuffs the paper in a trashbin and then they walk a bit further down the street towards Plaza Venezuela and they look in the shop windows at the swan-necked mannequins in evening gowns and elbow-length gloves and choose the dress Tony's going to wear when Jack takes her dancing at the Country Club.

When they're tired of window-shopping they stop for a drink in a sidewalk café. Jack orders a beer and a Coca-Cola for Tony and they sit at a round metal table under a striped umbrella and watch the world go by. Crowds of people are strolling up and down in the bright sunshine. There are students from the university – the men in baggy suits with wide shoulders the girls in tight sweaters and skating skirts. Bobby-soxers Jack calls them. There are secretaries in crisp white blouses and skirts so tight Tony's surprised they can walk at all.

There are people who work in banks and people who work in shops and people selling everything you can think of from shoelaces to wristwatches. Most of it junk Jack says but that's the only way these people can make a living poor devils.

An old man drags a cart full of lemons up and down calling out in a cracked voice to the passers-by. When he turns the big iron wheel it crushes the fruit to a pulp and the lemon juice runs out. You mix it with sugar and crushed ice and drink it right there in the street. The sharp smell of fresh-cut lemons is wonderful Tony thinks but Jack says you don't want to drink that stuff. God only knows what goes into it he says.

A man with a thin moustache like Señor Hernández's walks past their table carrying a briefcase. He's wearing a creased white linen suit and a white Panama hat and his eyes are hidden behind dark glasses. Tony catches Jack's eye. 'Leg-man for a gang of bootleggers,' he says quick as a flash.

'Think so?'

'Either that or he sells insurance.'

'He looks nasty.' She looks around for another subject. Nothing but co-eds and business people. Nobody interesting. Then she sees the old woman. In that crowd of people in summer clothes she stands out a mile. Her greenish-black two-piece and ratty fox-fur with glass eyes make her look like a witch. Her hair is a strange colour too: a bright artificial orange. She's wearing a hat with a spotted veil and her withered lips are painted a vivid scarlet. As she hobbles towards them leaning on a cane Tony nudges Jack. 'What about her?'

He doesn't glance round or give any sign that he knows who she's talking about but as the old woman moves out of earshot he leans across the table towards her and says softly, 'She's a Russian countess down on her luck. She fled the country after the Revolution, taking only a diamond necklace with her. Now she gives dancing lessons at the Academy. Every time she hits the skids, she sells another diamond.'

Tony stares at him. 'How do you *know*?'

Jack taps the side of his nose. 'I just know. Now finish your soda pop and we'll go visit the General . . .'

The General is the most handsome man in the world. His dark eyes glow with passion and his black hair falls in soft ringlets around his ivory forehead. A superb horseman he is seen to best advantage in the saddle: his cloak flung back as he reins in his rearing steed one hand holding the plumed hat he has swept from his head in the excitement of the moment. It's the way he must have looked on the field of battle urging his troops on to victory – or on the Andean heights with the world at his feet.

Just now the General isn't looking his best – with pigeon shit staining his cloak and the gold-laced front of his dress uniform. There's even a pigeon perched on the General's head – but the General's dignity is such that it withstands even this sacrilege.

'Quite a guy, that old General,' says Jack. 'A bit of a ladies' man too . . .'

'Tell me about the General and Manuela Saenz.'

'Manuela? They met at a dance in Quito. She was married, of course, but that didn't bother our hero. She was some girl, that Manuela. Crack shot. Rode like a man. Saved the General's life a couple of times. The Liberator's Liberator, he called her . . .'

'But the only one he ever really loved was his wife, who died,' Tony prompts him. This is how the story always ends when Jack tells it; only today he seems distracted.

'That's right,' he says cutting short the part about the General going to Europe to forget his sorrow and coming back a revolutionary. 'Say, Tony – there's something I gotta take care of. Why doncha take a walk around the museum for a little while, and I'll come and find you when I'm through?'

Angelina sits in front of the mirror, looking at her beautiful self. The pink silk robe which her new friend bought her last time he visited falls open to show the armour beneath. A brassière like a breastplate, with cone-shaped cups stitched in concentric circles, to lift and separate her breasts. A satin girdle, reinforced with strong elastic, to compress her soft round stomach. Her legs are shiny with the grape-bloom of nylon. Fussily, she checks to see that the seams of her stockings are straight.

Twelve o'clock. In half an hour he will be here. She flips open her silver-gilt compact (the gift of a former admirer) and checks her make-up, even though she already knows it is perfect. All traces of shine on forehead, nose and chin obliterated with thick white powder. Eyebrows tweezed into elegant winged shapes. Eyelids painted green, like jewelled geckos. Lips a deep purplish-red.

Angelina smiles at herself, turning her head this way and that to get the most flattering angle.

She likes this one, she is thinking. She likes him a lot. Maybe today he will bring her another present. Some perfume, this time – or that bracelet she saw in the Calle Real de Sabana Grande. Yawning, she gets up and stands for a minute, admiring the shape of her legs in high-heeled shoes. She opens the wardrobe. The red dress or the blue? He likes her in the red.

In a spirit of perversity, she starts to put on the blue. As she is reaching round for the zip, the doorbell sounds, loud in the heavy silence of the late-nineteenth-century apartment.

'*Momentito . . .*'

Frowning, she takes off the blue dress and throws it on the bed. Slips the red one off its hanger and deftly slides it over her head without disturbing the gleaming dark permanent waves of her hair. He's early today, she thinks. Impatient. She likes an impatient man. Humming softly under her breath, she slides the dress down over her hips. Zips it up. Then, bestowing one last smile on the apparition in the mirror, she saunters slowly to the door.

In the museum there's a painting showing the signing of the Declaration of Independence. The room where it hangs and the room where it was painted are the same: the chapel of the municipal palace. There are the same stained-glass windows and painted ceiling; even the red velvet chairs on which Simón Bolívar and his fellow signatories sat have been preserved. Tony looks at the red velvet chairs and at the table on which the Declaration was signed and at the Declaration itself in its glass-fronted case. Half-closing her eyes she tries to imagine what it must have been like to be here in that room on that day with the General and his illustrious associates sitting around the table in their black coats the way the artist has portrayed them in the painting.

At the head of the table with his arms spread wide as if he is making a speech stands Bolívar the visionary. *There have been three great fools in history: Jesus, Don Quixote and I ...* To his right sits Andrés Bello – philosopher and poet; to his left Francisco Miranda – soldier and man of the world. After the General himself Miranda is Tony's favourite. He isn't as handsome as the General but there's a twinkle in his eye which makes her think he must have been a man with a lot of stories to tell about his travels around the capitals of Europe and his encounters with George Washington and Catherine the Great. In the painting he is sprawling back in his chair looking up at the ceiling – as if he has just remembered a pressing engagement somewhere else.

Tony stares and stares at the picture willing it to give up its secrets. But it's no good. However hard she tries she can't get beyond the painted surface.

She pokes around the room a little longer looking at its other relics – all of which she's seen lots of times before. There's the map of Caracas as it was in 1580-something and the flag from Cortés's second expedition – now worn to papery thinness – and a woodcut showing the martyrdom of two Franciscan friars by the fierce Caribs they had been sent to convert. One of the friars has been tied to a stake while a row of naked Caribs with painted faces throws poison darts at him; the other is having his arms and legs cut off. He's looking up at the sky as if he's surprised at what's happening to him. Maybe he's wondering why God doesn't come down and save him.

She leaves the chapel and walks slowly around the cloister to the other side of the museum. There are palm trees growing in the courtyard their feathery tops reaching high above the roof of the building. The marble fountain in the centre is guarded by four marble lions. Each lion rests its paw on the rim of a giant shell. The lion is the symbol of the city Jack says – which is strange Tony thinks because there aren't any lions here. Jaguars and leopards and ocelots and panthers but no lions. The shell is like the shells you find on the beach at Chichiriviche – only bigger of course. It's the same shell you can see on the sides of the company's tankers and on the tops of the scarlet petrol pumps along the roadside. *Go well with Shell.*

Tony loiters for a while in the criss-crossed shade of the palm trees – leaning on the edge of the fountain and listening to the cool sound of water trickling from its marble basin into the pool below which is stained bright green with moss. She feels a strange sensation which might be hunger or sadness: she can't tell. She wonders if Simón Bolívar sat where she is sitting after the Declaration had been signed and the toasts to Liberty drunk and if he felt sad the way she does now – perhaps thinking of his dead wife and of all that might have been.

There are doors around the cloister leading to different rooms of the museum. Tony chooses one at random. After the brightness of the courtyard it seems very dark, and at first she can't make out what there is to see. As her eyes get used to the gloom she sees that the glass-fronted cases around the walls are filled with dolls. Their glass eyes wink at her.

These aren't the kinds of doll you can play with: they're just for looking at. Some of them are dressed like Indians from the *pueblo* in *liqui-liqui* and sandals; others wear the costume of Negro slaves. There's a model of an Indian hut thatched with palm leaves with an Indian family inside it. The mother Indian is grinding corn helped by her two children. The father sits at the table with his legs sticking out stiffly in front of him – the way dolls' legs always do. On the table is a doll-size pitcher with a doll-size tin mug beside it. The last time Tony came here with Jack he told her the pitcher had rum in it – which is why the man was the only one not doing any work. Drunk as a skunk Jack said.

Thinking of Jack reminds her that he's been away a long time. She wonders if perhaps she should go and look for him but decides to give him a bit longer. Maybe he'll take her for ice-cream sodas at the soda fountain in the basement of Macy's. The thought makes her hungrier still.

She leaves the room with the dolls and goes into the next one. Here there are models to show you how the city looked hundreds of years ago. In the first one it's just a village with a square surrounded by low whitewashed buildings and a church. The only way you can tell it's the same place at all is by looking at the mountains. Whoever built them must have spent a long time getting the shape just right; you have to look quite close to see that it's only painted plaster.

The next model shows the city at the time the Declaration was signed. There's a model of the building in which the ceremony took place and in which Tony is standing at this moment. She wonders if perhaps there's another model inside the one she's looking at with another model inside that – each getting smaller and smaller until it's too small for the eye to see. Resting her hands on the glass case so that the cardboard walls of the buildings inside tremble as if from a miniature earthquake she lowers her face until it's level with the diamond-paned windows. But there's nothing to see inside except dust and dead spiders.

After this she looks at the model showing Caracas at the turn of the century – when Guzmán Blanco built the golden-domed Capitol building and the opera house with its wedding-cake façade – and at the model showing the way the city looks today. Even this model isn't very up to date: the newest buildings like the Tamanaco and the Chrysler building aren't built yet and the tiny cars in the tiny streets have an old-fashioned look. As Tony looks closer she sees that some of the model people have fallen over. A smiling blonde woman lies in the street in the path of a moving car; a man reading a miniature newspaper has toppled on to the tramlines.

It strikes her at the same moment that the view of the city shown in the models and the view from the window of the museum must be the same. In the later models there's even a tiny replica of the General's statue in the centre of the square. She goes to the window and looks down.

Sure enough she can see the statue and the plaza with its *araguaney* trees and ornamental lampposts. It looks just the same as the one in the model except that the trees are much bigger in proportion to the buildings and the people are moving around. At least most of them are. Some aren't moving at all but are sitting on the benches around the square. On one of the benches Tony can see an old man reading a newspaper and a woman with a baby; on another she can see Jack sitting next to a lady in a red dress. As she watches the lady gets up and starts to walk away from the bench. Jack gets hold of her hand and after a minute she sits down beside him again.

Vivienne is driving down the straight red road which leads to Maracaibo. Red because the red dust kicked up by passing trucks and the laden tankers moving between the oilfields and the docks forms a fine layer over the asphalt – treacherous to drive on in the rainy season, when dust and oil mingle into a slick sheen. Today there's no sign of rain, though – won't be for weeks yet, if she knows this country. *Hot as hell*, is Jack's description and, for once, she agrees with him.

A tanker is moving up behind her now: its bulk fills her rear-view mirror. One of ours, she thinks automatically. No mistaking that yellow and red, that distinctive sign. *How should I your true love know from another one? By his cockle hat and staff, and his sandal shoon* . . . The benefits of an English education, Vivienne thinks wryly: a quotation for every occasion.

The heavy vehicle is gaining on her, although she's doing fifty-five, is pulling out to overtake her. They simply can't bear to see another car in front – especially with a woman driving. As the gleaming silver cylinder of the truck streams past she sees that the driver is looking back at her, and hears, above the roar of the engine, his low whistle of appreciation. *Damn his cheek*. She glares at the road ahead, refusing to give him the satisfaction of an angry response; glad of the partial protection of her dark glasses and white silk headscarf.

The tanker disappears in a cloud of red dust. *Hellbent for election*, Jack would say. Thinking of her husband, Vivienne smiles, then frowns.

Flat fields of bare earth and scrubby grass stretch on

either side. Flat trees, blown into curious anvil shapes by the wind. Flat-roofed adobe houses, where chickens scratch in the dust and barefoot children stand and stare. The lake in the distance, a blurred line of silver; a forest of derricks rising on the horizon.

Nearing Altagracia, she takes the turning which leads to the ferry. Here, the road is little more than a track, winding down to the lake and the jetty where the afternoon boat is already loading. Apart from a Jeep, and a truck full of bananas, hers is the only vehicle. The boat is crowded: groups of oilfield workers in sweat-stained khaki workclothes, older men in loose-fitting white suits and straw hats; old women in black and pregnant women carrying small children. A wedding party.

Vivienne negotiates the ramp and parks her car on deck. It's too hot to remain inside with the air-conditioning switched off, so she goes to lean on the rail with the rest of the passengers. She feels the throb of the engines beneath her feet, and the mild exhilaration of letting go, as the boat casts off and they move away from shore. The sun strikes the water. She narrows her eyes against its brightness.

Along the edge of the lake is a ragged line of mooring posts, on each of which sits a pelican, patiently waiting for the fishing boats to return with the next catch; a few of these birds, disturbed by the sound of the boat's engines, rise up from their posts with a noisy flapping of wings, circle once or twice, then settle once more.

Vivienne breathes slowly and deeply, feeling the warm breeze on her face, and smelling the distinctive marine smell: a mixture of fish, diesel, tar and salt, overlaid by the thick sweetness of fruit – bananas ripened almost to rottenness – ascending from beneath the truck's awning. She feels the roughness of the corroded iron rail, slippery with salt spray, beneath her fingers. Far out in the lake she can see the pale flame wavering from the tall chimney of an offshore refinery. Dark shapes of tankers crawl along the horizon.

In this state, her thoughts empty of all but immediate sensations, she feels happy for the first time in a long while. Weeks, months – perhaps a year. When was it exactly she knew things had changed between them? Strange that what had begun with such hope should have turned so sour.

And yet they'd been so happy.

Standing at the rail of the slowly moving boat, the wind ruffling her hair, Vivienne finds herself thinking of the little town in the mountains where she and Jack stayed after their wedding. A town like a thousand others and yet unique. A square, with a Colombian pine dropping its needles on the red-tiled plaza, mingling with fallen hibiscus blossoms. The inevitable statue of the Liberator. Whitewashed, red-roofed houses, with the window frames, doors and sills painted blue. A white church, with a bell tower, also picked out in blue: the same soft shade that was to be seen everywhere, as if pieces of the sky had attached themselves to the walls. EL MAESTRO ES AQUÍ Y TE LLAMA the legend over the door.

Inside the church, a blue and white Virgin presided over an altar covered with flowers – the calla lilies which grew wild along the streams here – and an iron staircase, also painted blue, gracefully spiralled upwards. Jack took a photograph of her standing in front of it – she has it somewhere. Resting the hand which wears the ring on the curving banister. Not quite smiling for the camera.

A sensation Vivienne has had before (but when? she can't think), of being a sleepwalker suddenly awakened, possesses her. *What am I doing here?* In the same instant she becomes aware that someone is watching her.

She looks around. Piet van Wel stands at the rail, a few feet away from where she is. He has just lit a cigarette. He nods at her through a cloud of exhaled smoke.

'Mrs Lindberg.'

'Mr van Wel.'

For a minute both are overcome by the embarrassment of unlooked-for encounters.

He is the first to recover his equilibrium. 'Please –' He offers her the pack he is holding.

'Thank you.' She takes a cigarette, allows him to light it. 'Well –' inhaling – 'fancy meeting *you* here . . .'

It's more coquettish than she intends: she finds it hard, sometimes, to strike the right note with men. Fortunately, the unintended nuance appears to have escaped him.

'A fortunate coincidence,' he says.

He smiles at her. The first time she has seen him smile, she realizes. It makes him seem younger somehow; more attractive too. His eyes are grey, she sees – a darker shade than his hair, which is almost white. Strange, in a young man. Hereditary, she supposes.

'Pretty view, isn't it?' she remarks, for something to say. There's a curious intimacy about the situation – being here with him, alone in the middle of this vast expanse of water – as if they were the last two people on earth. Although that's absurd, she tells herself – there's quite a crowd on board.

'Beautiful,' he agrees.

They talk of this and that. Their children. The party she is planning. *Very informal. Just a few friends. I do hope you and your wife can make it.*

All the time he is wondering what put that look on her face, the moment before she saw him.

Vivienne and Jack's party is a tradition carried over from Jack's bachelor days. About once a month the regular Friday night get-together at Jack's place for poker and a few cold beers gives way to a more elaborate event. This used to mean laying in a couple more crates of beer and a few extra bottles of Scotch. Since Vivienne took over the running of things the party has become a more serious affair.

Consuelo and Consuelo's younger sister Fernanda spend all day preparing food under Vivienne's exacting supervision. Hors-d'oeuvres of various kinds. Vol-au-vents. Bridge rolls. Cocktail sticks skewering cubes of cheese cocktail onions cubes of pineapple and green olives (the new American fad) are manufactured and set out on silver trays. Cold chickens are sliced and arranged on platters. Bowls of potato salad prepared the night before and chilled in the Frigidaire are decorated with paprika and chopped parsley. Avocados are diced for the green salad.

The drinks are Jack's department. Dry Martinis to start with the option of Gin and It for Sylvia Riley and ginger wine for Nancy Wilson who doesn't drink. Scotch for the men. Beer for those who are on the wagon. Tomato juice for tomorrow morning's Bloody Marys. Angostura Bitters for those who prefer a more radical hangover cure. Crème de menthe and Blue Curaçao and advocaat and grenadine and any other sweet-tasting brightly coloured drink you care to mention because sometimes one of the women wants to try a new cocktail – and in any case the bottles look nice ranged along the back of Jack's bar their sugary pinks and blues and yellows and greens catching up the colours of the women's dresses.

At six when Consuelo and her sister are having their meal in the kitchen Vivienne has her shower. At a quarter to seven Consuelo goes home to feed her baby and Fernanda changes into the black dress and white apron she will wear that evening when she hands round the canapés. At seven Vivienne does her face and nails and hair. Then when she has been to kiss Tony goodnight she lies down on her bed to rest for half an hour. It's going to be a long and tiring evening.

At a quarter to eight Vivienne starts to dress so that when the first of her guests arrive – fashionably late at a quarter past – she can be there to greet them poised and immaculate in her new midnight-blue shantung with the shawl collar a fresh cigarette in one hand the other outstretched in welcome.

'Marjorie, dear, how lovely to see you. Roger, hello. What lovely flowers. How sweet. You really shouldn't have bothered . . .'

And Jack in the doorway behind her a large whisky – not his first – already in his hand.

'Hey, Rog, you old son-of-a-gun, how's tricks? And who's this cute-looking gal? Don't tell me it's Marjie? It *is* Marjie. Marjie, you look terrific. You know for a minute there, Rog, I thought you must have traded in the old model for a new one . . .'

'Starting as you mean to go on?' Vivienne murmurs

under her breath as smiling brightly she relieves Marjorie Stevens of her wrap and hands it to Fernanda. It is common knowledge that the Stevenses' marriage has been going through a bad patch. Roger Stevens's predilection for younger women being only one of the reasons.

From where she stands behind the door Tony watches her mother greet the guests. Smiling in that way she has: amused and civilized. Her head tilted a little to one side as if weighing up the precise meaning of each detail. The small complacent smile with which Jean McBride glances up at her husband resting her hand on her spreading belly; the eggwhite-stiff waves of Nancy Wilson's new permanent; the fact that Sylvia and Frank Riley aren't speaking again. Vivienne smiles tilts her head smokes her cigarette with graceful gestures.

'Joan. Ronnie. So glad you could come.'

Clipped polite phrases fall like bits of glass. *How nice. So glad.*

More people arrive. The Johnsons – Babs and Ted. He's from Texas; she's a New Englander – a distinction sharpened by their exile. *My, what a darling room. I just love your drapes . . . Why can't we get drapes as pretty as these, honey?*

Vivienne smiles a shade automatically allowing Jack to perform the introductions. Break the ice. It's what he's good at.

'Ted, you know Roger Stevens, don't you? Roger's our top seismologist. One of the smart guys who's always telling us what's what, hey, Rog? Ted's from the Old Country – not yours, *old boy*, mine. Ted and I go way back, don't we, Ted?'

'Sure do,' Ted Johnson agrees taking the proffered

glass from his old drinking buddy. 'Well,' he says. 'Here's mud in your eye . . .'

The room fills up with noise smoke laughter. Sounds of ice chinking into glasses and of whisky bottles being unscrewed as Jack assumes his favourite role. *Scotch on the rocks, coming up. A dry Martini for the lady. Yessir* . . . Aloof from this convivial banter Vivienne circulates amongst her guests.

Seeming almost to float it seems to Tony in her hiding place behind the door. Midnight-blue skirts swaying above slender ankles; feet already poised for flight in their high-heeled shoes.

People are smoking – filter tips and mentholated – and drinking highballs and dry Martinis. The mood is relaxed; good-humoured. None of the evening's latent tensions have yet declared themselves.

Fragments of conversation reach her.

I say, old man – have you seen my wife?

If she's the cute redhead I was looking for her myself . . .

A group of men near the door are discussing the Brazilian strikes. Mr Stevens blames the Communists. *It's the thin end of the wedge. Once Rio de Janeiro falls, the rest of South America will follow, you mark my words* . . .

Mr Porter is of the same opinion. *It's the same every-where you look. Take Indo-China. Bally place simply overrun with Reds.* He puffs out his chest self-importantly toothbrush moustache bristling as if defying anyone to disagree. *And as for that bloody wog Nasser. The cheek of the man. What he needs is a bloody good hiding* . . .

Mrs Brown is telling Mrs Wilson about her problems

with her cook. *I really had to ask her to leave. It was starting to show. Well, I mean – you couldn't have her in the house, looking like that. Douglas simply put his foot down . . .*

Later Tony knows there will be dancing. She'll hear it as she lies in bed – the big band sound of Nelson Riddle; the mellifluous voice of Nat King Cole. And Cuban dance bands – José Fajardo's All Stars; 'Mongo' Santamaría and His Black Cuban Diamonds – playing sambas and rumbas and chachacha.

> *Yo vengo sacando candela*
> *Yo vengo sacando candela . . .*

'Sparkling Fire' – that was one of her favourites. Just hearing it made her want to dance. But she was too young to stay up late Vivienne said. She'd have to wait a year or two before she could join the fun.

In her mind's eye she can already see the way the full skirts of the women's dresses with their stiff taffeta petticoats will swing out as each dancing couple moves around the room forming patterns which constantly break up and re-form like the coloured mosaic in her cardboard kaleidoscope: circles which change into squares and squares into diamonds.

Lying awake she'll hear voices under her window. Somebody's wife with somebody's husband. A stifled gasp. *Oh, darling. Darling, please. Darling, no.*

The music will get louder. Voices will be raised in drunken altercation. Someone (probably her mother) will turn the music down.

Whatthehell . . .

Please, Jack . . .

153

Later still there'll be the sound of car doors slamming tyres on gravel. Shouted farewells then silence. Jack's voice: *Hey, look at me. You're not angry with me, baby, are ya?*

And then Vivienne's – cold with anger: *Don't be absurd.*

Through the crack in the door the colours click and shift.

Vivienne giving some instruction or other to Consuelo catches sight of her daughter. 'Antonia, you're supposed to be in bed.'

She shakes her head reprovingly then relents. 'Come and say goodnight, then.'

Draws her by the hand to the centre of a laughing circle. Faces looking down at her through a haze of smoke. *What an angel. Vivie, I swear she gets more like you every day* . . . A musky smell of warm flesh overlaid with My Sin tickles her nose as Mrs Porter swoops to kiss her. *Night-night, duckie.* The sticky print of lipstick left on her cheek.

'Say goodnight to Jack. Then bed.'

Since the trip to Caracas Tony has kept her distance from Jack. Their contact limited to the briefest exchanges. Hi, kid. How's tricks? he'll say and she'll say, Fine. Keeping her eyes lowered to conceal the panic in her eyes. She avoids being alone with Jack these days – and once when he asked her if she wanted to go to the factory with him she invented a stomachache. If he has noticed her reticence when he is around he has given her no sign of it. Preoccupied perhaps with his own conflicting desires.

On this occasion there is no good reason not to speak to him. He won't notice her anyway the mood he's in.

Eyes very bright and tie loosened he's leaning on the bar surrounded by the crowd which always surrounds him on these occasions. As she pushes her way through the acres of billowing skirts and scarcely less voluminous trouser legs she can hear his voice – *Goddammit, that sonofabitch took off so fast he didn't even stop to pull on his pants* – and then the burst of laughter which greets his story.

As Tony moves closer her progress impeded by the crush of bodies around the bar she becomes aware of a slight change – a shifting of atoms no more – in the room's constitution. An atmospheric pressure drop.

A few people fall silent. Someone laughing at a joke sounds unexpectedly loud. Conversations are resumed with unnatural suddenness.

Hemmed in by swirling fabric and the solid bodies it contains Tony can't at first work out what has made this difference. Until she hears Vivienne say above the conversational babble, 'Why, Piet. And Sofie, isn't it? So glad you could come. How nice . . .'

And now Tony by judicious manoeuvring slips through the narrow gap between Mr Riley's navy broadcloth back and Mrs McBride's voluminous lilac satin. She hears Sylvia Riley murmur 'My *dear*! That *dress*.' And Jean McBride's reply: 'Whsst! She'll hear you.'

There isn't anything wrong with Mrs van Wel's dress that Tony can see – although it certainly isn't the kind of dress that Mrs Riley wears. But there's a look on her face which makes Tony think perhaps she doesn't want to be here; and she's holding on to Mr van Wel's arm as if she's frightened he might suddenly abandon her on the threshold of a room full of strangers.

'Sofie, do let me take your wrap,' Vivienne is saying as she draws the new arrivals in. 'Such a pretty one, but I don't think you'll need it. It's so warm tonight . . .' This last remark is delivered as if warm evenings are rather the exception than the rule here.

She removes the shawl from Mrs van Wel's reluctant grasp and hands it to Fernanda who bears it away to the bedroom. Mrs van Wel watches it go with unhappy eyes.

'Piet, buddy – what'll it be?' says Jack behind the bar.

Piet requests a small whisky and a soda water for his wife. When she takes the glass from his hand she glances fearfully inside it as if afraid its contents might poison her.

'Let me introduce you to some people . . .'

Vivienne is trying hard Tony can tell. It's one of the things she's good at putting people at ease. Tony has heard Mrs Riley say this so she thinks it must be true. 'Vivienne never *condescends*,' Mrs Riley says. 'She treats everyone exactly the same. Which, in my opinion, is a mark of good breeding . . .'

Tony can see that Vivienne's good breeding isn't having much effect on Sofie van Wel. So far she hasn't said a single word. Clutching her untasted drink she stares at the floor in front of her as if she wishes it would open up and swallow her.

Vivienne introduces her guests to Sylvia and Frank Riley who contrive to shake hands with the newcomers without acknowledging one another's presence in any way. 'So you're the new man,' Tony hears Sylvia say to Piet van Wel. 'We've heard *such* a lot about you . . .'

Jean McBride admires Sofie's dress. 'What a pretty frock, Mrs van Wel. Did you make it yourself?'

Sofie gives a small pained smile but makes no other response.

'So how do you like Casigua?' Frank Riley gallantly interjects. There is a brief silence. Sofie stares at the floor. A short laugh escapes her. Before she can speak her husband answers for her.

'We find it rather –' he pronounces it *rahzer* – 'different from Holland.'

Frank nods his head vigorously. *Couldn't agree more, old boy.*

'It is, perhaps, a little bit . . . hotter.' Piet accompanies this remark with a humorous grimace to show that it is a joke. Ironic understatement. The thing northern Europeans have in common.

Frank Riley laughs immoderately. 'A little bit hotter, I like that. Yes, I suppose you could say it was a little bit hotter. Infernally hot, I'd say. Still, you get used to it. Beats the jolly old British winter . . .'

'We have winters in Holland too,' Piet says drily.

So he's got a sense of humour, Vivienne thinks – well, that's something. Funny how much more attractive a man looked once you put him in a dark suit – even one that had clearly seen better days. Pity they couldn't have managed a new dress for Mrs van W. She was sure she had any number of things she could let her have – the trouble was people like that were so proud, she'd see it as charity.

Tony thinks Sofie van Wel has the whitest face she's ever seen – whiter even than Mrs Wilson's with her red hair and freckles. Skin so pale it looks as if it's never seen the sun. Her hair is dark. Not as dark as Consuelo's – that blue-black glossy mass – or even Mrs Riley's raven curls. Heavy lustreless coarse black hair parted severely

157

on one side and fastened with a clip. Her straight dark eyebrows drawn together in the middle make her look angry and anxious at the same time.

She is wearing this expression as Vivienne takes charge of her husband drawing him across the room to where a group of his colleagues are standing. Sofie looks as if she would like to follow but before she can do so her path is blocked by Betty Brown. 'I don't suppose you know who I am,' says Betty, shaking her finger roguishly in Sofie's face, 'but I know who you are . . .'

'God help us,' murmurs Sylvia.

'I called on you a while back,' Betty explains to the bemused Sofie. 'But you were out. At least . . .' She wrinkles her brow in feigned perplexity. 'I *think* you were out . . .'

'Now I suppose she'll drag up the bloody cake,' mutters Sylvia.

'Did you say something, Sylvia?' says Betty sharply.

'Not to you, darling,' Sylvia replies. 'Do tell us,' she says addressing Sofie, 'is your husband as clever as he looks? He has such a clever face. I do love a man with a clever face . . .'

'I didn't think it was men's *faces* you were interested in,' says Betty with a snide little laugh.

Sylvia opens her eyes very wide. 'What a vulgar remark. Even for you, Betty.'

'Excuse *me*.' Betty has gone bright red. 'I think I see my husband over there . . .'

'Suburban little cow,' Sylvia murmurs not quite *sotto voce*.

'And how's your little girl – Annetje, isn't it?' Jean McBride asks Sofie to fill the silence created by this exchange. 'Over the worst now, is she?'

At the mention of her daughter's name Sofie looks startled. Her eyes dart to where her husband is standing separated from her by a wall of men. She opens her mouth as if to speak but no sound comes out. Her eyes fill slowly with tears.

'Oh, dear.' Jean glances at Sylvia who is watching them both with an expression of sardonic amusement. 'Did I say the wrong thing?'

'Darling, you have an *instinct* for putting your foot in it. It's your Scottish forthrightness.' Sylvia yawns delicately. 'Although what possessed him to bring her, I can't imagine. Talk about a fish out of water . . .'

Vivienne appears at Sofie van Wel's side. 'Do let me get you something to eat,' she says with great gentleness. 'You must be starving. Antonia –' acknowledging her daughter's presence as if for the first time – 'get Mrs van Wel a plate and a napkin, will you? Tell Fernanda to bring one of those trays of sandwiches. And then get to bed – you should have been asleep hours ago . . .'

She turns the pages of the book, looking for something – she isn't sure what. Some kind of definition, perhaps.

Columbus believed the world was not a perfect sphere but slightly squashed – like an orange or a woman's breast. At the top – or nipple – of the world, lay paradise. It was this he thought he had found when he anchored that day, sick with fever, in the Bay of Parian. He wrote in his Journal:

I believe if I were to sail beyond the Equator, I should find increasingly greater temperance in the climate and variation in the stars – though I do not suppose that it is possible to navigate there, where the world reaches its highest point, not for any man to approach, for I believe that there the earthly Paradise is located, where no man may go, save by the grace of God.

Amerigo Vespucci wrote a book about his travels in Venezuela before he had even visited the place. It was he (although some say it was in fact Ojeda) who gave the country its name – which means 'Little Venice' – because the houses on stilts in Lake Maracaibo reminded him of that city.

Ojeda wrote his memoirs, which have been lost. Their title was Alonso de Ojeda, the Unfortunate.

Raleigh, who failed to find El Dorado, wrote a History of the World.

The Quiriquire Indians were regarded as cannibals by the Spanish, who burned a 'C' into their flesh with hot irons. Writing of a different stripe.

Around her, under the blue dome, other readers stir as if in troubled sleep. A sigh like that of a light wind on a summer's day, which is the sound of turning pages, moves around the room.

5

It is a season for parties, everyone is having them – you'd think it was a patriotic duty Sylvia Riley says. Dinner parties where roast beef and Yorkshire pudding are consumed in the heat. Fancy dress parties where everyone wears red white and blue. Mrs Porter as Britannia in a cardboard breastplate and Mrs Wilson in a paper ruff as Good Queen Bess.

At the clubhouse that afternoon people are wearing their best clothes. There's an air of solemnity – like being in church Tony thinks. She and Vivienne are among the last to arrive because Vivienne has been trying to persuade Jack to accompany them. It'll look bad if he doesn't she says but he says it's not his kind of thing. I'm an American citizen in case you didn't know he tells her and she says as if I could forget. Just as long as you don't forget who won the war for you Jack reminds her and after that she doesn't say anything only tells Tony to hurry up it's time to go.

The room has been decorated with red white and blue bunting and a large portrait of the new queen hangs in the middle of the wall. Benches have been set out in rows in front of the portable screen. The front rows have already been filled. Small paper flags have been handed out at the door.

Mary McBride looks round and pats the empty seat

beside her. 'Guess what?' she says as Tony sits down.

'Don't know,' Tony says. 'What?'

'Stuart and David are back next week.' Stuart and David are Mary's brothers. Stuart's fourteen; David twelve and a half. They're both at boarding school in England. Tony doesn't see them that much any more – although when they were kids she used to play with David.

Now her voice betrays only the mildest interest. 'Are they?'

'Yes.'

'Oh.'

'Peter Riley's back too,' says Mary.

'I know.'

'And that stuck-up Kate . . .' She puts on a high affected voice which sounds nothing like Kate Riley's. 'Don't you *adore* lacrosse?'

Tony suspects she's only saying this because Kate says people who are Low Church are common and Mary's father's a Presbyterian minister. Mr McBride says people who drink and smoke and practise fornication have sold themselves to the Devil. Kate says everyone knows Christ preferred the publicans and sinners. And what about Mary Magdalene? She must have practised fornication like billyo. Kate's High Anglican – the same as Tony. Vivienne says you should say C. of E. if anybody asks you.

The lights go down. The white screen is filled with dazzling light. Then a few frames of flickering nothingness. Then numbers: 9, 8, 7 . . . And the screen is suddenly alive with moving figures: crowds lining a wide street. The film is in colour. *Oh, look*, Tony hears someone whisper. *It's raining. How perfectly typical.*

There's a burst of static from the loudspeaker in front
of the screen and then the sound of recorded cheering
fills the room. The commentator's voice is heard – a
little out of sync with the images being shown – as the
gilded coach draws up in front of the Abbey steps.
Then the cameras move inside the building to where the
doll-like figure stands almost crushed by its heavy robes
of state awaiting the signal for the ceremony to begin.

Karel sits and stares at the empty page in front of him,
and at the board on which his teacher has written the
words she has asked him to copy.

If I should die, think only this of me . . .

He picks up the pen once more. He traces the words.
Slowly the letters appear, an inky snail's trail across the
white.

If I should die . . .

The trail, which had proceeded smoothly thus far,
expires in a shower of blots. A deep wound, where the
pen nib has gouged the paper. The desk's surface is
uneven, scored by generations of penknives until it
resembles a palimpsest. He lifts the paper and reads
the names inscribed beneath it. P. J. Horrocks. A. L.
Wickham. R. O. Smythe. It is one of these who has
tripped him up, as effectively as if he had stuck out a
foot in the playground.

Squaring up the foolscap so that it is perfectly aligned
with the sheet of blotting paper on which he has been
resting, Karel makes another attempt. Lightness and
speed, the qualities he aims for, elude him now as always.
Words, when he tries to hold them, slip out of reach.

If I should die, think only this . . .

Intent on achieving the perfect line, Karel neglects

to dip his pen at the appropriate time. The flowing contour of the sentence breaks and dwindles to ugly scratching.

He gazes at the spoilt page through a blur of unshed tears. From where he sits, the world is reduced to a square of brilliant blue, seen through the screen of leaves and scarlet blossoms which half-obscures the view from the window. The peppery smell of wild tomatoes drifts in on the warm breeze. Doves call from the jacaranda tree. *Por favor, por favor*, they say over and over. Karel's throat aches with longing.

'How are you getting on?'

She glides from behind the desk where she has been sitting all this while, red pencil in hand, calmly going through a pile of exercise books. *What I Did in My Holidays* is the theme: his is amongst the pile.

In my holiday I stay home, he had written. *Mine sister she stay home too.*

'Very good, Karel,' says his teacher, looking over his shoulder. 'Now see what you can do with the next line . . .'

He's still labouring over the intricacies of this – *some . . . corner . . . of . . . a . . . foreign . . . field* – when a slight sound in the room behind tells him someone else has come in. He doesn't need to look around to know who it is.

'Come in,' he hears his teacher say. 'We're just finishing off an exercise.'

'I can wait outside,' says his father.

'No – please. Take a seat.' Then, as she sees him try to squeeze himself behind one of the antiquated desks, she laughs. 'That is, if you can . . .'

'Better if I stand,' he says, with a rueful grin.

There is silence – broken only by the scratching of Karel's pen.

Karel's father clears his throat. 'I will ask a favour,' he says. 'But maybe it's too much to expect . . .'

'I can't tell you until I know what it is,' his teacher says.

'I don't speak so good,' his father says. 'But I studied English in school three years.' He shrugs. 'I can read – not good, but a little. I thought maybe if I could read sometimes with Kareltje we could learn together . . .'

'That's a very good idea.' Karel's teacher smiles at Karel's father over Karel's head. 'What kind of book should it be? An adventure story, I think. What do *you* think, Karel?'

He is so startled at being addressed that he drops the pen, smudging the still-wet lines. He mutters something, but his teacher is no longer listening.

'A story about pirates perhaps,' she says, stacking the scattered books in front of her into a neat pile. 'Or explorers. Antonia might have something. I'll see what I can find.'

'You are very kind to take so much trouble,' says Piet.

'It's no trouble at all,' Vivienne says.

After this neither of them says anything for a while.

The smell of burning was the first thing he noticed. A singeing smell, as of scorched feathers; charred bones. The smell was accompanied on occasion by related phenomena. Smoke – or not smoke, exactly, but the darkening of the atmosphere smoke leaves in its wake. A film of grit on a windowpane; a smear of blackened grease. Curls of ash drifting on the air.

The wind was in the wrong direction: that was his

father's explanation. Smoke from the refinery was blowing inland. It was this which turned everything black.

Karel knew different, of course – but what good would it have done to say so? Better to keep quiet about this as about all the other things.

These were various and not in themselves alarming. Arrangements of harmless objects: a handful of stones, set out in a circle; feathers; flower heads; candlewax. One of Annetje's games, he'd thought at first; though when he asked her about it, she just looked blank. The marks on the doorsill were harder to account for: crosses, scratched in charcoal and what looked like blood.

Then there was the day Karel came home from school and found his mother talking or rather not talking but only listening to the old woman he'd seen once before in the back kitchen of the English house.

It had only been for a moment – he and the girl had been passing through, the girl talking as usual – but he'd known he was in the presence of someone powerful. Such an old, old woman, with such white hair, and such a lined dark face. The maid, Consuelo, said his name. The old woman stroked his cheek with her hard brown fingers. Her black eyes never leaving his face, as if committing all she saw there to memory.

Now he sees her again, drinking sweet black coffee in his mother's kitchen, her legs tucked under her long black skirts so that she resembles a roosting bird. She gives no sign that she and Karel have met before, but her black eyes move from his mother's face to his and back again in one swift look.

Sofie pays no attention to her son – perhaps she doesn't even know he's there. She stares instead at the plaster effigy which stands on the table between her and her strange guest: the figure of a woman in long white robes. At first glance, it's no different from the statues you see everywhere here – on the dashboards of cars and in the roadside chapels to the memory of accident victims – except that the robes the woman wear are red, not blue; her hair black, not golden like the Virgin's. The figure's eyes are blue and she wears a crown on her head: gold, studded with jewels. A queen, then – or at least a princess, Karel surmises.

As he watches from the doorway, hardly daring to breathe, he sees his mother stretch out her hand towards the figure; she doesn't touch it, but only spreads out her fingers, as if warming herself at a fire.

His mother has gone away, he doesn't know where – he thinks the old woman must have taken her. In her place has been left a smiling stranger. She's quiet and gentle and kinder to him than before; but something about her eyes makes Karel afraid. It's as if she's looking not at him, but through him – as if he had suddenly become transparent, a ghost.

Once, he wakes to find her standing at the end of his bed looking down at him. She doesn't speak but just goes on staring, as if she has no idea who he is or what he's doing there. He's heard her talking to someone in the next room when he and she are the only ones in the house.

There are days when she seems just as before: the way she used to be when Karel was small, before they came to this place. He remembers that time.

There was the house where they lived with Oma and Opa, with the big dark rooms that smelt of the stuff

Oma used to make the floor shine and whatever they'd had for dinner and the verbena water Oma wore, all mixed up in one smell. There was the room with the big square table covered with the red and blue carpet, where Karel liked to sit, hidden by the dusty folds that hung down all around. If you lifted a corner of the carpet you could see the room rising above you, through forests of chair legs and tables with silver-framed photographs of people in old-fashioned clothes, past the mantelpiece with its pewter candlesticks and the blue Delft plates on the wall to where, almost lost in the gloom, the brass lamp hung on its chain.

Sometimes when Karel had been under the table a while his grandmother's voice would say, 'Where's that little mouse? He's very quiet down there, under the floorboards.' And then he'd make a noise like a mouse and Oma would say, 'Come out, little mouse, and see what you can find . . .' And he'd come out, and there would be *speculaas* shaped like windmills and sheaves of corn, and honey cake cut in slices and spread with butter, and tea in tall glasses with a spoon to stir the sugar.

Oma used to let him wash the kitchen floor. You squeezed the mop against the side of the bucket and then swept it over the tiles, leaving soapy islands. When it was dry, you tied dusters over your feet and skated up and down. Oma learned how to skate when she was a girl. On wooden skates too – not the kind you have nowadays. She'd grown up in Friesland, on her father's farm. You had cold winters there. The canals froze right over. You could skate all the way to the Zuider Zee without ever leaving the ice.

Opa was blind; he sat in a chair. His eyes had no

colour in them at all. When you came into the room he knew who it was from the sound your footsteps made. He held out his hand for you to hold; sometimes, very lightly, he touched your face with his fingers. That was the only way he could see you, Oma said.

Opa had been a captain in the merchant navy. He had been to the Far East – to Java, Sumatra and Singapore. In the glass-fronted cabinet where he kept his pipes and tobacco pouch was a shrunken head, as brown and wizened as a dried apple. There was a knife with a mother-of-pearl handle, and a conch shell you could hold to your ear to hear the sound of the sea. The best thing was an ivory ball, no bigger than an orange. It was carved with tiny figures of men and tigers and elephants; there were houses and boats and palm trees and a smoking volcano. A complete world: when you held it in your hand you couldn't believe how light it was.

Karel doesn't remember much from before Annetje was born, but he does have one memory of Sofie. She is standing in the doorway of the room where he is sitting on his father's lap, and she is wearing a new dress. He knows it must be new, because of the way his mother is standing, with one foot slightly in front of the other, like a dancer, holding out the skirt with the tips of her fingers, for his father to admire. The dress is blue, with tiny white flowers. Karel thinks it must be the most beautiful dress in the world.

Before he went to sleep, his mother used to read him stories. There was one about a toad with a diamond in its head and one about a talking bird. The one he liked best was about the girl who climbed up the ladder to the moon, and every night she stole a little of the moon's fire; and on the last night the old woman who tends the fire sprang up and caught her.

He wonders if it is the same old woman who has taken his mother away.

In the street a man with white eyes stares after her as she passes, muttering a warning. A flight of birds went left to right across the sky. Her dead mother stood at the end of the bed and smiled sadly at her as if she would have liked to speak.

Sofie wakes with the taste of metal on her tongue. The face she sees in the mirror is not her own. If she sits very still and keeps her eyes to herself the other will go away. She knows better than to wish for this too much. It makes the other angry.

When the other is angry she does bad things. Once she tore the sheet from top to bottom with her nails. Another time she broke the bathroom window. Afterwards, they said it was the boy throwing stones – but she knew the real story. She thought it best to keep quiet about what she knew.

The other's thoughts are not her thoughts – they frighten her. Filling her head with terrible images. Flies crawling across a dead face: feasting on lips and eyes. Bodies of children broken and thrown on the fire.

The other makes her say things, sometimes. Cruel things, which make her children fear her. She feels the other's rage rise up inside her. Choking her, so that she has to vomit it up or die. At night the other crouches over her bed; tormenting her. Putting a whore's thoughts in her head and turning her body to stone.

She has tried reasoning with the other, but to no avail. She thinks maybe she will starve her out – or burn her.

The day of the window she took a long shard of glass from the debris and hid it in her clothes. Later, she sliced her hand open, hoping the pain would cure her. The other only laughed, as the blood dripped down. Smearing her face until it was masked with red.

She knew then the other was too strong for her – the other would never die, unless she herself died first. It was then she began to be afraid of what she might do. It makes her children afraid too, she can see it in their eyes.

The old woman is not afraid of her, she can tell that at once. She sits in her chair with her legs tucked under her skirt and her hands folded in her lap, and looks at Sofie with her small black eyes. She speaks softly in Spanish. Sofie cannot understand what she is saying, but she can tell from the sound of the voice that the woman is sorry for her, and that she will help her if she can.

All the time the old woman is sitting there, Sofie feels a great calm. She watches the old woman's moving lips, hears her soft voice murmuring gentle words. *María, María Lionza*, she hears her say. She knows that is the name of the old woman's god. María Lionza will heal you, the old woman tells her. Anything is possible for María Lionza.

There was the time she saw them in the street. Or thinks she saw them; she doesn't know for certain.

She was walking along Singel towards Bloemenmarkt, keeping her eyes down, not looking to left or right, not running and not dawdling. Making herself invisible.

She had been sent to get bread and had waited two hours in front of the bakery with all the others before the woman banged down the shutter and sent them away with a shrug. *Tomorrow, maybe.* She remembers the hunger sharpened by disappointment; the pain took her breath away so that she had to stop, her hands pressed to her side.

It was then she saw them.

Two ranks of men in black uniforms, their prisoners walking between. Ten or twelve of them, at a guess, of whom some were old, some young. Nothing special about them, in fact, except the fact that they were there – in that place, at that time. Some shuffled along, staring at the ground, all resistance gone; others seemed more aware. Looking about them as they walked, as if the opportunity to do so might not come again.

As she watched, one stumbled and would have fallen if another had not caught him.

She saw the face of the first man: it was torn and bloody, the lips a bursting pulp, the eyes mere slits in swollen flesh. If it was her brother Sam, his own mother would not have known him.

The other man, the one who had helped him, passed close enough to where she was standing for her to have reached out and touched him. To this day she does not know if he saw her or not. Her brother Jacob.

There was a moment, she thinks, when their eyes met and something – recognition, perhaps – passed between them.

It is this which returns to her most of all, so that there are times when her thoughts seem no more than an endless prolongation of that memory: his startled look, instantly checked. His knowledge, her betrayal.

She dreams of drowning. The water closing over her head; mud filling her mouth. A roaring in her ears like the moment before blacking out, when you feel yourself begin to fall and you know there's nothing you can do to save yourself.

Breathe. She can't breathe. She tries to scream but no sound comes.

Something brushes her cheek. It's a child's hand, the fingers grey and swollen; waterlogged.

She wakes in the dark, her heart pounding. Visions of a wasteland, covered with water, are what she sees. Bloated bodies of dead cattle washed up on a sandbank. Drowned trees, sticking up out of motionless tracts of water.

When he told her, she hadn't believed it at first. Then he showed her the photographs in the newspaper. The sheeted corpses laid out in rows. People crouched on rooftops. The flooded fields a gigantic mirror, reflecting a white sky.

What had happened seemed an inversion of everything she had known. That the sea could be controlled and the land increased was something she took for granted. Every child knew that – it was what you learned in school. They had colonized the sea, because there was not enough room in the world for their restless desires. It was what had made them great – their restlessness, and their refusal to be daunted by the impossible.

The whole country was an improbability: a mechanism for the redistribution of water. You could walk about on land which had once been at the bottom of the sea. Most improbable of all was the city. 'A water clock,' her father called it, explaining the way the canals worked. They harnessed the tides with an intricate system of sluices which, when opened, let fresh water in and flushed bad water out, and when closed prevented flooding. 'A water clock or an open sewer,' her father said. 'Think of that – a city built on a sewer . . .'

The Dutch had never had enough land – that was well known. And what you didn't have you had to take. First they'd taken as much land as they could from the sea and then they'd gone over the sea in search of more. When the Verenigde Oost Indische Compagnie was at the height of its power, they'd been the richest nation on earth.

They were good enough at getting hold of land, Sofie's father said, but they weren't so good at keeping hold of it. They'd lost New Amsterdam to the English – that was a bad bargain, if ever there was one. Now there was nothing left – a handful of small islands. Surinam. Curaçao. Remnants of a Golden Age.

Sometimes it's as if her father is in the next room. She can't believe he won't walk in the door at any moment and resume their interrupted conversation.

There are times when she hears his voice, speaking softly, the way he always used to do. Telling her things, explaining things, as his hands moved tirelessly among the scattered cogs and watchsprings on his workbench. Holding her breath, she'd watch as he picked up the delicate fragments with his tweezers, examining them for flaws through his jeweller's glass. Discarding what was beyond repair. Assembling what was salvageable into a working mechanism.

The sun is the worst thing. Sometimes she thinks the sun will drive her mad.

Everything is much too bright: the yellow sun, the red earth, the blue sky. Where she comes from, you never see such colours, except maybe on a cheap calendar tacked to a kitchen wall.

There are no shades of grey here. It is like being all the time in the full glare of noon. It is the light which has made her ill, she thinks.

Sometimes she wakes with the pain already starting behind her eyes. A knotted cord, slowly tightening. Her tongue feels too large for her mouth.

When she was a child, she used to have fevers. She remembers her father sitting beside her bed all one night, while she told him what she could see. A white desert, smooth and featureless as a taut sheet; nothing for miles in all directions. Whether it was sand or snow, she couldn't be sure. All she knew was that it was endless.

Hush now, said her father, but she said, Wait – that isn't the worst thing. The worst thing is the darkness which comes afterwards. You can't shut your eyes and make it go away, she tells him, because the darkness is there. Everywhere you look, she says – even inside your head. That's the worst thing.

Now she looks in the mirror and sees half her face has disappeared. Soon her blindness will be complete.

The pain settles down in her skull like an old friend come to stay.

When the old woman came to see her the first time, it was because she had heard about the pain. Someone – the Englishwoman's maid, perhaps – had told her, and so she came. Sofie opened the door and there she was, in her black dress. She didn't move or speak, waiting for Sofie to invite her over the threshold.

Piet knows he is lucky to be alive; and yet there are times when his survival seems like a peculiarly malevolent joke. To have endured so much for this. Some days he wonders if things wouldn't have been better all round if he had died with the others; or if he could have changed places with one of them that day – de Jong, say, whose wife was expecting. A life for a life.

Then he remembers his children and feels ashamed of the thought.

But still it fascinates him, the randomness of the thing. Why had he been spared, and not one of the others? They had all been no less guilty – or no less innocent.

He has an idea it had something to do with the letters of the alphabet.

Thirteen were chosen. Abelmann but not Beukers, Cuyp but not Dekker. The same scrupulous fairness applied all the way down the line, even where a letter was represented more than once – Hofstede was taken, but not Huisman – or where letters were not represented at all. Thus J was taken for I, P for O, R for Q. In his own case, the absence of U meant that V was passed over. His neighbours, Tauber and Winkelman, were told to step forward.

His task accomplished, the officer with the clipboard had dismissed them with an indifferent wave. All but those whose names he had called.

It has occurred to Piet since that, strictly speaking, he should have been chosen instead of Winkelman. Van Wel only counted as V not W if you read its initial letter as upper, not lower case. Which the officer had done; a fortuitous misreading, for him if not for Winkelman.

And in the end, what did it signify, that one of them had died and the other been saved? Saved for what, was what he sometimes wondered.

His mother would have had no difficulty in answering the question. But then his mother believed all such things were predetermined. There was nothing accidental about it: you were either one of the Elect or you were damned. In this respect, his mother would have seen eye to eye with the German officer.

Marriage to Sofie was apparently part of his destiny. So too was the fact he had ended up here, in this foreign land.

Meeting Vivienne Lindberg might also be regarded in this light. A stroke of luck as improbable as a pencil moving down a list, hesitating over a name, then moving on.

The moment when he first saw her and the moment he knew he was in love with her were separated by several months – and yet, looking back, he finds the two experiences have converged in his mind, so that he cannot now recall one without the other. It was as if the past were being constantly altered by the present: re-evaluated, in the light of that one revelation. All his past words and actions leading up to that moment; everything before and after it changed for ever.

It was that time on the boat, a little way offshore. He remembers the sun beating down on his head and the taste of salt on his tongue. Then seeing her, standing beside him. Her dreaming face, that moment before she saw him. Her startled look, as he said her name. She'd turned, and he knew he was lost.

He can't remember what it was they talked about that day. All he recalls is the way she looked, in her white dress against the blue. The wind blowing her hair back off her face as she stood, gazing out at that glittering immensity. The sun turning her hair to gold. Her eyes. Her smile.

He first met her, of course, at a party. It was the third or fourth he had been to in a week, which was that of his arrival. He was the excuse for this, and the previous three, although there could just as easily have been any number of other reasons – somebody's birthday, somebody else's return from leave, or the fact that there was an 'r' in the month. Looking back, the thing which struck him most about his first few months in the tropics – more than the heat, about which he had at least been warned – was the endless partygoing.

You'd arrive at a strange house where a party was already in progress – had, in fact, been in progress since the late afternoon, when those who'd been up since dawn knocked off work; a drink would be thrust into your hand by someone you'd never met, who would urge you to 'have a good time' and would then disappear; in pursuit of this elusive good time you'd stand around for a while trying to make your drink last, until someone else, out of some misplaced feeling of pity, told you you really *had* to meet some people.

It had been on one of these occasions that he'd met Vivienne. At the time, it had seemed no more significant than a dozen other such encounters with company wives – women in fashionable gowns, who smelled of perfume and American cigarettes, and looked at you with amused curiosity or polite indifference, before resuming more interesting conversations.

If Vivienne stood out from this crowd at all, it was only because she was Lindberg's wife. Not exactly the kind of wife he'd have expected, from what he knew of Lindberg. Oh, she was good-looking enough, if those kinds of looks were to your taste. A cool blonde, with no warmth in her smile; pale eyes meeting his for an instant then glancing away. In retrospect, he knows it was shyness, not coldness, which conditioned her response. Her apparent indifference a mask for its opposite. He wonders now if it wasn't precisely that – her initial resistance – which attracted him; although at the time he thought her merely rude.

Now, with the special pleading of hindsight, he reinterprets the moment, drawing meaning from insignificance. The thought that, at that moment, they were nothing to each other is something he finds hard to believe – that she might so easily have remained just another woman – an imperfectly remembered face, a name.

He sees now that he and Sofie were also casualties of a kind. It was true that neither had died, or suffered more than an average amount of pain or distress – and yet the more he thinks about their present situation, the more it seems to him that the war was to blame.

He remembers Sofie Silberman from the days when she and Lena were both in pigtails and short frocks. Lena used to make fun of her then, calling her the 'white mouse'; and there was certainly something mouse-like about her, with those big dark eyes and long narrow nose. Not pretty exactly, but refined and delicate-looking. The kind of looks which stayed in your mind.

She was very much her mother's girl in those days, he recalls: hanging around the back of Tante Sara's chair until told to go and play with the rest of them – which she did only after repeated tellings, because (he realizes now) it terrified her. She'd stand by the wall and watch them as they played in the street – games of tag and football, at which Lena, who could pass and tackle like a boy, excelled. Sofie never joined in – even when, to tempt her, they switched to the more decorous game of catch. You'd have thought growing up with brothers like those Silbermans would have inured her to rough behaviour. Even at ten or eleven they already had a reputation in the neighbourhood.

But Sofie was different. A sensitive plant. When you spoke to her she shrank back, as if at an unkind touch. She'd been delicate as a child – always ill with one thing or another. He wonders if it hadn't been one of these illnesses – brain fevers they called them then – which had made her the way she was.

He remembers one time when they were all still kids seeing her with Lena, walking down Utrechtsestraat arm in arm. Girls with secrets. He'd been struck by the difference in their heights – Lena towering over little Sofie – although there was only a year or so between them. He remembers thinking how much he'd have liked to be in Lena's place, with Sofie's arm linked through his and her head resting up against his shoulder. He supposes he must have felt protective towards her, even then – she seemed so gentle, so shy. He wonders how he could have got her so completely wrong.

Making love to her is like fucking a corpse; she's rigid, dry. Her arms clamped to her sides all the time he's on top, her face averted.

Moonlight floods the room with its damned light. A tear (does he imagine this?) slides down her face. Not a single word escapes her clenched lips. He knows better than to attempt a kiss.

Her flesh, as he enters her, his engorged prick like a

thing of wood or stone, has a charred smell, a stink of burning feathers.

He begins to move. He wants to flood her, irrigate her – bring the dead to life. Failing that, he wants to beat her black and blue. Make the blood come – anything to alleviate this terrible drought.

In the end her passive resistance proves stronger than his rage. She can take whatever punishment he can give. He can't break her. Nothing can move her. For all he knows (gasping, exhausted, after the pounding he's given her) she might be dead already.

Bloodless. You prick her and she doesn't bleed. Her blood, like her tears, dried up a long time ago. Now all that remains is a shell, a husk of a woman, a life-size doll he fucks and fucks, but can't possess.

Secret. She turns her face away. She's barely breathing it seems to him (feeling the jackhammer rhythms of his own heart); neither love nor hate can reach her.

Softly, in fear and trembling, he says her name. She doesn't reply. It is as if, at his most physical, he has become invisible to her. His seed leaking out of her on to the taut sheet. The intimate whine of mosquitoes the only sound.

Open-eyed in the hot night, watching the ceiling fan revolve, its currents stirring the net above their bed, he wonders how it has come to this.

He was in Amersfoort when the war broke out, doing his military service. Learning how to use a rifle and how to draw a sword without slashing his tunic to ribbons. The hussars were an old and proud regiment, with an attractive dress uniform – one of the reasons he'd picked them. He'd liked swaggering around in that uniform, with his boots and sword. Playing at soldiers. It makes him laugh to think they ever imagined they stood a chance against the real thing.

When the news came in that they'd bombed the airports, he was returning from an exercise with his platoon. There'd been a lot of wild talk amongst the men about joining forces with the French, but in the end they'd capitulated along with the rest. Later, they heard that a few had held out, in Zeeland. Seven days.

It was seven days more than his lot had managed. They'd been stripped of their weapons and confined to barracks for a couple of months, until their captors decided they were no longer a threat. Perhaps the most humiliating part of the whole episode had been when they were told they could go home.

Before military service, he'd been with Shell Werkspoor, working in the machine shop during the day and studying marine engineering at night. When the Germans came they shut down the factory and fired all the workers. Then they rehired all those who wanted to work, and could prove they weren't Jewish, making shell casings for the German war effort.

He hadn't bothered to show up. A week later, as he was walking home after another fruitless attempt to find work he was jumped by two men from the factory, both NSB sympathizers. One held him while the other used his fists. When he was on the ground both used their boots. In between blows and kicks they told him precisely what happened to Jew-lovers, and to the mothers and sisters of Jew-lovers. Two days later he went back to his old job.

It had been in February the following year that Sofie came to live with them. Her brothers had been arrested after the disturbances. Her parents had also been taken. Later they heard they'd been amongst those deported to Mauthausen. Four hundred shot or hanged in reprisal for a single death.

When they'd heard that the dockworkers were coming out on strike as a protest against the killings, he and his comrades at the factory had downed tools in sympathy. The strike had lasted two days. At the end of it he'd been arrested, along with a lot of others. They'd been beaten and thrown in the cells overnight, and in the morning a few of them were shot. The rest, himself included, were sent home. What would have been the point of wasting bullets?

He'd known from the beginning this country had something to give him – had known the minute he'd picked up the pen to sign his name to the three-year contract. It would be a new start: a chance to leave the past behind. When he'd said this to Sofie she'd stared at him in blank dismay. We've nothing to keep us here, he'd told her with an edge of impatience, and she'd said, What is there for us there?

But he'd known it was the right decision. Those first few months he couldn't get over his luck. There was so much of everything here: there was wealth for the taking, if that was what one was looking for. For himself, he was attracted by the newness of everything: the freedom of movement. Europe was burnt out, smashed, a wasteland. Here, they were making a new world.

He thinks of the first trip he made into the jungle, a week or so after his arrival. He and the rest of his party had boarded the Kalamazoo for the journey to Palmira, along the La Solita pipeline, where they would transfer to another train and from there to a boat which would take them to Campo Alegre. The journey was slow – the little train's speed did not exceed twenty-five kilometres an hour – but it could have taken all day and he wouldn't have minded. On either side of the single-gauge track stretched a dense wall of vegetation: weeds and grasses inextricably entwined with the trunks of trees thrusting up towards the light; squat banana palms whose broad, flat leaves cast a greenish shade. Flocks of yellow and green butterflies rose up in shimmering clouds as the train rattled by.

They passed clearings with squatters' shacks built of mud and thatched with palm leaves – *Bella Vista* was the name on one, he saw; railway-sleeper bridges suspended over foaming torrents; men fishing from dug-out canoes; and once a family of basking caymans, motionless as logs on the sandbank. But what he remembers most about the journey was his own sense of wonder – the feeling of being the first person there to see it – although others, he knew, had been there before him; and yet somehow it didn't matter, it was all so new and strange, the feeling of inexorable movement, of rushing onward into a vast green silence.

Towards the end of the trip, they had boarded the company launch *Flor de Mayo* for the three-hour journey along the Escalante River. The sides of the launch were covered with a screen of chicken wire – too coarse to be effective against insects. He had made some humorous remark about it to Lindberg. What kind of mosquitoes did they get around here anyway? Lindberg had given him a curious look: half-amused, half-sceptical.

What kind of mosquitoes? I'll tell you what kind. The human kind. And they bite, believe me . . .

They were near the Colombian border – Motilone country, Lindberg told him. *They don't like strangers. Especially not gringos. One minute you're standing here admiring the view* – his gesture took in the flat brown river, the silent jungle beyond it – *the next, you've got a poison dart in the back of your neck.* His blow took Piet by surprise – a stinging slap across the nape. Jack smiled and held out his hand, the palm of which was smeared with the blood of the monster he had just killed.

All that afternoon they sat making gardens in the dust. First you make a fence of sticks then you fill it up with leaves then you put the flowers on top. Oleanders are her favourite; their thick sweet smell reminds her of churches.

They were going to swim but they couldn't swim because the boy had hurt his leg. So they made gardens instead. The boy wasn't good at it and all his gardens fell apart. After a while he said he wanted to go into the house. She told him they were supposed to stay outside but he wouldn't listen so she let him go.

She made some more gardens and then she took her rope. She skipped a hundred forwards a hundred backwards and a hundred with hands crossed. Then she was tired so she sat on the swing and swung herself backwards and forwards. It was cool in the shade and the sun falling through the leaves cast moving shadows on the ground.

She waited a long time for the boy to come back. She started to think that maybe he had got lost or that something had frightened him. Once a stray dog got into the garden and growled at him. He isn't brave when it comes to dealing with things like that.

He wasn't in the garden and so she climbed the steps to the veranda. It was very quiet and for a minute she thought there was nobody there. But then she saw him *sitting in one of the big cane chairs. He had been crying and there were dirty streaks all over his face where he had rubbed away the tears.*

6

When Tony arrives at the swimming pool the others are already there: the McBride boys – Stuart and David – and Kate and Peter Riley. They lounge on the edge of the pool – Peter stretched out at full length leaning on one elbow Stuart dangling his feet in the water. David is absorbed in the book he's reading; Kate idly watches the struggles of a half-drowned fly. Grouped as they are in various attitudes of indolence and repose they seem to Tony like beings from another world. Immortals.

As she walks towards them across the burning concrete she is conscious that her legs are trembling. It occurs to her when it is too late to turn back that maybe she should have waited until Mary and the others had finished changing. At least then there would have been safety in numbers; on her own she feels exposed to the possibility of humiliation.

Too late she wishes she'd worn her new swimsuit instead of the old one which is too tight across the chest and gets caught between the cheeks of her bottom. She wonders whether to let on that she knows about Stuart's being made Captain of the First Eleven and Peter's Latin translation prize and Kate's suspension for smoking. And if she should ask David to return her copy of *The Treasure Seekers* – lent to him last holidays – or if he might not like being reminded that he once enjoyed childish things.

For one dreadful second it seems to her they might not after all be going to acknowledge her presence. But then Kate glances up.

'Hello, you,' she says.

'Hello.' After a moment's hesitation Tony squats down on her haunches. 'When did you get back?'

Kate yawns. 'Yesterday night – I mean, afternoon. It felt like night. The flight was ghastly. Three-hour delay at Tenerife. Turbulence over Trinidad. David was sick . . .'

'I wasn't sick. I said I *felt* sick . . .'

'You looked pretty green to me. Then they lost our luggage at Caracas airport so we ended up missing the connecting flight and by the time we got to Maracaibo Daddy had decided we weren't coming after all and was just about to give up and go home . . .'

'An average sort of trip, in fact,' says Peter. He looks at Tony. 'So what's new in the tropical paradise?'

She shrugs to conceal the alarm she feels at being directly addressed. 'Nothing much.'

'Nobody dead, dying or divorced? How disappointing. You'd think somebody might at least have murdered somebody.' His green eyes have a disconcerting gleam. She finds it hard to tell when he is being serious. 'I must say,' he adds as if the thought has just occurred to him, 'I'm rather surprised my father hasn't murdered my mother . . .'

'Shut up, Pete,' says Kate.

'I mean,' he goes on ignoring this interruption, 'they were at it, hammer and tongs, again last night. Screaming the place down. You'd think they might have given it a rest on our first evening back, but no . . .'

'I said bloody well shut up . . .'

'If you say so, sister dear.' He rolls over on to his back squinting up at the sky through his long black lashes. 'I just wish,' he murmurs dreamily, 'that if they were going to murder each other they'd hurry up and do it, instead of dragging it out night after night in this tedious fashion . . .'

'At least your lot are interesting,' Stuart says with a glance at Kate who has turned her back on her brother and is humming tunelessly beneath her breath. 'Mine are so insufferably dreary. Do you know the first thing my father said to me when I stepped off the plane? "Time you had a haircut, laddie." I ask you, is that any way for a father to greet his long-lost son?'

'All sons have an obligation to kill their fathers,' says Peter yawning and stretching. 'Like Euripides. Or is it Sophocles? I forget. Anyone for a swim?'

Tony's eyes are closed but she isn't asleep. Under the sheet which is pulled up to her chin she's fully dressed. Ready and waiting.

As she lies there afraid to throw off the covers even though she's much too hot in case Vivienne should take it into her head to check if she's asleep she thinks about the General the night before Carobobo. Lying wakeful and sweating under the mosquito net his stomach taut with nerves – the way hers feels at this moment – his mind going over and over his plan of battle.

Thinking about the General makes her think about that time in Caracas with Jack. She doesn't want to think about this but now she's been reminded of it she can't stop.

Jack and the woman in red. Side by side on the bench

like strangers. Not talking; each seemingly unaware of the other. Tony looks intently at this image noticing all its details. The precise angle at which the woman's head inclines itself towards Jack. The position of her hands. Her crossed ankles. The way Jack stares straight ahead as if lost in thought. The space between these two figures. The oleander blossoms which lie scattered in the dust at their feet.

The golden light of late afternoon lies over this whole picture which projects itself on to the inside of Tony's closed eyes like one of Jack's coloured slides. She fixes her mind on the image trying to keep out the one which follows.

The woman rising – a sudden movement as if something had made her angry. Jack stretching out his hand to catch her wrist and pulling her down beside him.

The woman turning towards Jack. It's too far to hear what she's saying but she's saying something – you can tell from the way she's moving her hands around. Venezuelans always talk with their hands Jack says. Only Jack doesn't let her. He gets hold of her hands.

Tony screws up her eyes very tight to shut out the next part but it's no good – she still has to watch it happen all over again as if she were seeing it for the first time. Jack drawing the woman towards him. Leaning towards her. And then the thing they do next. Even from a distance this is unmistakable. Even Tony knows enough to know a kiss when she sees it.

An owl hoots softly outside her window: once; twice. By the third time she's out of bed and slipping on her shoes. She goes to the window. It's so dark that she can't see a thing. Taking her time so as not to make a noise she lifts the mosquito screen from the frame and leans it against the wall. Then she opens the window.

'Coming,' she whispers into the darkness.

She drops the short distance from the sill to the gravel. As she straightens up a figure rises up beside her; a hand closes over her mouth.

'Don't say a word,' says a voice in her ear although she wasn't going to. 'The enemy are all around us . . .'

It's Peter's voice but when she looks around he's gone. A dark shape moves swiftly across the grass which looks white in the moonlight.

She hesitates no more than a second then follows him on noiseless plimsolled feet. Her heart pounds so hard she can hardly breathe. She is overwhelmed by the feeling that at any moment someone will step out of the shadows and catch her; that a voice from the silent house will ring out suddenly summoning her back.

But no one sees her and no one calls. It occurs to her that in any case the sound of her flight would have been obscured by the noise of cicadas which rises all around her a shrill metallic wheezing. She knows better than to be afraid of this or any of the other night sounds she can hear – but she is glad nevertheless that she is not alone. It feels strange being out here in the dark looking back at the house. It looks different at night with its windows lit like a place she has never been.

As she watches a shadow falls across the living-room blind: a figure restlessly pacing.

Tony pictures although she cannot see the room with its lighted lamps its throw-rugs and scatter cushions its vases filled with flowers. The flowers she knows make Vivienne unhappy. They are so unlike the flowers you get at home. Gaudy Vivienne says; showy and artificial-looking. Their perfume reminds her of cheap scent. On evenings like this when Jack is late and Vivienne is alone the flowers are enough to make her weep.

Tony quickens her pace and catches up with Peter.

'Did you bring the smokes?' he wants to know.

She fumbles in the pockets of her grey school shorts which with the blue and white striped snake belt which holds them up are her most prized possession. The cigarettes aren't too badly crushed and only one or two are actually broken.

He inspects the proffered handful dubiously. 'What are they?'

She hazards a guess. 'Churchman's, I think.'

He takes one. 'They smell a bit stale. You should get your maid to empty the box more often. Got a light?'

'I couldn't find any matches.'

'Haven't you got a lighter? Mine's out of fuel, unfortunately.' He shrugs. 'Never mind. Raoul will have one. Raoul always has everything . . .'

She isn't sure if she knows who this Raoul is. Last summer there were some boys from the village who used to sit on the wall and throw stones. Stuart McBride had a fight with one of them she recalls. A stocky dark-skinned boy with black hair and the beginnings of a moustache on his upper lip. His name was Raoul too. A dirty fighter Stuart said. Kicking and punching a chap when he was down. That was against the rules – anyone could tell you that. She wonders if this can be the same one.

When they reach the gate David is waiting for them with the bikes. The others – Stuart and the mysterious Raoul – have gone on ahead he says.

For some reason this annoys Peter. 'Bloody hell,' he

says. 'I mean, bloody, buggering *hell* . . .' He is still holding the unlit cigarette. He stares at it with disgust then flings it away.

'Don't mind him,' David murmurs to Tony. 'He's been in a mood all day.' He helps her drag her bike from the bushes where she has hidden it. 'Did you get out without your people seeing?'

'Think so.'

'Oh, well done. You know what?' he says taking courage from the surrounding darkness. 'You're jolly brave for a girl . . .'

'Thanks.'

She doesn't feel very brave though as with headlamps dimmed at Peter's insistence to avoid attracting attention they pedal off down the dark uneven road. Around them the night erupts into deafening shrieks and cries. Once a huge powdery moth blunders against Tony's cheek – so that only the thought of losing face with the others prevents her from screaming; another time her front wheel hits a stone and she almost falls off into the ditch. Snakes she thinks with a shudder. Poison toads. Tarantulas. *Caribes*.

Although you wouldn't find *caribes* in stagnant water. They like it fast-flowing. In spite of this she can't stop herself thinking about one of Jack's stories. The day he and some of the guys from the bush camp went fishing in the river and someone stuck a fishhook in his thumb and before you could say knife his arm was stripped to the bone. It's the smell of blood which draws them Jack says.

'All right?' David asks breathlessly catching up with her. His bike – inherited from his brother – isn't as good as Tony's new Raleigh. 'You almost came off there . . .'

'I'm fine.' She finds it hard not to be irritated by his concern; and yet she knows he only means to be kind.

At the point where the track joins the main road to the village Peter waits for them straddling his bike. Frowning he scans the darkness as if looking for a sign. He looks all around; then waves them on. Hugging the edge of the road to keep out of the way of passing traffic – which at that time of night is nothing more than a *burro* led by an old woman and an empty banana truck with a drunken bunch of plantation workers dangling their legs over the tailgate – they descend towards the twinkling stars of the town.

In the village square beneath the statue of Bolívar they meet the others walking around. Stuart and the dark boy Raoul. Stuart is smoking a cigarette. He waves at them airily.

'Hi, kids,' he says.

'Kid yourself,' says Peter scowling. 'Where did you get to?'

Stuart winks and taps his nose with his forefinger. 'Ask no questions and you'll be told no lies.'

Peter shrugs. 'I don't want to know your stupid secrets. You stink of beer, by the way . . .'

'Do I?' Stuart emits a small belch. 'So I do. Maybe it's because I've been drinking.'

'You're pathetic.' Peter starts to walk away wheeling his bike. 'Come on, Tony . . .'

For a moment she is torn between allegiances. She has always looked up to Stuart. At fourteen he is the eldest of the group and until this moment at least the most dependable. Stuart had fixed the puncture on her bike and chased away the rabid dog they'd met on the road that time. He knew how to mend a fan belt and how to suck out the venom from a snakebite. And he'd promised to help her with her backhand this vac.

Set against these not inconsiderable facts is the realization that Peter's approval matters more to her than anything else.

After only the slightest hesitation – a glance of regret towards the flushed and now foolishly gaping Stuart – she picks up her bike and makes to obey the summons. Her throat aches as if she is going to cry although she would rather die than acknowledge this feeling.

'*Epa, chico* . . .' Her path is blocked. Raoul puts his hand on the handlebars of her bike. 'Nice bike,' he says. 'I can ride, no?'

Without waiting for a reply he takes it from her mounts and pedals off across the square. Their argument momentarily forgotten they turn to stare. And certainly Raoul is worth staring at. Too tall for the machine he compensates by standing up on the pedals his legs moving like pistons. A trick cyclist Tony thinks although she has never seen one. It's as if he was born on wheels. Even Stuart for all his prowess can't ride a bike like that. Leaning so far over as he takes the corners that it seems to defy gravity. Back-pedalling so fast that he seems to be standing still one wheel off the ground – like that time at the movies with Jack when the reel started winding backwards.

They watch him open-mouthed.

When he is tired of the game he jumps off and saunters back towards where Tony is standing with the others pushing the bike with one hand.

'Nice bike,' he says again as he hands it over.

'You ride really well.'

'Thanks, *chico*.'

'Well, I'll be damned,' says Stuart. 'Where did you pick that up?'

But Raoul only laughs and shakes his head.

'*Vamos*,' he says. 'We go see my fren', no?'

Raoul's friend works behind the bar at the *bodega*; he lets them in with a nod to the man on the door.

The place is packed. As they walk in Tony's senses are assailed by the heat and the smell – sweat and acrid smoke – so that her eyes water and she almost chokes. Raoul closely pursued by Stuart disappears into the crowd; with a shrug of disdain Peter saunters after followed by David. Feeling the way she does when a big wave is about to close over her head Tony plunges after them into the press of bodies.

Dodging between the tables where men are playing cards she catches glimpses of other actions: a woman laughing head thrown back red mouth wide open; a man in a white shirt open to the waist striking himself repeatedly on his bare chest as if to emphasize a point. Above the shouts and laughter of the crowd can be heard the sound of music: the liquid notes of the harp weirdly shimmering above the staccato drumming of guitars the sibilant whisper of maracas.

'Hey, *chico*,' comes Raoul's voice from somewhere above her head and she looks up to see his face and Stuart's grinning down at her. A staircase leads up to a first-floor gallery; it is here they are sitting their legs dangling down between the roughly carved posts of the balustrade. As she takes her place beside them Stuart passes her the bottle they have been sharing – beer she surmises – she sniffs it just to make sure takes a small sip for politeness' sake then passes it to David. She wonders where Peter has got to.

'Isn't this *prime*?' Stuart demands his beery expansive gesture taking in the room below with its busy knots of people its writhing clouds of blue smoke. 'Decent of Raoul here to arrange it.'

Conscious of Raoul's dark eyes upon her Tony murmurs in agreement.

'Is it a party or something?' she wonders.

'Oh, they carry on like this most nights, don't they, Raoul? Drinking and dancing and the Lord knows what. Jolly good fun it is too,' pronounces Stuart. 'Beats hanging around with the old folks. Noo then, laddie,' he booms in cruelly accurate mimicry of his father's Scottish burr, 'don't let me catch you playing with yersel' or I'll want to know the reason whhy . . .' Stuart hiccups loudly. 'Beg pardon. I say, Raoul old chap – any chance of another beer?'

Raoul ignores him addressing himself instead to Tony. 'See that man?' He points to the man in the white shirt she had noticed earlier. 'Tha's my cousin, Enrique. Tomorrow he gets married. So this is, how you say, his farewell to life . . .'

'Eat, drink and be merry, for tomorrow we die,' chortles Stuart. 'Too right, old boy. Who's the gorgeous piece in yellow? His fiancée, I suppose . . .'

'You kidding?' says Raoul. 'Tha's Mercedes. Enrique's girl. He ain't gonna marry *her*, tha's for sure . . .'

From this vantage point they can see everything – from the cards thrown down by the gamblers (not the familiar hearts and diamonds Tony sees but stranger configurations of swords and cups and coins) to the flaring skirts of the dancers. There is space for only a dozen or so couples on the floor but as the tempo of the music increases more and more people get up to dance seemingly oblivious of the crush their bodies jammed closer and closer to form what looks from above like a single heaving mass.

People aren't so much dancing Tony sees as simply moving in time bodies pressed so close they seem to be glued together the only motion possible in that cramped space the undulation of pelvis against pelvis feet shuffling in lazy two-step. Watching them gives her a funny feeling in the pit of her stomach like the first time she ever smoked a cigarette. A feeling like falling and then catching yourself just in time. She likes the music though – the way it swoops and soars and shimmies. It makes her want to move her feet and jiggle her hips and lose herself in its swirling patterns that repeat and fold back on themselves but never quite seem to end.

She and her companions are not she observes the only children there. A girl about her own age in a white dress stiff with lace and ribbons takes the hands of a much smaller boy a miniature man in long pants and a bow tie and draws him out on to the floor where they begin to dance their steps meticulously aping those of their elders. And on the far side of the room a woman sits calming feeding her baby – a sight Tony finds almost as disconcerting as that time in Caracas when she saw a man spending a penny against a wall and forgot to look away.

The music has changed to a pulsing rhythm that seems to Tony like the pounding of her own heart. Feet are stamping hands clapping and a different mood seems to have overtaken the dancers – one of urgency and recklessness. Someone makes a noise that sounds to

Tony like a bird's call – shrill and loud with the sounds rolled around on the tongue – and at once others take up the cry. The air seems charged – electric – like the night she was watching the storm from her window and saw the flash come down striking the ground so swiftly only the blue-black stain on her retina told her she hadn't dreamt it.

Only a few couples are left on the floor now. They dance with energy and concentration in which there is something fierce as if the dance were a way of hurting – a fight Tony thinks. Except it is more graceful than any fight she has seen. The men dance with little stamping steps barely lifting their feet from the floor all the movement narrowed down into the hips. The women move around them never facing towards their partners never moving outside the circle whose centre is the man.

Now there are only two couples left. One of these is Raoul's cousin the future bridegroom and the woman in the yellow dress. They are the best dancers in the room Tony sees – the man standing there so proud and cold in his white shirt with his arms folded his feet tapping out the rhythm the woman moving in close to him but never quite touching tossing her head and stamping her feet as if she were angry about something. Then as Tony watches holding her breath the woman in the yellow dress suddenly seems to grow tired of her partner and turns away skirts spinning into the arms of the other man which are open to receive her.

'Oh, oh,' murmurs Raoul. 'Tha's trouble . . .'

At the card table voices are raised and someone bangs down a glass so hard the whisky in it jumps up into the air.

'I tol' you.' Raoul smiles at her his eyes dark and shining. 'Big trouble . . .'

All Tony can think is how late it is and that they still have the ride home ahead of them. Her head aches from the noise and the smoke. David she sees has fallen asleep his face pressed against the wooden bars of the balustrade so that his cheek is striped with red pressure marks. She wishes Stuart would tell Raoul it's time for them to go but Stuart seems to have disappeared.

'I think it's time we called it a night, don't you?' says Peter's voice in her ear. 'That is, as soon as McBride's recovered from his funny turn . . .'

Tony is so relieved to see him she can't speak. 'Where were you?' she says at last.

'Oh, just walking around,' Peter says vaguely. 'I couldn't stand the noise.'

The night air is cool on their faces as they step outside. The moon is full and all the houses of the little town gleam white in its cold glare. Leaning against a wall they find Stuart now as pale as he was red before.

'I feel like death,' he tells them croakily.

'You'll feel worse in the morning,' says Peter. 'Come on. The ride'll clear your head . . .'

Nothing stirs in the deserted square. The chess-players and old women with rosaries who occupy its benches during the day have long gone; only Bolívar's statue remains – frozen in the act of drawing its sword.

There was a moment, Vivienne thinks, when I knew he no longer loved me the way he used to: it was that time in Caracas. We'd be sitting in a bar or café having a drink together and I'd see his thoughts were elsewhere.

I'd see his eyes follow some girl along the street and then he'd meet my eyes. *So I was looking, OK? So what? Is that such a crime?*

Then there was the time I found the handkerchief in his pocket smelling of some cheap scent. Gardenia. Tuberose. And there was a bite mark on his neck – he said he'd cut himself shaving when he saw I'd noticed.

The more lies there were the worse it got. What had once been love poisoned by suspicion. Passion cooled to polite indifference.

And yet it hadn't always been this way.

She'd loved Jack; still loved him, if the truth were told. It made no difference that he'd lied to her and betrayed her. What had gone wrong between them had been as much her fault as his. She'd expected too much of him – and now she had lost him. The worst thing was, she had only herself to blame.

Alone in her well-lit sitting room, Vivienne sits and broods, listening for the sound of a car. Although it's unlikely he'll be back tonight; he had some business to see to, he said.

Her thoughts go round and round in her head, giving her no peace. We were happy together, she thinks – we could be happy again. If we could only put the past behind us, everything could be as it was.

She has tried, once or twice, to get Jack to talk about the way things are between them. But he just acts as if she's accusing him of something.

My dear, I did warn you. A man like that – what did you expect? Vivienne can almost hear her mother's voice. Although all men were the same, in Laura Barrett's view. *Look at your father. Nothing but a great baby.* Vivienne's mistake, she knows her mother would have said, was to have let Jack see she was unhappy. *They simply can't bear it, d'you see? Makes 'em feel they're to blame.* You should always show a man a smiling face, was one of Vivienne's mother's maxims.

Even before she'd lost the child, things hadn't been right between them. It was as if they both spoke a different language – or rather, as if the same words used by one could mean something entirely different from what the other meant. It was more than the usual mis-understandings one got in any marriage. She felt there were times when he wilfully misinterpreted what she said, in order not to have to deal with what was left unspoken.

It wasn't like that, oddly enough, when the two people concerned actually spoke a different language. Then, one had to be all the more clear about what one meant; ambiguities only clouded the issue, and so one learned to avoid them.

She was a natural teacher, Piet van Wel said. The way she explained things, even he found it easy to follow. It was as if she'd unlocked a door in his head, he told her. Everything that had been shut away, unused for so long, suddenly made sense to him now.

An image of Piet's face flickers across her mind. The way she's seen him look at her lately troubles her more than a little.

She'd thought him cold, at first. Frozen, by whatever hell he'd been through before he came to this place. She'd seen men like him before, with the same look. A kind of blankness – as if life and senses had been atro-phied. There were different ways of dying, not all of them to do with the body.

*

At this time of year it rains every day at around the same time – usually between five and six. You can feel the heat building up and the humidity is extreme – like being in a Turkish bath, Jack says. For an hour or so before the storm breaks you can almost see it in the air – a blue mist of water vapour, blurring the edges of things. In this strange twilight, colours glow with the intensity of flame; sounds seem preternaturally sharp.

Then comes the rain. Heavy drops that fall with a sharp crack, soaking the ground in seconds, conjuring a flash flood from the parched earth. The rain falls without ceasing for exactly an hour (she has timed it). Falling so hard it raises bubbles on the surface of each glistening puddle, which burst and form again in an endless sequence of interlocking circles.

Vivienne is sitting on the veranda watching the rain and thinking about pouring herself a drink when she hears a car drive up. At first she thinks it must be Jack returned from his trip to Caracas – but then she sees it's the Land Rover, not the Chevrolet.

She watches as Piet van Wel gets out and runs towards her across the yard, the upturned collar of his shirt an ineffectual shield against the deluge. It is only a few yards from the vehicle to the house and yet he is drenched by the time he reaches her, his hair plastered flat against his scalp, his shirt soaked through.

She lets him in. 'I'll fetch you a towel . . .'

'No need.' He grins, shaking the drops from his hair. 'See? It's dry already.'

He reaches inside his shirt. 'Here.' Handing her the book he has placed there for safekeeping. 'I brought this.'

'So I see,' she says, amused. She hesitates no more

than a second before taking the book – her copy of *Robinson Crusoe* – so lately warmed by contact with his body.

'It's quite dry,' he assures her.

Vivienne suppresses a smile. 'Won't you have a drink? I was just about to.'

'If you're sure I'm not intruding . . .'

'Not a bit. You've saved me from the indignity of drinking alone.'

'In that case, how can I refuse?'

She mixes them both a gin and tonic. 'So,' she says, handing him the glass. 'You got through it all right? I mean, some of the language is a bit archaic . . .'

He shrugs. 'What I didn't know I had to guess. It wasn't too difficult.'

Vivienne sips her G&T with a thoughtful air. 'Such a *practical* book,' she remarks. 'Very much a man's book, I always think. All that making and building . . .'

'You don't think a woman would have done the same – to survive?'

'Oh, if it's a question of survival . . .' She lets the sentence tail off, as if the idea were not worth the bother of explaining.

'You think there should be something more?' he persists.

'Maybe.' She frowns. 'It's just that I sometimes feel he never really *looks* at the island. Except . . . I don't know . . . as a place to *use*.'

'And you – how would you look at it?' he asks her.

Vivienne laughs. 'How indeed? I suppose I'd sit on a rock and look at the sea, and hope that the ship that was going to rescue me wouldn't be too long about it . . .'

'I like your way better.'

'It's certainly a lot less work.'

They sit for a while in companionable silence. The rain has settled to a steady, musical drumming, like a waterfall; from the safety of their cavern, they watch it come down. Once a bolt of lightning strikes the ground not far from where they are: a spark flies up and Vivienne gives a little gasp – part fear, part pleasure.

'That was close,' she remarks to her companion, who has turned to look at her.

'A thunderstone, I think . . .'

'Thunderbolt,' she corrects him.

'Out of a clear blue sky,' Piet says with a faint smile.

What Jack feels for Angelina is nothing like love but still he can't get enough of her. She haunts his thoughts, his dreams.

When he closes his eyes she rises up before him, the way she looks when she's kneeling astride him, his cock thrust deep inside her, her body in its black satin cuirass rearing above him, avenging angel. Seen like this, she is formidable. Heavy white breasts swelling over the top of the low-cut corset, black hair falling over her face; those fierce black eyes. The hard red mouth she will never let him kiss, in case it smudges her lipstick.

He loves the taste of her. Blood and honey. The deliquescence of oysters on the tongue. How she hates it – protesting, as he spreads her legs, buries his face in her, that it is dirty, disgusting, a thing no decent girl should allow. He tells her he can't help it; he just wants to eat her alive.

She doesn't object so much to the other thing. Men are made differently, she says with a pitying shrug. Slaves to their *cojones*. If God had meant it to be a sin, he would not have given men pricks.

So that when he's lying there sated and tired, she takes him in her mouth and rouses him again. He loves the way it feels of course, that goes without saying. Her wet mouth sliding up and down his hardening cock; her encircling fingers slowly tightening their hold. But it's the way she looks as she performs these acts which excites him as much, if not more. The unselfconsciousness with which she swallows him – her eyes closed, their long dark lashes brushing her cheeks like those of a child at prayer; her red lipsticked mouth stretched as wide as it will go.

What he likes most of all is to fuck her from behind. There's an element of perversity to this act which adds to the pleasure, he finds.

First he gets her to undress – an inversion of her usual professional role, but one to which she brings the same kind of expertise. Removing certain garments – her dress, her slip, her hat, her gloves – and retaining others, according to direction, with the calm detachment of the born mannequin.

Depending on Angelina's mood, and on the number of garments she has to shed, this performance can take quite a while. Not that he cares. He could watch her for hours as she poses and preens, admiring herself in the long glass with an expression that's the nearest thing he's seen on her face to love; peering closer, to check the perfection of the image; repairing slight or imagined flaws with the aid of powder and lipstick.

Occasionally, she will pause in the middle of these private rituals to dreamily finger a nipple, just visible above the rim of satin; or to refasten the rubber button on a loose suspender. These things are done with an air of polite boredom – as a concession to his presence, he suspects.

When she is sufficiently but not entirely naked – still wearing her corset, stockings and high-heeled shoes – he positions her on the bed. Makes her kneel with her back towards him and her ass raised. Her legs a little apart, to allow him access. Then he has to decide whether to enter her first with his tongue or with his fingers; sometimes he does both. Although this makes her angrier still. Twisting away as she feels his tongue circle her asshole; kicking out at him with her sharp heels.

The only thing she really likes is to feel his cock inside her. That's normal, she says; it's what God intended. He pushes it in and she gives a soft gasp of pleasure. *Madre de Dios.* As he begins to move slowly in and out of her, holding her by the hips, his eyes meet the eyes of the tortured Christ on the wall above the bed.

With Vivienne it's different. When they made love it was like dying – it scared him the way she got sometimes. Her face all wet with tears her parted lips gasping, *My love oh my love.* Once she'd said as if it were a joke, You could kill me, you know. It wouldn't take much – and you know I wouldn't resist.

He'd laughed then and told her she was more likely to kill him, the way she drove him wild in this heat, but he'd felt uneasy afterwards, thinking about it. *Kill me now. I'd rather die quickly than slowly.*

Sometimes he thinks it might have been better for both of them if he'd taken her at her word. At least then they might have been spared this process of slow attrition

– their love declining by degrees until nothing was left but the memory of what had been.

He doesn't exactly know when this started to happen (he isn't a man who thinks about such things) but he knows things were never the same after the baby died. She'd been so happy when she knew she was pregnant – so full of plans for the way their life was going to be. He'd wanted her to give up work of course; even the doctor had advised it. Vivienne thought she knew better. In this respect she was no different from all the other women he had ever known.

Afterwards it had been months before she had let him touch her. As if in some way what had happened were all his fault. It was nobody's fault, the doctor said. Just one of those things that happened. A quirk of nature.

At the club that afternoon Tony is sitting on the edge of the pool dangling her legs in the water when Peter Riley surfaces at her feet. He hauls himself up on the tiled rim until his face is level with hers. Water streams down his face and chest his wet hair is plastered to his face in glistening strands like pulled toffee. He shakes his head from side to side like a wet dog and the water flies off stinging Tony's hot skin with icy droplets.

'Sorry.' Green eyes gleam with laughter under the flicked fringe. 'Have I made you wet?'

'You did it on purpose.'

'I swear –' He puts one hand on his heart. 'It was an accident. Besides,' he says, 'you'll be coming in, won't you?'

'I might . . .'

'Well, if you're going to be *iffy* about it . . .'

He lifts himself further out of the water taking his

weight on his arms tendons standing out beneath the skin taut as wires. He leans forward so that his stomach is pressed against dry land and heaves himself out writhing like a landed fish.

'Behold,' he gasps. 'The evolution of the human race . . .'

He lolls beside her leaving himself in outline on the hot concrete – a shadow form which evaporates in seconds. His eyes are closed their wet lashes spiky against his sunburnt cheeks. Eyelashes wasted on a boy Kate says. He and Kate are a lot alike. They have the same eyes and the same-shaped mouths. Thin lips that curve in a sly smile like a cat's. On Peter's upper lip is a faint shadowing of dark hair. Otherwise you might almost think it was Kate lying there . . .

He opens his eyes and sees her looking at him. He holds her gaze unblinkingly a slight smile on his lips. This is a game he's good at. As ever she's the first to look away.

'Are you going to the McBrides' tennis party?' she asks him in a voice that sounds as if she has swallowed a fly.

He doesn't answer at first but goes on watching her still smiling his hateful smile.

'I might,' he says at last. 'But then again, I might not . . .'

'Oh.'

He yawns – stretching himself. 'I suppose I shall have to make the effort,' he says wearily. 'Although, frankly, the prospect doesn't appeal. I'm bound to be paired off with Stuart – and Stuart, as he never tires of telling us, is a much better player than I am. When he's finished running rings around me on court and my humiliation is complete I'll doubtless be given the task of lobbing easy serves to the kiddiewinks.'

'I'll have to help with the teas,' Tony says sulkily.

'Oh God, yes. Ginger pop and fairy cakes. There's something about those people,' he says with sudden violence, 'that makes me want to *spit* . . .'

'Mrs McBride's quite nice.'

'Nice.' He gives a studiedly mirthless laugh. 'Och aye. I'm no' denyin' it, hen . . .'

'I thought you and Stuart were friends,' she says – conscious that this is dangerous ground.

He opens his eyes so wide that she can see the white all round the pupils. 'Whatever gave you that idea?'

She does not reply focusing her gaze on the scintillating planes of water whose shift and dazzle hurt her eyes. Shouts of children playing in the pool float towards her but she doesn't hear them. All her senses are attuned to the person sprawling beside her: the slouch of his shoulders the insolent pout of his underlip. The sourish smell of his sweat pricks her nostrils.

'I grant you,' his voice continues in the same airily aloof 'mocking' tone he habitually adopts when speaking of something which matters to him, 'that's how it might seem. Such a good *sport*, Stuart. Such a decent *chap*. Captain of the rugger team. Captain of the cricket team. Captain of just about every bloody team, in fact. Have you any *idea*,' he says vehemently, 'what the past two years at that school have been like?'

A shadow looms above them blotting out the sun.

'What are you gassing about now, little brother?'

She is in tennis whites – standing with her legs a little apart calf muscles braced weight balanced evenly on the balls of her feet. In contrast to her sibling's indolent pose she seems fired with energy; swiping the air with her racquet as if impatient to begin play. Squinting upwards Tony catches a glimpse of slim brown thighs disappearing into a vortex of sharp white pleats.

'None of your business. Oh, I *say* –' He rolls on to one elbow the better to look her up and down. 'You *do* look the part. Getting in some practice, are we?'

'I don't know what you mean,' Kate says huffily.

'Don't you?' His eyes gleam. 'Don't ... you ... *just*.'

Kate flushes. A dark painful-looking red like a port-wine stain.

'Unspeakable beast,' she hisses.

For a moment it looks as if she may be about to hit him. The racquet is in her hand and he is on the ground at her feet. She looks from him to the racquet and back again. Evidently thinking better of her violent impulse she turns and stalks away.

'Better work a bit harder on your backhand,' Peter calls after her. 'If you want to beat him, that is . . .'

He rolls on the ground clutching his sides in exaggerated laughter.

'What did you say to make her so angry?'

Tony's question sets him off again.

'Don't you know?' he asks between gasps. 'I thought everyone knew. My sister's in love with that buffoon – has been for years . . .'

'You mean Stuart?' Tony can't believe her ears.

'The McBride of McBride. Who else?' Peter wipes his eyes. 'Trouble is, the poor kid doesn't stand a chance . . .'

She looks at him – still more puzzled. He raises an eyebrow. Suddenly – teasingly – enigmatic.

*

Picture this: an English tea party in a tropical landscape. Ladies in straw hats and ankle-length skirts sip tea from bone china cups on the smooth-rolled lawns beneath spreading acacia trees and towering palms admiring the bright un-English blooms in densely planted borders. Clipped English voices exclaim politely. *How pretty. How nice.* The tennis courts have been freshly swept and sprinkled with water to keep the dust down. Small girls in pastel cotton frocks play tag in the shade. The sky is a hot clear blue.

Jean McBride – now grown too unwieldy to move very far without effort – lies on a rattan lounger fanning herself with a two-month-old copy of *The Times* in which she has been reading the details of the sensational murder trial which was scandalized them all this season. From time to time she groans softly.

'Oh, this *heat* . . .'

She wouldn't miss it for the world she tells anyone who will listen – it's so nice to see the young people enjoying themselves. She turns back with relish to descriptions of bodies trussed with washing lines and stowed in kitchen cupboards.

On the courts the young people are having what Jean calls 'a bit of a knock-up' before getting down to more serious play. There are frequent outbursts of hilarity.

'Oh, I say, Hard *luck* . . .'

'Match point, I think . . .'

Tony watching from the sidelines can't deny that Stuart is the better player; although Peter has more style. Kate plays well when she wants to; but she's a poor loser given to displays of petulance. David plays tennis the way he does everything: quietly stolidly without flair.

As for Tony herself – she's good enough. She'll never be as good as Vivienne though.

Vivienne has said she'll play – although when Tony last saw her she was sitting in the shade talking to Mrs McBride. If she wants to take part in the women's doubles she'll have to get changed soon Tony thinks.

Jack hasn't showed up yet. He hates this kind of thing. Any game that doesn't involve a deck of cards or a roulette wheel is a waste of time as far as he's concerned. Years ago when he was a kid he used to play softball. And baseball – sure. But that was then.

Kids' games. She can almost hear his scornful tone.

What would he say Tony wonders if he could see Mr McBride – 'the Reverend' as Jack calls him – in his tennis shorts? Bony white legs protruding from baggy off-white breeks. The line where his sunburn stops half-way down his neck – now revealed by his Aertex singlet and the absence of his dog collar.

Mr McBride fancies himself as something of a player. He was champion three years running in the Christian Fellowship tournament and has installed this court at his own expense. He allows the Sunday School to use it on alternate weekends but the main beneficiary is himself. For the past six weeks since the season started he has been out there every night after evening prayers practising forehand smashes and backhand swerves with his cook José.

It is Mr McBride's party and Mr McBride's chance to shine. Although there will be stiff competition from some of this afternoon's guests. Mr Wilson for example – dashing in immaculate whites – is well known on the company circuit. It's rumoured that he only got his recent promotion by allowing the chairman to beat him in the inter-departmental match.

The women have also turned out in force. Mrs Brown – girlish in pleats – is protesting she's forgotten the rules. Mr Wilson will have to explain them to her she says. Mrs Riley displays her shapely legs in shorts cut so high and tight they are barely decent. *Exhibitionist* Tony hears Mrs Brown whisper to Mrs McBride.

Mrs McBride is busy supervising the teas – which she does from the cushioned recesses of her lounger: sending Luisa in one direction with trays of lemonade Constanza in another with supplies of tea and hot water; commandeering a stray child or two to hand round the cakes. She simply hasn't time to listen to Mrs Brown's jealous mutterings.

'Sylvia's so vivacious isn't she?' she merely replies. 'How she does it in this dreadful heat I can't imagine . . .'

When tea is over the playing can begin. The young folk must go first Mr McBride magnanimously insists. An elimination match followed by another for the adults. The winner of one to play the winner of the other – to find the 'Man of the Match'.

'Or the woman, you pompous old fright,' Kate mutters in Tony's ear. 'Odious counter-jumper,' she breathes. 'Mummy says they're quite common, really. Grandfather McBride was a clerk in a railway office. Can't you just imagine buying your ticket from Holy Joe?'

Stuart and Peter are the first to play. A match which draws the eye – if only for its pairing of opposites. Tall blond Stuart – at fourteen as tall as his father; a head taller than slight dark Peter who has inherited his build and his good looks from his mother. From the start the outcome of the match seems a foregone conclusion.

Stuart is so much the better player: strong and graceful at once; making it look quite effortless. Moving around the court in a series of feints and lunges that make Tony think of fencing or dancing or any of those physical acts requiring the perfect coordination of hand eye limbs.

Peter is no match for him. Although he is no mean player. What he lacks in grace and skill he makes up for in cunning. A tactician like the General Tony thinks her heart quickening. Relying on the element of surprise to achieve his ends. Lulling the enemy into a false sense of security – then springing the trap. More than once in the course of the match he succeeds in disturbing Stuart's imperturbable poise – leaving him blinking good-humouredly at the nets as a well-placed serve is returned with unexpected savagery.

When Stuart has beaten Peter – as everyone had known he would – it is time for the girls to play. On the other court Mr Wilson is effortlessly destroying Mr Brown as their wives look on from the sidelines. Sandy pugnacious Brown has never been much of a hand at tennis. Women's game he calls it. He's more of a rugger man. That Wilson with his crooner's looks – all eyes and teeth – has always struck him as a bit of a pansy. Women fell for that type – but then what could you expect? The weaker sex.

With sweat-soaked crotch and armpits Brown soldiers gamely on.

Tony has been drawn against Kate. The thought makes her feel rather sick. She has a wild impulse to say she isn't well – that someone else can take her place – but knows this will only make it worse. Better to get it over with.

She has played against Kate lots of times in the past of course but never like this. In public – with everybody watching. She grips her racquet so hard she can feel her knuckles crack. Then she steps out on to the court in a blaze of light.

Kate loses no time in establishing her advantage: her first service smashes over the net raising a small cloud of dust and provoking a ripple of admiration from the watching crowd. With a burst of effort Tony returns the service. Kate slams the ball back over the net placing it so that it is just out of Tony's reach.

'Well played!'

Kate permits herself a *moue* of satisfaction.

Waiting for her adversary's next service Tony grits her teeth. Her palms are so slick with sweat she can barely hold the racquet. The best she can hope for is death with honour. If she can just hold out for another few volleys she can avoid complete humiliation.

Drawing on hitherto untapped reserves of determination she returns the second service. Irritated perhaps by this effrontery Kate sends the ball back with considerable force – this time aiming it straight at the younger girl's head. Tony tries a side-step but isn't quite quick enough. The shot ricochets wildly off her racquet and hits the net. Tony reminds herself of the General hiding out in the jungle after his first defeat – dishevelled and sick at heart but indomitable. *Death or Liberty* the inscription on his flag a skull-and-crossbones his insignia.

'Death or Liberty,' she mutters squaring up for the next assault.

Looking back she can't work out what it was that happened. One moment Kate was winning the game with her usual insouciance – as if she couldn't really be bothered but might as well finish what she'd started –

the next her game had gone completely to pieces. It wasn't that Tony was playing any better but that Kate was suddenly playing a lot worse – failing to return the easiest shots and hitting the ball all over the court like an absolute beginner. In the end she'd had to concede game set and match flinging down her racquet in a sulk and complaining that the sun was in her eyes.

It was only when Tony hardly daring to believe herself the victor was walking back towards the house that she saw what had put Kate off her game. For there was Stuart – the tennis courts no longer holding any interest for him – deep in conversation with his new friend Raoul.

Tony's drinking a bittersweet glass of Mrs McBride's home-made lemonade and thinking about going back to watch the mixed doubles – Mrs Riley and Mr Wilson against Vivienne and Mr McBride – when Peter detaches himself from the crowd of onlookers and comes over and sits down beside her.

'You played a good match,' he says.

'Thanks.' She feels herself flush with pleasure. 'I wasn't that good. Kate was off form, that's all.'

'My darling sister is her own worst enemy. She lets herself be ruled by her passions – always fatal, in my experience . . .'

'I expect you're right,' says Tony. She finishes her lemonade savouring its last sugary traces. 'Coming to watch the match?' she asks getting to her feet.

Peter seems in no hurry to move however. He tilts his head so that he is looking up at her his green eyes narrowed against the glare of late afternoon. 'Tomorrow night,' he says.

'What about it?'

'It's one of their festivals. A carnival or something. Raoul's been telling Stuart about it. We're all going.' Something glitters in the dust at his feet. A *bolívar*. He swoops to pick it up tosses it high in the air and catches it in one fluid movement. 'You can come too, if you like,' he says carelessly.

'What'll I say to them at home?'

'No need to say anything. It starts quite late. They'll all be sozzled by then. No one will know you're gone.'

'I don't know. I'll have to see . . .'

'Suit yourself.' He whistles a snatch of 'Chattanooga Choo-choo'.

She finds the photograph when she is going through her mother's papers, sifting what is to be saved from all the rest of the stuff: receipts, used chequebooks, letters from people she's never heard of, postcards from places she's never been. You can't keep everything.

The photograph is tucked inside an old envelope. She is about to discard it, but then she sees the deckle edge sticking out of the top. The print is a faded one; its once-sharp blacks and whites have acquired a sepia tinge.

Her mother stands in front of a building which must be a church: its arched doorway rises over her and there are words – perhaps an inscription – just visible above it. She is wearing the white linen two-piece she wore at her wedding in the Mexican border town where they had been married by a justice of the peace a few days before; looking closer, it is just possible to make out the ring on the third finger of her left hand.

Light from the arched doorway falls on her face and dress; a figure cut out of light, she seems to hover against the darkness of the vaulted space. Her face (eyes hidden behind dark glasses, red lips faintly smiling) already betraying uncertainty.

7

She's in bed not asleep but listening for the sound of a whistle when she hears their voices raised in angry altercation.

'You're crazy, you know that?'

That's Jack. And then Vivienne says something she can't hear and Jack says, 'The hell with it. I'm not sticking around to hear any more of this . . .'

'You never did like hearing the truth,' Vivienne says.

Then there's a silence during which Tony can picture them glaring at one another across the room: Jack angrily stubbing out his cigarette in the cut-glass ashtray; Vivienne saying nothing just looking at him her eyebrows raised in that way she has as if she were angry and sad at the same time.

'Aw, the hell with it,' Jack says again.

There's another silence followed by the banging of the screen door. A few minutes later she hears the Chevy's engine burst into life and guesses he's taken off for the club. It's the only place *to* go. Although sometimes he told her once he just drives around. Mile after mile along the empty mountain roads with the radio playing softly and nothing but the stars for company.

After this it goes quiet for a bit. She lies very still thinking about what she's heard when the smell of cigarette smoke tells her there's someone else in the room. Through the white veils of mosquito netting she can see Vivienne standing at the end of the bed looking down at her.

'Antonia? Are you awake?'

In the bright moonlight which floods the room her face is as pale as a plaster madonna's in a roadside shrine. It's hard to make out her expression but it sounds as if she's crying. Tony breathes slowly and evenly feigning sleep and after a little while her mother goes away.

The red Chevrolet is already parked outside the club when Piet drives by. Lindberg starting early, he thinks. Although it's not that early: he and Sofie have already eaten what passes for a meal in their house, the children are in bed and Piet has said he won't be gone long – an hour or so at the most.

He isn't sure if Sofie hears him or not – these days it's hard to tell how much attention she pays. She doesn't answer him – merely shrugs and gives him a blank look, as if nothing could matter less to her than where he's going or who he might be with. She turns back to her sewing – a nightdress, to judge by the colour. At least it will keep her busy, he thinks with a twinge of guilt.

Things are easier between them since he moved out of their room to spend his nights on the living-room put-you-up; now she no longer flinches every time he comes near her. It's too small a house for two people to live separately – but they do the best they can. Most days, he leaves the house before she gets up, and by the time he returns at night she's usually already asleep.

Once or twice he's tried to talk to her about their

marriage, and what it has become, but without success. Sofie looks at him as if she doesn't know what he's talking about – as if he's suddenly started talking in a different language. In the end, it's easier to leave things as they are. She isn't happy here, he knows that – but then, she wouldn't be happy anywhere. He's no better and no worse for her, he supposes, than any man would be.

He's been going to see her for some weeks now; timing his visits so that they coincide with Lindberg's absences – which isn't hard to do: the man's out most nights, it seems. Not that it makes any difference to the hours he puts in at the oilfield: Lindberg is evidently one of those men who can stay up half the night drinking and playing poker, and still be at work before anyone else. Maybe he's one of those people who doesn't sleep, Piet thinks. One thing's for sure: he doesn't spend much time with *her*.

Piet justifies his behaviour by such thoughts, even though Vivienne herself has never complained of her husband's neglect. Piet wonders what she has said to Lindberg about his visits – or if, indeed, she has mentioned them at all. Once or twice, running into Lindberg at the oilfield or in the factory canteen, Piet has been conscious of an uncomfortable feeling – as if he ought to feel guilty for something. Whereas in fact all he is doing is trying to improve his English. Certainly, his grasp of the language is a whole lot better since Vivienne has been giving him lessons. The boy's too, he reminds himself.

And of course no one knows the truth of the matter except him – even Vivienne, he feels sure, has not guessed it. If he is in love with her, that is his affair. And as long as nobody else knows, it can't do any harm, can it? It isn't as if you choose these things.

He knows – to the minute – when he first felt this way; as to why – well, that's not so hard to understand. She's everything he's ever wanted: beautiful, gentle, kind. Her only flaw – a tendency towards melancholy – is something he knows that, given the chance, he could cure.

He turns into the long drive which leads to the Lindberg house. This is the time of night when he's most likely to find her alone, he guesses – with Jack at the club and the child asleep. He has the book they have been reading together with him. There are only a few pages left to go; they'll finish it tonight.

He switches off the Land Rover's engine. There's a light on in the living room: she must be waiting for him. They have made no arrangement and yet it's understood between them that he will come. He walks across the gravel towards the house; climbs the steps; rings the bell.

A shadow moves across the screen and a moment later she stands framed in the lighted doorway.

'Oh,' she says, stepping back to allow him to enter. 'I wasn't sure you'd make it this evening . . .'

'Forgive me. My wife . . . There was a meal to cook.'

He had arrived home to find everything just as it had been when he left that morning. The dirty dishes still in the sink, the refrigerator empty. He'd sent the boy out to buy eggs and milk and he'd made *pannekoeken*. Mummy wasn't feeling well, he told the children; they had heard this explanation before, and it passed without comment.

'Please don't apologize.'

She turns and walks back into the room. After no more than a second's hesitation, he follows her.

'Would you like a drink?'

'Thank you. I . . .'

'Gin, isn't it?' She walks over to the bar in the corner, pours him a shot and hands it to him.

'Cigarette?' She pushes the silver box on the glass table towards him, after taking one herself.

Something about the way she performs both these actions – with the air of someone merely going through the motions of civility – makes him look at her more intently. The hand with which she holds the cigarette is shaking. Averting her gaze from his, she reaches for the heavy table-lighter; flicks it ineffectually once, twice, three times.

'Damn.' She weighs the object in the palm of her hand as if it is a missile she's about to hurl.

'Let me . . .' He gives her a light.

'Thanks.' She glances at him quickly over the flame. 'So,' she says with determined brightness. 'How did you get on?'

'Better, this time. More than fifty pages.'

'That's good. What did you make of it?'

He shrugs. 'Some things I don't understand. The part when they lock the girl in the room. Who would do such a thing to a child?'

'I always hated that part too.'

'And then later . . . the part in the house . . . with the mad woman. I don't see . . .' He frowns over what he is trying to say. 'Why does he not cast her out and marry the other one?'

She smiles at this and shakes her head. 'He can't do

229

that. He's married to her, you see. Divorce simply wasn't a possibility. The only way he can escape is with her death . . .'

'It happened a long time ago, this story, I think . . .'

'A hundred years or so,' Vivienne says. 'And yet I'm not sure people have changed as much as all that . . .' She picks up the book. 'Let's go on with it, shall we? Do you want to start reading or shall I?'

'You start.' He sits down on the arm of the chair in which she is sitting so that he can look over her shoulder while she reads.

She opens the book at the place he has marked. 'Ah, this part.' She smiles. 'I remember this part . . .'

Hesitantly at first, then with increasing confidence, she begins reading aloud, underlining the sentences with her finger so that he can follow; pausing from time to time to allow him to catch up. Distracted by her nearness, he finds himself listening more to the sound of her voice than to the sense of what it is saying, although the story is absorbing enough and under other circumstances he would be interested to find out what is going to happen, now that the protagonists are face to face again after undergoing so many trials. But with his senses aroused by other aspects of her presence – the light falling on her hair; the smell of her perfume – his mind will not focus. The words she is reading might as well be in an unknown language, for all the sense he derives from them.

'Choose then, sir – *her who loves you best*.'

'I will at least choose – *her I love best*. Jane, will you marry me?'

'Yes, sir.'

'A poor blind man, whom you will have to lead about by the hand?'

'Yes, sir.'

Her voice catches in her throat. Looking at her, he sees that her eyes are filled with tears. 'Oh, dear,' she says, between laughing and crying. 'You must think me awfully stupid . . .'

'Not so. I wish,' he says recklessly, 'you would tell me what makes you so unhappy.'

She does not reply at once and he wonders if he has offended her.

Then she smiles. 'Oh, I couldn't do that,' she says. 'I hardly know you . . .'

'You know I love you.' The words are out before he has time to think.

There is a brief silence.

'I think you'd better go,' says Vivienne calmly.

She makes a move to rise. The book falls from her lap to the floor. 'Damn,' she murmurs. She goes to pick it up at the moment that Piet reaches down for the same purpose. There is a slight collision.

In the ensuing confusion, he finds his face inches from hers, so that he is looking into her eyes. The moment lasts no longer than a heartbeat, but he has time to observe the colour of the irises – a pure intense blue – and the bluish gleam of the whites surrounding them.

Then, with the hand with which he has failed to retrieve the book, he reaches out and touches her face.

Karel's in bed but he's not asleep. The room is filled with moonlight, it comes through the thin curtains and wakes him up. Annetje's in the bed next to his; she talks in her sleep – he's used to it now. The first few times it happened he thought she must be awake the words were so clear and matter-of-fact.

'Tell the man to go away.'

From the way she'd said it he'd thought there really was a man in the room; he'd looked around quickly but the room was the same as always.

'What man? There isn't a man,' he'd told her, not that she could hear him.

Another time she talked about a big black dog. She made Karel promise to chase it away.

Now she lies peacefully enough, one arm flung up over her head. The hair around her face is dark with sweat. She breathes through her mouth – a soft buzzing sound, as if an insect were trapped in her throat.

Karel hears his mother's voice in the next room. She's laughing and crying, the way she often does when she's alone. His father went out some time ago – he doesn't know where. But Karel knows he won't be back for a long time.

There's a sound he can't identify: a tapping or scratching. At first he thinks it must be the wind – but there is no wind tonight. He gets out of bed, even though he's afraid of what he might see. He goes to the window and looks out.

There are people standing in the road outside the house. Two men dressed in white and a woman in black, with a black shawl over her head. In the bright moonlight the men's faces are clearly visible. One of them is dark; cruel-looking, with a heavy black moustache. The other is younger – not much more than a boy.

The woman's face is hidden by her shawl, but something about the way she stands strikes Karel as familiar.

He's seen her stand like that – feet firmly planted, arms folded across her chest – in the kitchen of the other house. When she turns, it's no surprise to see it is his friend the maid – the one who gives him biscuits and handfuls of raisins to eat when no one is looking. The moonlight flashes on her gold earrings.

As he watches, they are joined by two others: an old woman and a young one. The first Karel has also seen before. Her witch's face and sharp black eyes haunt his dreams. The other one is his mother, wearing a white dress he has never seen her wear.

He stands at the window, his face pressed to the glass, to see them turn as if at a signal and walk away with his mother amongst them.

Vivienne sees herself as if from a distance – a figure on a brightly lit stage. She watches as a man who is not her husband and with whom she has, until that moment, had no exchange that was not entirely blameless, takes her in his arms and kisses her.

The kiss seems to her – watching from her private auditorium – to go on for a long time; certainly, neither of the participants shows any inclination to break free. If the woman offers any resistance at all, it is in the passivity of her response: allowing herself to be embraced, but not herself embracing the man whose desire she has awakened.

The kiss ends at last – but the figures remain in their positions: the woman standing, gazing up into the man's face; the man with his hands resting lightly on her shoulders. This would have been the moment to have moved away, she sees – to have placed a distance between herself and what has happened.

But instead she stands there, waiting for what will follow.

Then he brings his mouth down to hers once more, sliding his hands from her shoulders to her breasts, and this time she brings her arms up to embrace him in return.

The lights are all still on at the front of the house but she doesn't think anyone's heard her leave. Noiseless as a wildcat she runs across the grass to where the others – Peter and Stuart – are waiting. They watch as she drags her bike from its hiding place.

'You'd better go first,' Peter tells Stuart. 'Tony can follow you and I'll follow Tony.'

She's grateful for this piece of courtesy – dreading as she has been the ride ahead of them. It isn't that she's afraid of the dark – only of what it conceals. Hazards which by day would seem insignificant are magnified out of all proportion after nightfall. Sounds – she finds sounds the worst thing. A twig snapping suddenly; a cough; a scream. Worst of all the sound of someone or something breathing close at hand. A sound which in daylight you wouldn't even hear.

Half-way along the track which leads to the main road a figure steps out of the trees – so abruptly that Stuart has to jam on his brakes to avoid a collision.

'*Buenos noches*,' says Raoul.

'Christ. You didn't half give me a turn.'

Stuart regains his balance with some difficulty.

'Where are we going, Raoul?' Peter wants to know.

But Raoul only shakes his head. His teeth flash white in his dark face. He motions for them to get off their bikes. 'No good now,' he grins. He shows them where to stow the bikes under a heap of dead branches. He indicates that they should follow him.

The path runs steeply down through the trees growing steadily darker the nearer it gets to the bottom of the ravine. Tony knows this path or thinks she does – it's the way down to the stream she's done it in daylight lots of times. At night everything looks different – rocks leaves creepers blotting out what light there is until there is nothing but darkness. Tony feels rather than sees as the ground beneath her feet gets more precipitous – changing from a broad stony track to a bare earth trail through flattened undergrowth.

The thin beam of Raoul's torch dances ahead of her, making the darkness darker.

Sounds seem louder too. The soft crunch of dead leaves beneath their feet. A nightjar's call. The dry rustle of bamboo. She knows these sounds and yet they terrify her. This headlong descent into unknown territory seems suddenly like madness. Only the thought of going back alone is worse.

Behind her Peter stifles a cry as a branch whips back across his face.

In the intense blackness pierced occasionally by the flare of Raoul's lighter as he takes his bearings Tony can barely make out the shapes of things around her. Gnarled tree roots rising higher than her head creepers tangling around her feet. The breathing stillness of the forest floor.

She stumbles on. Something rushes past her brushing against her legs – she feels its rough coat its heat. Too shocked to scream she stops dead causing Peter to run straight into her. Something touched me she wants to explain but he covers her mouth with his hand. Below them through the trees lights are moving.

The scene shifts from the brightly lit drawing room to a place no theatre she has been in would ever show. Instead of bright lights, there is darkness, illuminated only by the glow of a shaded lamp. In the room across the hall from the bedroom she shares with Jack, Vivienne watches herself betray him.

The bed has not been made up since the last time the room was used when the boy was here, she notices with the part of her mind that is detached from what is happening: seeing the bedcover pulled back to reveal the striped ticking of the mattress; the man and woman lying down together, still fully clothed – reluctant to break their embrace even for the brief time it would take them to undress.

She sees herself lying shamelessly with her dress around her waist to show her stocking tops, and the man bending to kiss her there, and her hands twisting themselves in his hair as his tongue enters her.

Karel doesn't hesitate. He wakes Annetje and makes her put on her slippers. She's so sleepy he ends up having to do it for her. Then he tells her they're going out to find Mama and she doesn't protest any more.

Even though he's been as quick as he can there's no sign of their mother and the others when they get outside. They turn in the direction he has seen them go and before long he and Annetje encounter more people – some alone, some in small groups – all going the same way. No one seems to notice the two children – or if they do no one seems surprised. Karel notices that most of the men are dressed in white pyjamas – like his, only his are striped; the women wear long white nightdresses like Annetje's, only without the flowers.

A few people are carrying things in baskets – one holds a trussed-up chicken. There's a smell of cigar smoke and candle wax and a heavy sweet smell Karel can't name which reminds him of churches.

By the time they have been walking a little while, quite a crowd has collected. Angels, says Annetje suddenly, clutching her brother's hand. In her wide-eyed sleep-walker's stare he can see the reflection of the white-clothed multitude – an angelic host like the one in the picture Oma sent to remind them to say their prayers.

After a while there are no more houses – only the road stretching ahead in the darkness, with the forest on one side and the ravine on the other. If it were not for the white shapes of the people walking in front of them, they would have lost their way a long time ago. Karel keeps on walking, pulling Annetje after him. She doesn't complain any more – in fact, he wonders if she is still awake. Her eyes have a vacant, tranquil look; her mouth hangs slightly open.

Several times Karel thinks he sees his mother in the crowd, but when he draws level with her it is always someone else. Is Mama an angel too, Annetje wants to know. He tells her there are no angels, but she doesn't seem convinced.

In the soft light their naked bodies have a powdery, golden sheen – as if flesh had been transformed to precious metal.

He kneels above her, kissing her feet, her smooth round belly, her breasts.

Ik hou van jou, he murmurs. I have you and hold you.

From where they stand they can see down into the clearing as if looking at a stage set. Around the edge people are standing – a rough circle. Flares stuck in the ground cast a flickering light on those assembled perhaps fifty perhaps a hundred people it's hard to tell. Women in white dresses hold lighted candles. The flames light their faces from beneath so that each appears distorted – mouth and chin illuminated eyes glittering from a mask of shadow. Someone is speaking or chanting in a low voice and there's a low continuous sound like humming or praying.

Raoul holds up his hand to caution them to keep still as a man leads a small black goat to the centre of the arena. The animal is tethered and bound. The chanting grows louder. Tony feels as if her head is filled with the sound – a languorous murmur like the buzzing of many flies.

A woman steps into the light. She is wearing a red cloak over her white dress and her long black hair falls down to her waist. She raises her arms above her head and at once there is silence. It's so still Tony can hear her own heart beating.

Something flashes in the firelight. Blood spurts from the kid's severed artery and splashes on to the ground. The crowd stirs and sighs like a troubled child in its sleep.

The woman in red begins to speak: a loud harsh voice that sounds as if it belongs to someone else. Tony can't understand much of what she is saying but she can make out a few words. *La reina* – that means the queen; *diablo* – that's the Devil. *Santa María* is the Virgin Mary of course – although this isn't like any church service she's ever been to.

The woman's voice has changed: it's higher and more like singing than speaking. She calls out what sounds like a list of names: *Felipe, Gregorio, Constanza.* As each name is called the crowd shifts to allow someone to pass.

An old man steps forward guided by many hands. The woman speaks to him and he replies: her guttural tones counterpointed by his reedy treble. Then she stoops; when she straightens up again her hands are covered in blood. She draws one across the old man's eyes then down over his forehead leaving a bloody cross.

Another man obeys the summons. Tony sees it is José – the McBrides' cook. Mary has told her José suffers from fits. Once he fell down in their kitchen and scalded himself on a hot pan. When he came to he didn't remember a thing Mary said.

The woman touches José on the forehead. Suddenly his eyes roll back in his head and he falls at her feet like a stone. Tony knows he isn't dead but she can't help feeling scared. She can't bear to watch and yet she can't tear her eyes away. She feels as if something terrible is going to happen.

The woman is chanting: *María María María.* Other voices take up the refrain and soon the whole crowd is making the same sound syllables blurring into unmeaning with repetition.

A strong smell of perfume fills the air. It makes Tony think of that time at the Rileys' house. A crash from the bedroom. Mrs Riley's angry voice. *You bastard. You did that on purpose. My favourite scent.*

José opens his eyes. He gets to his feet and the crowd

239

falls silent once more. Then José begins to speak. The voice which comes out of his mouth isn't that of a man but the light clear voice of a child. *Sofía*, it says. *Sofía.*

'Why did you marry her?' It is said in a detached tone. Her expression gives nothing away either.

'I was all she had in the world.'

She considers this. Her face in profile on the pillow beside him is enigmatic, a tranquil mask. Hard to believe that only a few minutes before he had seen the way she could look when the mask was off – her mouth soft with desire, her eyes closed in passionate abandon. 'Did you love her?'

'I . . .' He is momentarily at a loss for words. 'We cared for each other,' he says at last. 'There was nothing else you could do, in those times . . .'

'I know.' She sighs. 'I'm sorry,' she says. 'I shouldn't ask such questions. It isn't fair.'

'You must understand,' he tells her, 'I thought I could help her. You don't know the things she went through . . .'

'No.'

'She wasn't always this way,' he goes on. 'So silent. So full of anger . . .'

'Maybe you should talk to her.'

'Oh, I have, believe me.' He laughs: a harsh sound. 'She says I'm trying to make her crazy. I want to kill her, she says. I want to take away her children. It's no good talking to her,' he says. 'Talking to her only makes it worse.'

She turns over on to her side, propping herself on one elbow. Light from the shaded lamp defines the gleaming curves of her naked back. She reaches for the packet of cigarettes on the bedside table, lights one and hands him another.

'Have you thought about talking to anyone else?' she says.

He frowns. 'What do you mean?'

'I mean a doctor. Someone who knows about such things. There must be people – even here . . .'

'Who knows what they might say? They might put her away somewhere. I can't do that to her . . .'

'No, of course not. I see that,' she says.

There is something shocking about her coolness – the matter-of-factness with which she lies there, calmly discussing his domestic situation. It is as if she has already set aside what happened between them – placed it in some separate compartment of her mind. I must go, he says after a while, and she says, I suppose you must. Can I see you again? he asks her, and she says, I really don't know.

He can't see anything at first because there are too many people. They're looking at something; he can't see what it is. He pushes forward, worming his way between close-packed bodies, drawing his sister after him.

When they are almost at the front of the crowd he sees her.

In the white dress with her hair loose around her shoulders she could be a dark angel. Her eyes look at him but don't see him; he knows that look from before. Beside her stands the old woman and a third he also recognizes. It's the lady in the red cloak with the golden crown. She isn't wearing the crown today but he knows it's the same one. She looks fierce and proud: a warrior queen.

The old woman is speaking – explaining something. He doesn't know what it is but he hears his mother's name. Then the queen starts to speak: it sounds as if she's giving orders. Her hands are red; she strokes his mother's face with her red hands.

When she feels the warm blood on her face Sofie begins to scream.

When he has gone, she is left with the knowledge of what she has done. She trembles all over with the shock of it, as if she were suffering from fever. Mechanically, she begins to remove the signs that he has been there: the two glasses, the ashtray. She carries these through to the kitchen and rinses them, then puts them back on the shelf behind the bar. In the sitting room the book – cause of her present confusion – lies on the floor, its pages crushed. She picks it up and smooths away the creases.

In the room where they have been her clothes are scattered on the floor. She gathers them up, throws them in the linen basket, and twitches the bedspread straight. Then she switches off the lamp and pulls the door to behind her – softly, so as not to disturb Antonia, who sleeps across the hall. She doesn't glance into the child's room, as is her habit – perhaps reluctant to bestow a kiss on an innocent cheek with lips that have so lately betrayed that trust.

The shower is as hot as she can stand it. She stands blind with tears under its scalding jet, letting the water wash over her until all trace of his smell, his touch has been erased, and her skin feels as if it has been flayed from her body.

*

They could wash away sins in the Blood of the Lamb they said it was all the fault of the Jews anyway it was well known they killed babies ripped from the womb red and slippery skewered on sticks their sins would find them out they said they had infallible ways of knowing you could tell by the smell some said it was in the blood a certain look in the eye the way he had looked at her that day he knew without words she was the one marked for death they said murderers knew their victims she let him pass without speaking she knew he was bound to return in the end there was no escape his blood was on her hands running down her face the smell it was the smell however hard she tried she'd never wash it off . . .

Tony doesn't know how she got home that night all she knows is she must have been running because in the morning her legs are covered with scratches. She can't bring herself to undress she gets under the covers trembling all over at the memory of it.

The woman screaming and then the little girl. Running out from the crowd crying, *Mammie, Mammie*, the boy tried to stop her but she was too quick for him. There was blood on the woman's face and on the child's nightdress she hid her face in her mother's skirt she clung to her and wouldn't let her go.

Then someone in the crowd began to sing it sounded like a hymn and before long the rest of them were singing. Someone was throwing flowers red petals falling through the air like confetti and all the time Sofie was standing there with her dead white face her black eyes staring as if she were looking at something a long way off.

Falling asleep one night in front of the television she finds herself transported to another place. It reminds her of somewhere she knows, she can't at first recall where. Something about the colours — those pearly pinks, steel blues, primrose yellows, greys — makes her sit up and take notice. Those broad, tree-lined streets look familiar, and the big smooth shapes of the cars — Buicks and Cadillacs — which glide, stately as ocean liners, along the boulevards.

And then there's the drive along winding mountain roads. A glimpse of the sea. Waves crashing on the rocks below.

A conversation about death. A woman in a white swagger coat with the collar turned up walking away between the trees.

There's the Spanish town, baking in the noonday heat. Deserted, like all such places. The church with its white tower that endlessly seems to fall. The rising whorls of the staircase.

And she knows, at last, what place this is and what she has come to find.

8

When she sees the others again it is as if nothing has happened. It isn't until nearly two weeks later in fact because everyone's too busy getting ready for school – Tony most of all since the uniform which arrived last week from John Lewis has had to be altered. For days it seems she's been doing nothing except stand on a chair wearing clothes two sizes too big for her while Vivienne and Consuelo crawl around her with tape measures and mouths full of pins.

Now – although she finds it hard to believe the time could have gone so quickly – it's the last weekend of the holidays the end of summer. Last year she was one of the ones left behind when the others went back but now she'll be leaving too. She and Jane Wilson and Mary McBride will be travelling together and Michael Brown who's only eight poor little mite says Vivienne what can that woman be thinking of. When they get to London they'll be met by Mary's grandmother who lives in Ruislip Manor quite handy for the airport. Next day she'll put them on the train at Victoria and they'll be with all the other girls making the journey to the south coast with their trunks and hockey sticks and fading memories of warmer climates.

Ruislip. Victoria. Worthing. There's something exotic about the names of these places Tony thinks. They belong to a foreign country – a green and pleasant land – of which improbable as it seems she knows herself to be a citizen. She knows it will be colder there – she can tell from the itchy feel of the navy school skirt about her knees and the weight of the blue serge blazer with *Veritas* and *Fidelis* embroidered on the breast and the thick wool stockings she can hardly bear to touch and the heavy shoes the hat the scarf the tie.

Seeing these garments laid out upon the bed is like looking at another self. An older more experienced version of the person she is now – for whom these stiff uncomfortable clothes and the alien weather for which they are designed will seem as natural and familiar as those she is leaving behind. In a month's time these clothes and the Sunday dress with the puff sleeves and plaid collar will have acquired the patina of wear – like the scuffed sandshoes kicked off under her bed and the creased and shiny shorts she is growing out of.

For the moment she would rather not think about this. All that matters is what remains to her of the place which has been her home. The endless summer coming to an end.

Today – because it's the last chance before the kids go back – they're spending the whole weekend at the beach. Everyone is going: the Rileys and the McBrides and the Wilsons and the Browns. They're going to sleep in a bunkhouse on the beach and when they're hungry they'll go fishing and catch a whole lot of fish to cook on the fire Jack says. They'll have a cooler full of beer and a house full of pretty women and they'll play cards and drink and dance the night away.

By the time they get to the beach on Friday it's late afternoon. Already it's cooler and in an hour or so it'll be just right but the sand still feels hot enough to burn the soles of their feet as the whole bunch of them children and adults strip off their clothes and run screaming across its glittering expanse towards the sea. Most of them the women especially content themselves with just a quick dip not even getting their hair wet before shaking the water off and heading back for the shade.

Tony's different though; Tony likes to swim. She doesn't hesitate for a second doesn't stop to think about jellyfish she just runs straight in feels the warm waves lap at her thighs plunges deeper until she's up to her waist then dives into the swell lets it lift and take her. She swims a few strokes then drifts for a while face down on the water. Through its glassy surface she can see her own shadow moving like a ghost over the seabed whose sandy ripples are starred with pink and white shells. A shoal of tiny silver fish darts across her field of vision escaping the lurking monster overhead.

She swims a few more strokes surrendering herself to the motion of the waves. With almost no effort at all she's being drawn further out. If she keeps on going she reflects dreamily she'll soon be out of sight of the land. She swings around so that she's looking back at it: the long curving beach with its fringe of ragged palms; the figures now reduced to insignificance of her friends and family. It wouldn't be hard to leave them all behind.

While she is still considering this thought she hears herself breathlessly hailed. A red head bursts from the water.

'Hello,' gasps David. Without his glasses his face looks naked – sleek and blind as a drowning kitten. Cautiously treading water he gulps down air. 'You're a long way out.'

'I know.'

'I'm going in in a minute,' he says. 'Are you coming?'

'I might swim for a bit longer.'

'Mum said I should have my swim now if I'm going to have it,' David says gamely his teeth chattering although you couldn't have said it was cold, 'because we'll be eating soon.' He glances back towards the beach where a plume of black smoke is already rising against the sky. 'Kerosene,' he says pointing it out to Tony. 'My dad says it's a waste because it makes the wood burn too fast but your dad says there's plenty more where that came from and anyway he's so hungry he could eat a horse.'

'I'll come back in a minute.'

Tony turns so that she is parallel to the shore and swims a few strokes against the incoming tide David floundering along in her wake. They're so far out and the water's so deep you can't see the bottom; the sea is a deep green shot through with darker colours purple indigo black. Tony thinks about all the creatures that live in the sea – sharks and jellyfish and starfish and flying fish and those strange fish with lights on stalks growing out of their heads that never see the sun. She thinks how cold and dark it must be at the bottom of the sea and is glad she is a creature of the warm surface twisting and turning in the sparkling waves.

'Come on,' she says to David. 'I'll race you –' and together they swim back towards the inviting shore where the fire is already burning brightly. Shadows are lengthening across the firm wet sand. *I say, you chaps. Who's for a game of cricket?* The tide recedes. The red sun drops like a stone into the sea.

Tony can't believe there can be anything more

beautiful in the world than the way it looks now with the sky all fiery streaked with purple clouds the sea like molten gold. She watches it fade red turning to rose turning to deepest violet each change reflected in the darkening water. Night falls with a suddenness that never fails to take her by surprise. She would delay it if she could just to savour those last few moments of warmth and colour – but within a few minutes the light has gone and there is a chill in the air that was not there before.

Then there's a shout from further down the beach and she sees Stuart waving to her. The boats have returned with the men bringing the catch for tonight's supper. Silver tuna yellow dorado and rose-pink red snapper tumbled together at the bottom of the bucket. She runs to help carry them back.

Later when the fish have been cooked and eaten and the beers broken out the children sit on the sand with their backs against the low-leaning trunk of a coconut palm and watch the party. The fire has burned down now so that it gives off more heat than light and in its faint glow and that of a million stars couples are dancing to the music of a wind-up gramophone. Circling slowly with a soft-shoe shuffle on the sandy dance floor bumping into each other from time to time as the tempo changes each accidental collision provoking whoops of laughter. Every so often when the music starts sounding slurred and fading someone rushes to crank up the machine setting the heavy black discs spinning faster.

Some of the records are new: the Cuban dance music and American big-band sound which Tony will always associate with this place; others are of the same antique vintage as the record-player. Quaint old-fashioned tunes with a scratchy sound to them. Reedy voices crooning sentimental words:

> Blue moon,
> You saw me standing alone,
> Without a dream in my heart,
> Without a love of my own . . .

She hears a movement in the dark beside her and knows without turning to look that it's Peter. Since that night at the *santería* meeting she's seen him no more than a couple of times – once at the club to see *The African Queen* and once at the pool and on neither occasion had there been a chance to talk. Although she suspects he might not have wanted to talk even if there had been a chance.

She wonders if like her he finds it hard to believe that what happened really happened. When she thinks of that night it seems like a confused dream. Things seen but only partially understood; things heard and imperfectly deciphered.

Peter's face in the torchlight: the sweat on his upper lip. The way he'd clutched her arm. *My God. Let's get out of here.* And then the moment when they'd realized the others had left them. Blundering back up the steep track in the dark, slipping and sliding in the mud, tearing their hands on branches. *That bastard*, he'd said almost weeping with rage. *I'll kill him. That bloody bastard.*

On the beach that afternoon they'd been playing cricket he and Stuart and the rest of them – Stuart's team had won – and then they'd sat in the shade and played Beggar my Neighbour until it was time for supper. The talk had been of school and home and of England winning the Ashes. There'd been an argument about whether Len Hutton was as big a hero as Edmund Hillary – Stuart said he was because he had proved that England was tops at everything just as Hillary'd done by climbing Everest. Peter said on the contrary neither of them could be described as a hero in the true sense because what they'd done was perfectly useless. It had ended up with both of them rolling over and over in the sand Stuart on top saying over and over, *Say it. Go on. Say it.* Peter red-faced and breathless. *I'll see you in hell first.*

Watching them Tony is reminded of a time when they were all much younger it must have been several summers ago before any of them went away. Stuart had been angry with Peter because he'd borrowed his knife without asking and broken one of the blades. There'd been a fight and Peter's nose had started to bleed. She remembers the blood running out of his nostrils in two bright streams over his mouth and chin staining his teeth red as he stood there smiling not making any attempt to wipe it away.

In the half-light it's hard to tell who anybody is or whether people are drunk or sober or naked or clothed. Above the noise of the party the music and the shouting and the clinking of bottles can be heard the sound of the sea softer and more insistent than any of these. A man and a woman are dancing stumbling around in ever-diminishing circles to a rumba beat. In the dim glow of the firelight they can see it's Jack and Sylvia. She has her head resting on his shoulder her arms limply hanging by her sides a sleepwalker's trance.

'God I hate them,' Peter says with passion. 'The whole stinking lot of them. Doesn't it make you sick the way they carry on?'

It doesn't seem as if he expects a reply and so Tony says nothing. Moonlight shimmers on the water the breeze rattles the dry fronds of the palm trees and the fireflies endlessly chase each other round and round in the air.

A figure looms out of the gathering darkness.

'I say, you chaps – isn't it about time you were in bed?'

It's Peter's father. They smell his pungent breath part whisky part nicotine.

'It's not that late,' Peter says tonelessly.

'No arguing, old man. Chop-chop. Is that young Tony with you?'

'Hello, Mr Riley.'

'Beddy-byes for *you* too, miss. Night-night, all . . .'

He wanders off into the trees, trailing the red coal of his cigarette after him.

'*Hate* them,' Peter whispers in Tony's ear. 'Hypocrites,' he murmurs. 'Liars. Swindlers. Cheats.'

In bed that night in the girls' bunkhouse with Mary on one side Kate on the other Valerie Jane and Jennifer on the floor at their feet Tony lies awake for a long time listening to the music and the laughter as if she already knows this is something which has to end.

Then for a while it's as if Karel's mother has come back, and everything is as it used to be. She's quieter perhaps than she was before; but she doesn't cry so much and there are days when she almost smiles. He goes into the kitchen, where she is waiting every morning, not saying anything, just sitting in the chair with her hands folded, watching as he eats his breakfast. He looks up from time to time and meets her eyes.

254

At bedtime, when she has kissed him goodnight, she stands for a few minutes at the end of the bed, as if there were something more she wanted to say.

One day she stops him as he is about to leave for school.

'How old are you?' she asks with a faintly apologetic frown, as if this information has momentarily slipped her mind.

He tells her: nearly ten.

'You're a big boy now, Kareltje. Soon you'll have to be the man of the family and look after Mama and Annetje.'

He asks her – what about Papa? But she only smiles, a little sadly, and shakes her head.

Karel wonders if this means his father is going away. He knows there are times when the men go upcountry, looking for fresh deposits of oil and minerals. Maybe this time Papa is going with them, and no one has told him. Karel hasn't dared to ask him, in case it turns out to be true.

School is different too, now that Antonia and her friends have gone. There are some new children, much younger than Karel. The boy wet his pants because he was afraid to go *pipi* in the boys' hut after one of the others had told him about the snake they found curled around the pan. The girl sucks her thumb, and when she has to read to the teacher she tries to climb up on her lap like a little baby.

Karel's one of the older ones now. Next year he'll be going away to school with the rest of them. Papa wants him to continue his studies in England or maybe America. There's no future for any of them back home, Papa says.

Karel's father comes in from work in his khaki work

clothes – his shirt soaked under the arms and across the back his trousers spotted with oil and mud – and sits down in his usual chair. He's so tired he doesn't even look at the paper he's brought, just sits there with his head leaning back and his eyes closed. When Karel thinks he's not looking he watches him, studying the way he sleeps – his mouth hanging a little open to let out the whistling breath, his eyelids fluttering open from time to time as if to reassure himself that everything is as it should be.

Under the suntan his face has a greyish look, his lips bluish-purple with fatigue, dark shadows under his eyes. His hair, bleached whiter than before by the sun, contrasts strangely with his dark face – the opposite of Karel's mother, whose pallor seems all the more extreme by contrast with her black hair.

Mrs Lindberg's hair is light, the colour of butter. It shines in the sun as she sits in her garden, surrounded by flowers. There is a magazine in her lap, which she is not reading. Her eyes are closed.

As she hears the crunch of their footsteps on the gravel she opens her eyes.

'Why, Karel. This is nice. Would you like some tea?'

She is talking to him but all the time she is looking at his father, who stands beside him, holding out a book. It is the one she has lent him; Karel has watched him poring over it in the evenings, with the dictionary open beside him.

'Did you enjoy it?'

'More than the other one . . .'

'It's a charming story.' She yawns. 'I love happy endings, don't you?'

She sits smiling up at him, one hand idly turning the

pages of her magazine, the other pushing the thick blonde waves of her hair back from her forehead. He regards her without speaking. It's as if they've forgotten Karel's presence.

'You must see it's impossible. There are too many things – I mean, people – to consider. And besides . . .' She hesitates, wondering how she can say this without hurting his feelings. 'I don't know if I feel . . . the way you feel.'

'It doesn't matter,' he says calmly. 'I don't expect you to love me. All I ask is to go on seeing you . . .'

'I don't know what to say,' she says, thinking aloud. 'Things are different now – don't you see?'

'How different?' he wants to know. 'The only difference is we know where we stand . . .'

'You might,' she says sadly. 'But I'm not sure I do . . .'

She lets him in quickly; they kiss with an urgency born of desperation – neither wants to be the first to break away. They stand in the confined space behind the door their bodies pressed together, breathing the same breath. Her skirt is around her waist his fingers already inside her but she says *No. Wait*. She draws him towards the shuttered room its shifting patterns of darkness and brightness. She lies down on the bed and pulls him down to her. A slanting band of light falls across the wall.

There is no one in the house but themselves – she has contrived it. It seems she has a talent for subterfuge. Lying has become as natural to her as breathing – as essential too: a means to a desired end.

He touches her and she shudders as if the spirit left her body. He enters her and it feels like a kind of death.

257

She knows she wants nothing more than for this to continue: for time to stop. *This room, this moment.* But the light climbs up the wall and the shadows move around and soon it will be time for them to part – each parting foreshadowing the next. There is an inevitability about this, as there is about their meetings, each of which resembles all the others, until they merge into a single occasion.

When she comes to look back on this time, she will be unable to distinguish one from another, or indeed to say how many meetings they had – a hundred or only one? What she will recall is the unvarying afternoon light, the touch of his mouth, his face. Years later she will start from sleep, imagining she hears his voice.

For days after he has been to see her, the world seems transfigured: a paradise. Colours are brighter, sounds clearer. He knows what it is to be alive.

Towards his children, he feels a rush of affection: how beautiful they are. Their skin is smooth and golden, their eyes a clear, bright blue – like her eyes – the whites shiny with health.

When he gets in from work his boy comes shyly to meet him; stands there waiting as if he wants to say something, or ask a question maybe, but can't find the words. *Dag, Kareltje*, he says and the child smiles back at him, ducking his head in embarrassed pleasure as his father ruffles his hair.

His little one, Annetje, climbs on his lap. His face is all rough, she complains, when he tries to kiss her. She shows him the picture she has made at school. A house, with two windows and a door in the middle. Four people standing in front. 'This is you, Papa –' pointing to the largest of these, a grinning giant with hands like bunches of bananas. 'This is me, this is Kareltje – and this is Mama . . .' The last a stunted figure all in black, with a downturned mouth and eyes from which teardrops fall like a hail of bullets.

There's a dead tree in the school yard and one day Karel arrives to find it painted white and covered with ribbons. Red and green paper streamers flutter against the blue December sky; on the topmost branch a star, cut out of tinfoil, glitters in the bright sunshine.

One day a crib arrives in the classroom. Plaster figures of the Holy Family – Joseph with his bald head, Mary with her blue gown – stand on a bed of moss in the miniature stable, whose roof is made of woven palm and whose walls are of bark. A tinfoil star, with an electric bulb concealed inside, illuminates the scene. In the centre of the stable a matchbox filled with cotton wool denotes the manger, which is empty, at present – because the Baby Jesus hasn't yet been born, their teacher says.

Karel stares and stares at the empty box. Something about it troubles him. The sense of something about to happen. An event whose conclusion is already known.

All over the camp, coloured lights are being strung from trees. Coloured paper figures – snowmen and *Sinte Klaas* – appear in the windows of the general store, where Karel stands in line with the list of groceries his mother has given him, waiting for the storekeeper to finish his conversation.

The store is painted blue, like most of the stores around here, with a wooden shutter that folds back so that the front of the shop is open to the street. Inside, it is also blue, with shelves up to the ceiling. These are divided vertically as well as horizontally, so that the effect is of a room full of boxes stacked one on top of the other, or of a large cupboard with compartments – each containing a different item.

Karel lets his eye wander over the shelves, with their neat stacks of cans and jars and packets and bottles: red tins of Oxo, cans of sweetcorn, red beans, condensed milk and golden syrup. Bottles of different kinds of beer – Polar with the blue label, Solero with the yellow – are arranged in rows side by side with scarlet-labelled Coca-Cola bottles, Vimto with the rubber stoppers, orange bottles of Kia-Ora. There are blue packets containing matches and white packets containing lard. Pepto-Bismol. Sunlight soap. And cigarettes: Belmont, Lucky Strike, Camel and Senior Service.

The person in front of Karel in the line to whom the storekeeper is talking is Consuelo, the maid from the English house. When he walks in she stops what she is saying a moment then starts speaking again very fast. He doesn't understand what she is saying of course, but from the way she keeps looking over her shoulder at him he thinks he himself must be the subject.

On the counter in front of him is a box holding Christmas cards. Some depict wan-faced madonnas and pious shepherds; others are more festive. Tables covered with white cloths and sparkling silverware. Cut-glass decanters filled with ruby liquid. Platters heaped with food: glossy haunches of venison, roast turkeys glistening as if freshly varnished. In the background: blazing log fires and windows half-shrouded in velvet, through which snow-covered landscapes can be seen.

'*Pobrecito*,' he hears Consuelo say, glancing in his direction. '*Desafortunado*.'

The sound of the words makes Karel shiver. He trembles beneath the relentlessly pitying gaze of Consuelo's black eyes. He hasn't seen her since that night in the forest – the night he'd rather not think about. The way she'd looked at him then and the way she is looking at him now are the same: as if she knows everything that is going on in his head.

The storekeeper takes the list out of Karel's hands. '*Papas*,' he translates, weighing potatoes floury with earth into the bag Karel holds open for him. '*Pan*' – taking the still-warm loaf from the tray – '*arroz*.' The storekeeper tips a shovelful of smooth white grains into the metal dish on the scales. The arrow climbs higher and higher, until it reaches the red 1,000 mark. 'OK?' says the storekeeper in English. He winks at Karel, tipping the rice into a white paper cone which he twists shut. He puts it in Karel's bag with the other things. Karel gives him the money and he counts out the change into the child's open palm, talking to him all the while.

'Boston Red Sox,' he says. 'World series.' He nods and smiles. 'You betcha.' Karel doesn't know what to say so he nods and smiles in return. This seems to please the storekeeper. As Karel starts to leave, he shouts, 'Hey, fella . . .'

Karel turns, and the storekeeper takes a handful of sweets from a jar and presses them into Karel's hand.

There are days when Sofie seems almost like her old self. She gets dressed, makes breakfast, talks to the children about all the things they're going to do with their day. Towards Piet, her behaviour is cordial enough, but no less guarded than it's ever been. Sometimes he catches her looking at him thoughtfully, as if she knew more of what was going on in his mind than she lets on.

He knows he should feel guilty for betraying her and, for what it's worth, he does. She's his wife; he's let her down – there's no getting away from the fact. And yet he can't regret what's happened. Falling in love with Vivienne Lindberg is the best thing he's ever done. Until that moment, he'd thought all that side of him – his capacity for feeling – had been extinguished; knowing he can feel this much for someone is like coming back from the dead.

It was only three months she was away but in those months things happened which changed it all irrevocably.

In any case she had other things to occupy her mind. She had never slept in a room that was not her own before. She had never been surrounded by so many people she did not know. In the face of such immediate realities everything that had gone before had no more substance than a troubling dream. It was something that had happened to someone else, in another life.

It was only much later that she got the whole picture – and by that time just about everyone who had been involved and who knew what had happened was already dead. So that afterwards when she tried to piece it all together, she found there were gaps in the story; inconsistencies – so that the nearest she could get was no more than an educated guess, an approximation.

9

The plane comes in to land over a sea so calm it looks from where Tony sits like rumpled blue silk. She peers through the oval porthole which lies between her and the sky for a first sight of land. *Silent, upon a peak in Darien.* Except that it isn't a peak but a plane which gives her this vantage point; the peaks are what she is looking down upon.

As the plane dips towards the shore and turns away again in ever-tightening circles the mountains too advance and retreat their green slopes soft as fleece in the warm light. Huge clouds the size of mountains roll down the slopes to the sea. From this distance it is hard to tell which is which clouds becoming mountains becoming clouds in the blink of an eye.

They begin their descent and the mountains close around them. The ground approaches. The sea dips behind the horizon and then there's the bump as the plane touches down. They're still travelling very fast blue sea red earth green trees rushing past red and white chequered control tower and white airport buildings getting nearer and nearer. They slow to a halt and the steps are wheeled into place. The doors open.

Tony is the first to step outside shading her eyes with her hand against the light as she descends the steps into air so hot it's like walking into a furnace.

*

Jack is waiting for them at the arrivals gate – Tony picks him out easily even though there must be a hundred others dressed as he is dressed in tropical whites and Panama. For one dreadful moment it occurs to her he might not be alone; the thought stops her in her tracks so that Mary McBride who is behind walks slap-bang into her clumsy idiot but then she sees it's all right. In that sea of brightly coloured clothes and smiling faces there's no sign of the woman in red. Jack sees her and waves. *Hey, girl.* The way he smiles fills her with such confusion she doesn't know how to respond just stares right back at him as if seeing him for the first time.

Luckily Jack's so busy getting their bags he doesn't seem to notice Tony's strangeness. All he says is she looks as if she could use a good night's sleep.

She wants to tell him she feels as if she is already asleep – locked into one of those dreams where you know you're dreaming but can't wake up – but she doesn't want to say this in front of Jane Wilson. Jane will wait until Jack isn't looking and then she'll tap her finger against her forehead and make that face she always makes when anyone says anything she thinks is stupid. 'You're barmy,' she'll mouth her eyes round as buttons. 'Completely bonkers.'

But it is like a dream Tony thinks as they step out into the December heat. She can't believe she's really here at last.

Faces of people come towards her out of the crowd – they are every colour from deepest black to palest gold. In England the faces are all one colour. She shivers in spite of the heat afraid she may be going to wake up after all in the long dark room she shares with the other

266

girls in that ugly red brick building on the edge of the English Channel.

Fragments of sound reach her. Snatches of conversation. *Cómo estás? Muy bien* . . . Laughter. Honking of horns.

In his white suit Jack strides ahead of them through the crowd of arrivals and those about to depart weeping women small children holding out their hands – *Señor, señor* – taxi drivers touting for trade waving them all away as if they were troublesome flies.

It is as if nothing has changed. The drive back from the airport the view of the lake the heat the dust the light are all as she recalls them from before.

She's wide-eyed – preternaturally wakeful – in spite of the fact that she hasn't slept for days or what seems like days she doesn't want to miss a thing.

Things are as she remembers them and yet she feels as if she has never really seen them before. The billboards on the tops of buildings. *Firestone. Johnny Walker.* The pastel colours of the houses as they drive across town. Pink houses blue houses – yellow green mauve. The colours strike her as astonishing; bizarre.

And the cars – why hasn't she ever noticed the cars? The cars you see in England are all one colour like the faces only black not white. Here they are all colours; shiny reds metallic blues. Cars bristling with fins and glittering with chrome; cars whose radiator grilles resembled grinning mouths.

All these things she has taken for granted now reveal themselves to her stripped senses. Guajiro women in long vividly coloured dresses standing in the road with their babies in their arms; moving without haste to get out of the way of the car. They think white people are devils Consuelo says.

Men hanging around outside a roadside bar. Squatting in the dust at the edge of the road drinking beer and throwing dice. In England the only people you saw sitting in the street were cripples like the man she'd seen selling matches outside Waterloo Station. *War veteran with five mouths to feed. I did my 'bit' now please do yours.*

A little girl in a torn dress peering shyly from behind the wrought-iron grille separating her front yard from the street. The dark bright eyes looking back at her make Tony feel suddenly she is a stranger here. A white devil.

Trinitaria the shocking pink of painted toenails drops its blossoms on the roof of the car as they pass. Vultures feasting on a dead dog scatter at the noise of the engine then regroup like a coven of witches around the carcass.

Then they're out of the city driving very fast along the new highway Marcos Pérez Jiménez's gift to the citizens of Maracaibo Jack says a road going from nowhere to nowhere. Tony's eyes want to close but something stops her from going to sleep every time her eyes snap open it's to see the blacktop stretching away in front of them a dead straight line ruled across the wilderness.

This is so like a dream she's had she's almost convinced she must have slipped unknowingly into unconsciousness – but then Jack asks her how she's doing and she knows this must be real. Although Jack himself has been part of her dream life lately – sometimes walking ahead of her with his arm around the waist of a woman in a red dress; sometimes sitting in the driver's seat beside her as he is now while the road unrolls in front of them mile after endless mile.

Tony sees it all: the flat burnt yellow scrubland with its stunted *saman* trees the bare red rocks the wide blue sky. Sun flashing on the blades of a windmill. There is something reassuring about such monotony. She would be happy to go on sitting here for ever.

But before long they turn off the highway and start heading inland into a different kind of country. The road grows narrower and steeper and the trees taller and closer together. Soon they've left the coastal plain behind and are climbing higher and higher up a road barely wide enough for two cars to pass which zigzags up the mountainside. Tony knows they have to get up the mountain and down the other side before they can get to where they're going; it's a journey she's done a hundred times before but this time for some reason the thought of it fills her with dread.

Everything is of gigantic size in this landscape – the trees the rocks the waterfalls which tumble down the mountain threatening to wash away the road. After the muted greys and blues of the country where she has spent the past few months the colours here strike her as too intense – too real somehow. And the road – the road terrifies her. Instead of going straight ahead the way a road should it twists and turns back on itself like a demented snake hurtling towards nothingness then pulling back in the nick of time as the car seems about to go over the edge.

Chicken chapels are to be found all the way along this road – she remembers trying to count them once when she was small and running out of fingers. They pass the wreck of a bus wedged into a crevice in the rockface its front smashed in its engine and seats ripped out. *El Tren del Amor* is the name painted on its side wreathed with hearts and flowers and birds of paradise.

'You OK?' Jack asks her perhaps noticing she has been quiet a long time. She tells him yes and he says it's not long now. She's a tough cookie for staying awake so long he says although he's the same he can never sleep either. The road winds and winds and then Mary wakes up and is sick out of the window all down the side of the car. The smell of it coming back in makes even Tony feel bad and she's never carsick. Jesus H. Christ Jack says and Tony wants to laugh knowing how much Mary's father disapproves of swearing taking the Lord's name in vain he calls it although Tony doesn't see how it's different from praying.

Pretty soon they start to descend through groves of bamboo sunlight flickering through its gently swaying leaves reminding Tony of the films she's watched at the club which have the same slightly grainy flicker with the sound always a little out of sync. Then at last the road levels off and is no more than usually winding or uneven and they leave the jungle behind and come out into broad daylight. And there's the familiar red dirt road leading down to the camp and the familiar shapes of its outlying buildings: the pumping station and the office and the bachelors' bunkhouse and the streets and streets of small identical houses which make up the married quarters.

They drive past all this and then they reach the slightly larger houses on the outskirts of the settlement where the managers and accountants and surveyors live. VIPs and sky pilots Jack says because this is where the Wilsons and the McBrides live. Jack lived here once himself before he was married to Vivienne. All the houses have the same layout inside – a larger version of the ones in the married quarters. A box for each of the workers and a bigger box for the boss. That's the American way says Jack.

They drop Mary off at her house and Jane off at hers and then they climb back in the Chevy and drive to La Soledad. All the while they're driving Tony's wondering whether anything's changed since she was last here all those weeks ago. She doesn't say anything to Jack but when they pull off the road on to the drive and they see the red roof of the house appear through the trees she feels her heart beat so fast she can hardly breathe.

But the house looks the same as it did the last time – its red roof and white walls just as she remembers them. The windows with their gauze screens still make her think of eyes behind dark glasses.

And then the door opens and Vivienne comes out of the house and walks towards her over the gravel. And Tony sees that something has changed after all although she finds herself unable to say what it is.

When it comes to him Jack can't believe he hasn't thought of it before, it's so simple: he won't see her again. He doesn't have to explain, he simply has to act – or do nothing, in this case. No need even to write or telephone, because it would only upset her – and if there's one thing he can't stand it's women's tears. Of course he's been careful not to give her his address. They've always met in hotel rooms or at her apartment – places which hold no associations, or not for him. And of course they live in different cities. There's no way she could track him down even if she wanted to.

That's the advantage, he tells himself, of a long-distance affair – the thing that offsets all the disadvantages. When you decide you've had enough, you can love 'em and leave 'em. Sometimes you have to be cruel to be kind.

It was fun for a while, what he had with Angelina – but now he's made the decision he can see it's the right one. What matters is his marriage; Angelina was just a distraction. To tell the truth, she was starting to bore him a little.

Vivienne. Thinking about her, he feels a rush of pity. Poor kid, he's been neglecting her lately. Work, and the thing with the girl, have been taking up too much of his time. But he'll make it up to her. Flowers. Presents. Women liked those kinds of things. And no one was going to tell him he didn't treat his women right.

Although she's been acting pretty funny herself these past few weeks. Kind of distant – as if she were upset about something. Not that there was any way she could have known he was seeing another woman – he'd been so careful. But women had instincts about these things. Although if the truth were told, a lot of what had gone wrong between them was her fault.

He was a man, wasn't he? He had a man's needs. A man couldn't go without a woman for all those months and not find himself going crazy. He'd been a little bit crazy, he sees that now. But all that was over. He knows what his priorities are.

At the sound of the Chevy's engine, Vivienne glances up, wondering what's brought him home this early. Maybe the poker game was cancelled.

'Hiya, baby.' He stands in the doorway, his smile a shade abashed.

'Has something happened?' Her tone is one of polite interest. 'I wasn't expecting you this early . . .'

'No,' says Jack. 'Nothing happened. I just felt like seeing you is all.'

'Have you had dinner?'

'No, I haven't. Vivienne . . .'

'I'll tell Consuelo.' She moves towards the door.

He steps in front of her. 'Vivienne, look at me . . .'

'Jack, what *is* this about?'

'Look at me.'

'I'm looking,' says Vivienne.

For a minute they stand face to face, confronting what each has done to the other.

'I'm sorry,' Jack says at last. 'Whatever I've done, I'm sorry for it . . .'

'Really, Jack . . .'

'No, I mean it,' he says. 'You have to believe me. You know you mean more to me than anything else in the world . . .'

Vivienne is silent, studying his face, as if trying to find the answer there to all that is troubling her. Then she sighs. 'I believe you,' she says.

Jack brushes his fingers lightly across her cheek. She flinches slightly at the gesture. 'Can't we try again?' he says softly. 'It used to be so good between us – remember?'

'I remember.'

He draws her close to him, kissing her closed eyes, her shut lips. 'Oh, baby,' he murmurs. 'You know I'll never love anyone the way I love you . . .'

*

'Do you love him?'

'I don't know what I feel any more. I suppose so . . .'

'He's wrong for you.'

'Maybe . . .'

'You know he is.'

'Nobody's perfect. Jack's been a good husband, in his own way . . .'

'Not good enough. Not for you. You deserve better . . .'

'Don't say that. Don't say anything . . .' She is weeping now. 'My God. What a mess I make of everything,' she says.

Driving home one day from Casigua, she takes a wrong turning – she can't think how, she must have been dreaming – and finds herself in front of the house. She knows it instantly – even though she's only been here once, dropping off some of Antonia's cast-offs for the little girl – besides which all these houses look the same. The steps up to the porch, the wrought-iron grille over the glass door; even the front gardens are identical, with their stiff ranks of scarlet gladioli.

On an impulse she can't afterwards understand, she slows the car to a halt; idles the engine. *This is where he lives. The place his life goes on.* She finds herself imagining what it would be like to see him, engaged in this other life – the one he leads when he isn't with her. As if catching him unawares might tell her something about him she didn't already know.

But it's Sofie that she sees. Sofie's face, gazing out of the window with an expression so perfectly blank it makes Vivienne think of a statue. Frozen behind the wheel, Vivienne returns that gaze, which both sees and does not see her, for a moment which seems to her to go on for ever. Then Sofie turns from the window and lets the curtain fall.

It's the festive season and everybody's having parties. Jack and Vivienne's is the week before Christmas followed by Babs and Ted's the next night and Nancy and Roy's the night after that. There's a carol service at the mission hall with drinks at the vicarage after and on Christmas Eve Sylvia and Frank are having open house. Christmas Day will be spent either in the bosom of the family – for those who have families – or else recovering from the week's excesses. The bachelors' Christmas Night party will carry on well into the small hours of Boxing Day when those sober enough to attend will join Betty and Douglas for a pre-lunch sherry to be followed by lunch at the club lasting effortlessly until the cocktail hour.

Three days of relative sobriety will be followed by the grand finale of the New Year's Eve party which will be held as usual at the club. This year for the first time Tony is allowed to stay up and see the New Year in. She has a new frock for the occasion and she is allowed one glass of champagne. Kate and Peter and Stuart and the others will be there as well. Watching the grown-ups getting plastered Peter says but Tony is looking forward to it. She's got her New Year's resolutions all worked out. She's going to be a nicer person work harder at school and do at least one good deed every day.

Drinking starts in earnest at five with an aperitif gin and tonic for the ladies Scotch on the rocks for the men no more than a couple of drinks before dinner which is early today because of getting ready for the party. At eight o'clock or thereabouts people start dropping round for a pre-party snifter one or two drinks to get you in the mood no point in turning up stone cold sober.

By nine or half-past most people are drifting towards the club where Jock the barman is already setting them up for the usual suspects. Bachelors mostly who've finished their dinner in the mess hall and are settling in for the night. No one's dancing yet but there's music. 'White Christmas' booms over the Tannoy. The bar is festooned with paper-chain bunting left over from the Coronation festivities and in the corner is a silver tinsel Christmas tree fairylights glowing eerily through a spun-glass shroud of angel-hair.

Because it is New Year's Eve and the company is throwing the party some of the Venezuelan employees are invited. Ramón Hernández is there with his handsome wife and the eldest of their five daughters. Hernández's cousin Captain Mendoza – the local Chief of Police – has also stopped by for a drink. He stands very stiff and correct in his olive-green uniform with his cap under his arm listening to but not joining in the conversation.

People are dancing to the music on the club gramophone: a medley of seasonal favourites and the Latin sounds favoured by Jack and the American contingent. Watching from the sidelines Tony sees what Jack means when he says most Englishmen dance as if they've got a stick up their backsides. You've gotta move your hips Jack says. That's what dancing's all about. The music changes from 'When the Red, Red Robin Comes Bob, Bob, Bobbin'' to the latest number by Tito Rodríguez's Mambo Devils. It's one of Tony's favourites: when she hears the infectious rhythms of those bongos and saxophones she can't keep her feet still. Mr and Mrs Wilson evidently think otherwise. 'This music's all right in its place,' Tony hears Mr Wilson saying to his wife as they quit the dance floor, 'but it's quite impossible to dance to . . .'

> *Ven, ven, la Rumba buena te llama*
> *Ven, ven, la Rumba buena te llama . . .*

Across the room Tony sees Mrs Riley has persuaded the Chief of Police to dance. 'Is this rumba or chachacha?' she wants to know. 'Such a wonderful sense of rhythm you Latins have . . .' Mrs Riley is wearing a figure-hugging dress of shimmering aquamarine whose sequins catch the light. She laughs and tosses her black hair and swivels her hips around. Captain Mendoza can't take his eyes off her.

'Pathetic, isn't it?' says a voice in Tony's ear. Peter's eyes are unnaturally bright. A lock of hair falls across his forehead giving him a somewhat *louche* appearance. 'God, if this is what being an adult is all about I don't think I'll bother . . .'

'Oh, don't be such a crashing bore,' says Stuart. He is flushed and jovial. He winks at Tony. 'I must say,' he nudges Peter, 'your ma's a real corker. Especially in that dress . . .'

'Don't be obscene,' drawls Peter.

'Only stating the obvious,' persists Stuart. 'She *is* a corker. So's young Kate, if it comes to that . . .'

'I say, do you mind leaving my sister out of this? Or I might just have to punch your head . . .'

'You and whose army?' jeers the blond boy. An ugly

note enters his voice. 'Maybe you're jealous – 's that it? Want to keep her all to yourself . . .'

'Just dry up, will you?'

'Or maybe you don't like women – that's more like it!' A slow grin spreads over Stuart's face. 'Always thought you were a bit of a nancy . . .'

'I said dry up . . .'

'Having fun, kiddies?' beams Mrs Porter appearing red-faced and breathless out of the crowd. 'It *is* a wizard "do", isn't it?' Smiling beatifically she weaves her way towards the lavatories.

'Who *is* that ghastly woman? Do I know her?' Peter inquires in penetrating tones. He takes Tony's arm. She can feel the warmth of his hand its slight but insistent pressure just above her elbow. 'Fancy an orangeade?' he says. A command not a question she understands from his tone.

'Get me another, would you, old man?' says Stuart all acrimony forgotten. 'Usual mixture. *You* know . . .'

Peter looks at him coldly. 'You've had enough,' he says.

Kate appears at that moment in a swirl of rayon pleats whose 'Ashes of Roses' shade makes Tony's maroon taffeta seem *passé* by comparison.

'Hello, darlings,' she breathes in passable imitation of her mother. 'This is a dull party, isn't it?'

'*Was* a dull party,' Stuart gallantly corrects her. 'I was just saying,' he smirks, 'how nice you look. That's a ripping frock.'

'Do you like it?' Kate shrugs. 'I wasn't sure about the colour . . .'

'It's a ripping colour. Awf'lly smart,' Stuart assures her.

'Sweet of you to say so.'

'Come on,' Peter mutters to Tony. 'Let's get out of here. Or I might very well be violently ill . . .'

Outside it is cooler now; and quieter. The sounds of music and laughter recede as by an unspoken accord they cross the patio towards the swimming pool which gleams in the light of the almost-full moon. They sit on the wall dangling their legs. Around them there is nothing but darkness. Palm leaves creaking softly. The phosphorescent glow of fireflies.

Peter lights a cigarette and tosses the match away. 'Sorry. Did you want one?'

'No, thanks.'

Moodily he inhales; holds the smoke in; lets it out in a long sigh. 'Can I ask you something?'

Anything at all she wants to tell him. She makes a slight sound indicating assent.

He is silent a while. Strikes another match and sends it spinning into the dark. 'Do you ever feel . . .' he starts to say, 'I don't know . . . as if you don't belong?'

'What – here you mean?'

He gives an impatient shrug. 'Here. Not just here. Anywhere. I suppose what I mean is . . .' He strikes a third match. Lets it burn until it is scorching his fingertips. 'Oh, I don't *know*,' he says angrily. 'Forget it.'

'I think I know how you feel,' she says in a small voice.

'Thought you might.' He takes another drag on his cigarette. 'Bloody, isn't it?'

Tony doesn't know what to say so she says nothing. They sit for a few minutes watching the moon in the water its silver disc shivering into fragments as the night wind passes.

Beside her Tony feels Peter grow suddenly tense. He grips her arm so tight she has to stop herself crying out. 'Who goes there?' he demands of the darkness. 'Friend or foe?'

There's the sound of someone laughing. A figure steps into the light.

'Fren', *amigo*. Who you thin'?' Raoul grins.

'It could have been anybody,' Peter says furiously. 'How was I to know?'

'If I wan' to cut your throat I do it already,' Raoul tells him smilingly. 'I let you hear me, no? So you know I am your fren' . . .'

'You shouldn't talk like that in front of her,' Peter frowns indicating Tony.

Raoul gives Tony a hard look. 'If I don' make a mistake,' he says, 'it's the boy with the nice bike, no?'

'She's a girl you fool. Haven't you got eyes?'

'*Sí, señor.*' Raoul inclines his head courteously. '*Me perdona, señorita,*' he says to Tony.

People are dancing and drinking and talking and then someone shouts it's nearly time. And they're laughing and pushing Jack towards the door because everyone knows you have to do these things properly and New Year's Eve wouldn't be New Year's Eve without a first footing. Don't forget the coal someone says and someone else puts a bottle of whisky in Jack's hand to keep out the cold while he's waiting around outside for the chimes to strike. Although it's not cold Tony thinks they've all been here so long they've forgotten what cold is like.

The chimes of midnight are striking on the World Service and everyone is hugging and kissing and singing 'Auld Lang Syne' when someone says where's Jack?

Typical of him to do a disappearing act just when he's needed. Better check whose wife is missing says somebody and everybody laughs. They're still laughing when the door flies open. You're supposed to knock first Jack old boy one of the bachelors shouts.

Then Jack steps into the room with somebody else behind him it's one of the men from the oilfield his face all blackened with soot his clothes covered in oil. And everyone goes quiet because you can tell from their faces that something's happened. Well fire at La Rosa Jack says. Started two hours ago. Luis and the boys have been doing all they can but they can't contain it. Guess they need some help from the rest of us.

Christ Almighty Tony hears one of the Texans say why'd they wait two hours the whole shebang could be burnt to a cinder in less. Ever seen one of those fires man you don't even want to think about the mess it can make. Somebody cut the phone lines Jack says quietly. Jesus Christ says another are you saying what I think you're saying? Maybe and maybe not Jack says with a shrug. We don't have time to discuss it right now.

Suddenly everything's moving very fast men stripping off their white tuxedos and rolling up their sleeves Jack shouting orders car doors slamming engines revving. Tony knows it's impossible because they're too far away but in her mind's eye when she remembers this afterwards she seems to see the sky lit up with flames. People in party clothes running around flakes of ash drifting on the air and everywhere a smell of burning.

When the men have gone it's quiet. The women stand around looking at each other and nobody says anything for a while. Then somebody says maybe they should do something. But nobody seems quite sure what.

It's a hangover from the war Vivienne thinks – no one wants to be thought a shirker. The boys are doing their bit so it follows that they – representing the home front – ought to be doing theirs. She goes to make some coffee. When she returns with a tray of cups she's managed to dig up from somewhere the others are talking tactics. Bandages Jean McBride is saying. They're bound to need bandages. And stretchers for those overcome with heat exhaustion. A soup kitchen Sylvia Riley murmurs what about a soup kitchen? I can just see myself dispensing soup in my Sunday-go-to-meeting frock.

The women sip their coffee and stifle their yawns. It's been a long evening. There are servants waiting up and children to settle. In the end everyone agrees that the best thing is to go home and await developments. There's nothing to be achieved by remaining here. There's a brief consultation while those with cars at their disposal offer lifts to those whose cars have been commandeered for the fire-fighting effort and then people start to drift away. Happy New Year someone calls as they are leaving and someone else says well at least it can only get better.

A mile from the camp the sky's all lit up like the Fourth of July – a dirty red staining the blackness. The stench of burning oil is the next thing that hits you. Its acrid taste catches your throat. Cinders sting your eyes so they stream with tears like a woman's.

He drives through the open gates and parks as near as he dares to the conflagration. Around him men are spilling out of cars and running around like ants in a broken ant hill. The heat is intense, like being inside a blast furnace.

It's Number Five that's gone up, although Four and

Six are in danger. Whoever's responsible – and he's got a fair idea – has done a fine job, Jack thinks grimly. The eighty-foot steel tower above the well is a roaring column of flame, shooting up 200 feet into the sky. It casts a fierce red light on everything around that seems, to his dazzled gaze, as bright as day.

Showers of red-hot sparks fly out all around, igniting everything within a 100-yard radius. The wooden shacks that house the winching gear are burning fiercely; as he watches, the roof of one collapses in on itself, bringing the walls down with it. The tin roof of another glows so hot it looks like molten gold. Beautiful – if it wasn't so fuckin' heartbreaking. The pumping station and the office buildings – although some distance from the main blaze – are also alight; he guesses they must have been torched separately. On the ground small fires flare up spasmodically as sparks fall on puddles of oil, turning their greasy shimmer to incandescence.

In the surging crowd he sees Luis, his face blackened with soot, his eyes and teeth gleaming weirdly in the infernal glow.

'*Epa*, Luis . . .'

'*Señor*.' Even in the midst of this pandemonium, the man's gaze is watchful, guarded. He knows something, Jack thinks.

'How bad is it, *hombre*?'

Luis shrugs. 'Not good. We lost *número cinco*. Maybe *cuatro* will be next. *Quién sabe?*'

The insolent offhandedness with which these remarks are delivered makes Jack see red. He moves a step closer to Luis, standing over him so that the difference in their respective heights is more marked.

'Now you listen to me, *amigo*, and you listen good,'

he says coldly. 'We're gonna stop that fire in its tracks and we're gonna stop it now. Otherwise I will personally bust your fuckin' ass. You get those boys of yours organized and I'll do the same for mine. *Comprendes?*'

'*Sí, señor.*'

There is a sullen look in the dark eyes now – a barely concealed resentment. By humiliating his foreman like this in public, Jack knows he has made an enemy. What the hell, he thinks. You got to let 'em know who's the fuckin' boss. Tomorrow, when the fire's died down, he'll get to the bottom of this business.

'Looks pretty bad, don't it?'

A face, red and shining with sweat, looms out of the crowd. It's Curly McGuire, one of the roughnecks, newly arrived from Phoenix. A nice kid, thinks Jack. Should do well out here, if he lasts.

'It's containable,' he says. 'If the wind don't change. First thing we need to do is make a firebreak. Start by pulling down those sheds. Get some of the boys to help you. Break out some axes. Dynamite, if that's what it takes. I don't give a damn as long as it works.'

'Sure thing, chief.' Curly's boyish grin is the last thing Jack sees of him, as he dives back into the crowd.

Nearer to the fire the heat is almost insupportable: his face feels as if it's burning up; his shirt is soaked through in seconds. But it's the sound that is the most terrible thing – a steady dull roaring that drowns out everything else. The sound of oxygen being sucked from the atmosphere.

Above this fierce murmur he hears his name being yelled. Ted Johnson's face, wild-eyed and sweating, is thrust close to his own. A yellow safety helmet is shoved into his hand. 'Jack. For Chrissakes put this on. You know the Goddamn rules. Or are you *tryin'* to get yourself killed?'

Jack laughs and claps the helmet on his head. 'It'll take more than a bunch of half-assed Commie saboteurs to bump off ol' Jack . . .'

Ted looks at him. 'Think it's sabotage, huh?'

'Let's put it this way – if it ain't sabotage, then that bolt of lightning did an awfully neat job of cutting the phone lines.'

'So who do ya think . . . ?'

Jack holds up his hand, cautioning silence, although the chances of their being overheard in this confused din are slight. 'Later,' he mouths. He claps Ted on the shoulder. 'C'mon. Let's get us some dynamite and blow this baby to kingdom come . . .'

It's nearly four by the time they're through but by then Jack's sure the worst is over. Number Five will burn for three days or more until it burns itself out but the rest of the wells are safe enough. Just to make sure, he'll double the guard on the gates tonight. Post-mortems can wait until the morning, he decides.

'OK, boys,' he says, looking round at the circle of soot-blackened faces whose exhaustion reflects his own. 'You did a grand job. Drinks on the house tomorrow night.'

It's tomorrow already, one of the Texans points out.

'So it is,' says Jack. 'And a Happy New Year to you too.'

It isn't long after she's gone to bed that Tony hears the car. Her room's at the side of the house and so she can't see who it is but she hears the scrunch of tyres on gravel then the slam of the car door and the sound of footsteps.

Jack's home already is her first thought but when she opens the door to the hall she hears the voices – Vivienne's and someone else's. A man's voice. Not Jack's.

Through the crack in the door Tony can see her mother sitting on the sofa. She's all hunched up and her voice sounds as if she's been crying. The man sits down beside her and puts his arms around her talking to her in a low voice Tony recognizes at last as Piet van Wel's. It's hopeless she hears Vivienne say don't you see it's never going to work. And all the time Piet is holding her and stroking her hair and saying her name over and over until both of them fall silent.

Jack's on his way home. He's dog-tired, half-drunk with the whisky he's had to revive him. His clothes stink of sweat and smoke. There's a rip in his dress shirt and as for his good trousers – they're beyond commercial repair. Oil is one stain that's harder to get out than blood.

In spite of all this, he can't help feeling a sense of exhilaration – a hangover from the mood of the past few hours. Watching that sucker go up in flames – that was some thrill. Like standing on the brink of an erupting volcano. In the day-to-day run of things it was easy to forget you were dealing with dangerous elements. You took it for granted – like the forces of nature. Only when things got out of hand did you realize what you were up against.

He looks at his watch. Three-forty-five. In another few minutes he'll be at La Soledad. He wonders if Vivienne is still awake. He won't disturb her, he decides. What he has to ask her will keep until the morning.

Nearing the turning, he thinks about the conversation he'd overheard at the party that night – it seems like a hundred years ago. It wasn't much in itself, just the tone of voice in which something was said, that made him sit up and take notice.

Betty Brown (a woman he'd never thought worth a second glance, although some guys found her attractive) had been talking to Vivienne. His beautiful wife, looking more beautiful than he'd ever seen her. God, he was a lucky guy.

How are you, Vivie dear? Such a long time since we've seen you. I suppose all those English lessons must take up a good deal of your time?

Vivienne had flushed and murmured something. And then Sylvia Riley had cut in (that dame always was one for saying what was on her mind, even when nobody asked her): *Why don't you mind your own business, you insufferable little prig?*

English lessons. Now he comes to think about it, she *had* mentioned something. He wonders now, as the lights of La Soledad appear through the trees, whether he should have paid more attention at the time . . .

Karel wakes with an acrid taste in his mouth and the sensation that there isn't enough air in the room. Things look different – their familiar edges lost in a haze of blue. He wonders drowsily if this is some new kind of darkness. He could close his eyes again with the greatest of ease, let this soft cloud wash over him, waft him to sleep more profound than any he's known. He wants very much to sleep – in fact nothing has ever seemed more desirable – but he knows he must not.

Karel's legs and arms feel clumsy – heavy – as if they don't belong to him at all. His chest hurts with the effort of breathing and his eyes are stinging so much he can hardly see. There's no time to wipe away the tears. Waking Annetje is hard at first, he has to shake her and shake her. She opens her mouth to cry, but chokes instead. Karel is choking too. The air is so hot it burns his lungs every time he takes a breath.

Karel wants to scream for his mother, but his throat is parched and swollen. Then he sees her standing in the doorway. She's wearing her best dress – the blue one – and the hat and coat she wore when they left Holland. Come, Kareltje, she tells him. It's time to go. She buttons him into his coat and does the same for Annetje. The suitcases are in the hall packed and ready. Come on, she says again. The kitchen is already blazing; soon the living room will follow. Already there are flames licking the door frame. Their heat scorches Karel's face.

In a minute or less the flames will reach them. Their mother does not seem worried. With a calm smile she opens the door. At once a jet of flame shoots across the room, engulfing everything in its path. Karel drags Annetje outside and runs pulling her after him, until his legs give way and they both fall down on the grass. When Karel looks back he sees his mother in her hat and coat, a suitcase in each hand silhouetted against a swelling wave of fire.

Much later Tony wakes with a start. Something – the cry of a night bird or the sound of wheels on gravel – has disturbed her. She lies there open-eyed in the darkness her senses alert. *Something's wrong.* She knows it as surely as if the words had been spoken aloud. Her heart beats faster. *Something's different.* She feels this acutely. But she can't put her finger on what the difference is.

It's late and everyone is surely asleep by now. She

closes her eyes and drifts back into unconsciousness. In the morning she will not remember this moment of revelation.

They think it must have been around four or five it happened. It was late; he was exhausted; he'd been drinking heavily earlier. He'd taken the corner too fast – the way you did if you'd had a few. Nine times out of ten you got away with it.

They reckon he must have lost control for a second – that would have been all it took. A moment's inattention and you were lost. Hurled into nothingness. It happened all the time.

These were treacherous roads – more like mountain tracks in fact; not built for automobiles at all. Narrow. Winding. Full of blind corners. Sheer rock on one side and a precipice on the other. A case of the devil or the deep blue sea.

They imagine he wouldn't have known much about it. A moment's shocked realization – *Sweet Jesus* – before the blackout. Or he might have been dead already: heart attacks at the wheel were common enough. Instant oblivion – the best way to go some said.

The car was a wreck when they found it at the bottom of the ravine. A burnt-out shell – its scarlet paintwork blistered beyond recognition.

*There would have been a distance between losing control
and oblivion. A point when he must have known that
everything was lost. How far he had to fall.*

*Did he think, then, what it had all meant – having
leisure for such a reflection as the wheels hit soft dirt
then spun out into the void and he found himself suddenly
airborne: spinning, tumbling, falling? Did her image (but
whose?) cross his mind then or at some other moment
between living and dying?*

*Something – the glittering stars, a bird's flight across
his path or merely a sudden loss of the will to continue
– distracted him. A split second – no more – but enough.
Take your eyes off the road for a second and you're
finished.*

*Sleep. He might have gone to sleep for a minute. Not
long. The flicker of an eyelid and all that's been waiting
to happen happens.*

10

For a while it seems her mother is mad with grief: she doesn't eat she doesn't sleep she walks from room to room crying and laughing and talking to herself. Oh no she says. Oh please. Oh God. Oh no. When she is calmer or just worn out from crying she sits in a chair and rocks herself to and fro hugging her arms around her as if she were trying to get warm.

Once when Tony walks in Vivienne is standing looking out of the window. She doesn't see Tony. Come back she is saying. Forgive me. I know you can hear me. Come back.

Just lately she has been spending a lot of time sitting at her desk with her pen in her hand and a pile of writing paper in front of her. She doesn't write anything but she fiddles with the pen for hours – unscrewing the top and putting it back on; straightening the loose sheets until their edges are exactly aligned. She sighs and presses her hands to her side as if something hurt her there. I can't breathe Tony hears her say. There's no air. I can't breathe.

Tony wonders what he must have been thinking of in those last seconds. Did he know he was going to die or did it happen too fast for him to know anything? She wishes he was here so she could ask him. What she does instead is to drive that last stretch of road for him.

It's a road she knows like the back of her hand – better if anything. She doesn't look at the back of her hand that often. Whereas the road from La Rosa to La Soledad is one she has driven along or rather been driven along hundreds of times. She knows every bend and twist in it every tree and bush along the way. She could drive it with her eyes closed – which is what she does night after night in the days after Jack is killed.

First the long straight bit through the cleared jungle then the steep climb between tall trees and bamboo groves rock falls across the road you had to drive carefully then the part where the road narrows so that only one car could pass. The sheer rock wall on one side the ravine on the other. Time and time again he'd said to her how dangerous it was. *One of these days when you're older I'll let you have a turn at the wheel. I wasn't much older than you when I started. Driving's a lot like life. The sooner you get out there and make your mistakes the better.*

The most dangerous place was the blind corner. Take it too fast and you didn't have a hope in hell. You'd ease off the gas at this point shift down a gear. Only a fool would try to wing it. Tony closes her eyes although she's still far from sleep. Picturing the corner. Jack getting nearer and nearer. The rocks jutting out into the road the dead tree as you rounded the bend . . .

But that's wrong she thinks he wasn't coming from La Rosa at all he was heading in the opposite direction the marks of scorched rubber on the road and the way the undergrowth was broken proved it. He'd been heading back down the mountain not up. Away from La Soledad. There were tyre tracks in front of the house as if someone had driven up and then suddenly had a change of heart. Reversing so violently they left deep scars in the gravel.

Vivienne is alone, as she often is since it happened – sitting in the dark as she often does, a cigarette in her hand and a drink at her side. She doesn't do much these nights just sits looking out over the dark garden; listening to the relentless calling of cicadas, the *flick-flack* as a moth throws itself into the blazing aura of the porch light.

A shadow falls across the floor as someone steps between her and the light. She knows who it is without turning round.

'I didn't hear the car.'

'I left it –' He gestures vaguely. 'Back a way.'

'Very wise.' There is a hint of dryness in her tone. Deaf to this nuance, he moves a few paces towards her.

'I wanted to come before,' he says. 'Only . . .' He shrugs – a gesture of helplessness.

'You did the right thing,' she reassures him, with no more than the slightest edge of irony.

This time he notices something. 'Believe me, I would have come,' he says, aggrieved she should have doubted him. 'You don't know what it's been like . . .'

'No,' she agrees, this time in all seriousness. 'I don't know. But I can imagine.' She allows a pause – no more than a beat – to elapse. 'How is your wife?'

He doesn't answer straight away. 'Please,' he says. 'May I sit down?'

'Do.' She indicates the open box on the table. 'Cigarette?'

'Thanks.'

In the lighter's flare his face appears out of darkness,

then disappears, leaving a faint afterimage. A ghost of a ghost, thinks Vivienne.

'You ask me about my wife. I'll tell you. My wife is very sick.' There is a tremor in his voice which was not there before. 'Crazy. My wife is crazy. Only a crazy person would do what she did. She could have killed herself. My children too. Lucky for her they're OK.'

'I know,' she says. 'Thank God.'

'*God*,' he says. In his mouth, it sounds like *Hot*. 'When I think . . .'

'Don't think. It's over now.'

Both are silent for a while, lost in reflection – considering, perhaps, the way things might have been if circumstances had been otherwise. The twin coals of their cigarettes glow and fade like fireflies with each inhalation of breath.

Vivienne rouses herself from these thoughts with a start. 'I'm sorry,' she says. 'Thoughtless of me. Would you like a drink?'

'A fast one, only. I shouldn't stay . . .'

'Help yourself.' She gestures towards the trolley with its array of bottles and glasses. 'There's ice if you need it.'

'Thanks.'

He gets up. Through the partial darkness she can see him moving about. There is the clink of ice cubes against glass, the sound of a bottle being unscrewed. She turns towards the sound.

'What will you do?'

He takes his time before replying. 'I wanted to see you,' he says carefully. 'To talk.'

He takes a drink, as if this will give him courage to say what he has to say. Dutch courage, she thinks, suppressing an impulse to laugh. She waits for what she knows will follow.

'My wife is sick. This country makes her crazy she says.' He laughs. 'I think she would be crazy anywhere. She says not. She will be better in her own country, she says.'

'So you're going back.' It's a statement of fact, not a question.

He seems taken aback. 'Yes. I don't want this, of course, but . . .'

'You don't have any choice.' Her voice is calm. She sips her drink, her hand perfectly steady.

'It's not what I want,' he says again.

'No. But you have to go.'

'Maybe for a little while, only . . .'

She accepts the lie with a polite inclination of the head, knowing it has been said to assuage her feelings. She is no longer sure in any case what those are. There has been too much damage. She doesn't know if she will ever feel anything again.

He finishes his drink, but makes no move to go. The silence prolongs itself, until it seems as if it will never end. They might sit here for ever, Vivienne thinks numbly – they might, but they will not. Because all things have to end. And so she is the first to break the silence.

'Will you write to me?'

'Of course.'

He says it with the same conviction with which he has earlier assured her of his return. The spell broken, he gets to his feet, but still seems unable to leave, hesitating in the doorway as if there were something more he had to say.

'I'm sorry for what happened,' he says abruptly. 'It

must have been terrible for you. When I heard I wanted to come but I was afraid . . .'

'You don't have to explain.'

'I thought you might not want to see me. I mean, after that night . . .'

'Don't talk about it, please.' Her voice breaks with tension. It's the first time she's betrayed any emotion at all.

'Forgive me,' he says.

'There's nothing to forgive.'

After her momentary loss of composure, she is calm again: her voice as matter-of-fact as if she were discussing the weather. She gets up – ever the perfect hostess – to see him out. 'Well, so long,' she says.

'So long – for now.' An inconclusive adieu.

Suddenly overcome with a rush of feeling, he reaches for her, kisses her mouth and eyes, her face, her hair. She neither responds nor resists. A dead thing, a husk, she thinks dully, feeling him start to move away – bestowing one last kiss on her brow, as one would to a beloved corpse.

They've taken his mother away, as he knew they would. She's very sick, they say; she needs to go away for a while until they can make her better. As soon as Mama is able to travel, they are going away too. Back to Holland, so that Mama can get well again. Papa says they'll be staying with their grandparents for a while, until they can find a place of their own. They can tell Oma and Opa about all the places they've seen.

Opa was a sailor once, Papa tells Karel – he went all round the world and back again. When Papa was a little boy he remembers his father walking up the street on his way home from one of his three-month voyages, carrying his sea chest on his shoulder and shouting out greetings to all the people in the neighbourhood. *Roost rust* was one of his maxims, which meant: he who rests, rusts. You can rest all you like in the grave, he liked to say.

His mother has gone, but his father is back. All day he sits in a chair and sighs, holding his head in his hands. He doesn't seem to hear when Karel speaks to him.

Once he tells Karel and Annetje to get in the car. Hour after hour he drives them along the mountain road. It's getting dark and Karel's starting to feel hungry. The lights of the nearest town seem a long way off. They've been driving for what seems to him like hours – Annetje has fallen asleep on the seat beside him – when their father pulls over to the side of the road, leans his head on the steering wheel and begins to cry. Karel sits very still in the back of the car, not daring to move or breathe, and after a little while his father starts the car up again and drives them back home.

Another time Karel's father takes him to the girl's house to play. He doesn't come in with him, just drops him off in front and drives away. The girl comes out when she hears the car. She doesn't seem pleased to see him but she doesn't tell him to go away either. They play for a while and then later the maid gives them biscuits and a glass of milk. They play some more and then it gets too hot to play so Karel sits by himself for a while.

He is sitting on the veranda when Mrs Lindberg comes out of the house. She doesn't see him and at first he thinks there must be someone else with her. 'I really don't know what I'm going to do,' she is saying. Then she catches sight of Karel. For a minute she stands there staring at him as if she's never seen him before. Then she smiles. 'Oh, Karel,' she says. 'You gave me quite a turn. Do you know,' she says, her voice sounding as if she's going to cry, 'I've mislaid something. My fountain pen. I don't suppose you've seen it lying around?'

When he shakes his head she sits down in one of the big cane chairs as if suddenly exhausted by her search. 'Oh, dear,' she murmurs her hands fumbling a cigarette out of the pack. 'I can't imagine where I could have left it . . .'

He sees the girl one more time after this – it was the last day. The boat was leaving for Curaçao and then they were going to catch the big liner which would take them all the way to Spain. Just like the conquistadores, Papa said – only they'd be travelling in the opposite direction.

Karel stands at the edge of the garden, looking in. Through a screen of leaves and purple flowers, he can see the girl. He hears her voice and at first he thinks she's talking to herself. But then he sees she's talking to her parrot, which sits in the grass at her feet.

'It's no good, you know,' she is saying. 'You'll have to do better than this. What will all the other parrots say if they see you can't fly?'

He walks towards her; clears his throat to alert her to his presence. She glances up. 'Oh, it's you,' she says, not sounding surprised. 'Look at stupid Pedro,' she sighs, pointing to the bird. 'He's forgotten how to fly. I keep trying to set him free but he just stays put. Lazy old bird,' she says tenderly.

She holds out a grape. The parrot takes the fruit

delicately from between her fingers and then crushes it to pulp with its strong beak.

'You're going away too, aren't you?' the girl says casually, wiping her fingers on the skirt of her dark dress.

He nods.

'I don't suppose we'll ever meet again.' She says this as if it is no more than a curious fact, not a matter for regret. She sits back on her haunches, ruffling the tame bird's feathers.

After a moment's hesitation, Karel sits down beside her.

'When are you leaving?' the girl asks. He tells her. 'Two days before me,' she remarks.

When she speaks there is the gleam of metal against her teeth. She sees him looking. 'Don't stare,' she tells him, and frowns.

Then for a while there is no sound but the wind stirring the leaves of the orange trees. He smells the sweet scent of their blossom. In the grass at his feet a column of fire ants is marching away.

'Is it true your mother tried to burn down your house?'

He shakes his head. 'It was an accident.'

'Thought it must have been.' She whistles a tune underneath her breath. 'Do you want some lemonade?' she says. 'I'll ask Consuelo . . .'

He would rather not see Consuelo just now. He scrambles to his feet. 'I have to go . . .'

'Don't go yet. I've something for you. Wait . . .' She runs towards the house.

Karel scuffs his feet in their worn black shoes, raising a small dust-storm. The scarlet and blue bird observes him with its sinister eye.

The girl returns, breathless. 'Found it,' she gasps.

'Here you are.' She holds out the blue and white striped belt; its clasp catches the light. 'Go on, take it,' she says. 'My snake belt. You can have it. I don't need it any more . . .'

They are leaving together on a flight only a week later than the one Tony would have been getting anyway to allow for the funeral. Not that Tony is going to the funeral it isn't something for a child Vivienne says although Tony would quite like to have gone. She can't get over the feeling that maybe Jack isn't dead after all. Seeing him being put in the ground even if it is inside a box and you don't know for sure it's really him inside might make her believe it's true.

But she doesn't say this to Vivienne. Vivienne has enough to think about – you can see from the distracted way she wanders around the house on the morning of the funeral still only half-dressed although the car will be here at any minute a worried frown creasing the space between her eyebrows until it seems certain to leave a permanent mark.

These days Vivienne is always restless never sitting still for a minute always jumping up and going in search of something – her gloves her bag her scarf – opening doors and closing them. It's as if a ceaseless wind blows through the house when she's around rearranging objects. *Have you seen my sunglasses?* she murmurs. *I'm sure I left them around here somewhere* . . . Vivienne's eyes are red and swollen she has cried so much. Tony hears her at night in her room when she thinks no one is listening.

The car arrives to take Vivienne away and the house is quiet once more. Tony sits on the steps eating an orange and spitting the pips on to the gravel and wondering what it's like to be dead. She squeezes her eyes tight shut until there's nothing to see but red darkness. Nothing nothing nothing. The taste of the orange is sharp on her tongue. She opens her eyes letting the light flood in. He's dead and I'm alive is all she can think.

When she'd woken that morning there was blood on her nightdress. She'd stared at it convinced she was going to die. But when she told Vivienne her mother had seemed more put out than worried. 'Oh dear,' she'd said her frown mark deepening, 'what a day to choose . . .' She'd given Tony a pink elastic belt and a box of thick white Kotex. 'Oh, don't worry,' she'd said seeing Tony's face. 'We all get it. You've heard of the curse, I suppose?'

In another week they will be leaving. Tony knows although nothing has been said that this will be for good. What will happen to the house she asks Vivienne and Vivienne says, They'll sell it I suppose. Either that or they'll pass it on to someone else in the company. It wasn't ours, you know, she says gently as if she guesses what Tony is feeling. Just a rented house. Temporary – like most things she says.

Tony can't bear to think about it – someone else living in their house. Some other family sitting around their table and sleeping in their beds. A thought more terrible even than these strikes her. Consuelo she calls running back through the house in a panic.

Consuelo is in the kitchen standing where she always stands behind the table. She is making sandwiches for the people coming back after the funeral. What do you want she says not looking up from what she is doing one hand holding the stack of sandwiches she has just made in place the other steadying the knife with which she is about to cut it.

Tony asks her: are you going to work for the other people? She's breathless as if she has run a long way instead of just the short distance from the veranda steps to the kitchen.

Consuelo looks at her. What people she says going on with her stacking and slicing.

The people who're going to live here after us. After Mother and I leave. Those people Tony tells her.

Consuelo says nothing for a while. She finishes cutting the sandwiches puts down the knife wipes her hands on her apron. I don't know nothing about no people she says at last. She looks again at Tony. A long hard look. Your Mama said you have to put on a dress she says. Because there are guests coming.

She places the sandwiches on the willow-patterned plate and carries it through to the dining room. Tony follows her. Waits until she has arranged the table to her satisfaction. It looks very nice she thinks. Apart from the sandwiches there are bowls of potato salad and trays of cold ham and chicken laid out in alternate stripes of pink and white. There are cheese straws and cocktail biscuits spread with anchovy paste and decorated with olives. It looks as if they are having a party Tony thinks.

What happens when you die she asks Consuelo. Consuelo smiles. You go to live with the angels she says. That's where your papa is now – and where you'll go too if you're a good girl and do what your poor mama tells you.

Does that mean that when I die I'll see Jack again Tony wants to know not entirely sure whether she believes this account of things. But Consuelo has no doubt whatsoever. Of course she says. You'll see your papa again. But in another world Consuelo says.

The cars arrive. People are getting out of them; walking towards the house. The screen door bangs. Consuelo and Fernanda in their black dresses and white aprons are dispensing drinks from silver trays.

Sylvia is the first to enter – elegant in a black suit black gloves and a chic hat with a spotted veil. She ignores the offered tray; walks straight across to where Vivienne is standing; embraces her.

'Oh, my dear. What can I say? I'm so sorry . . .'

Frank is a few paces behind. 'Anything we can do,' he says gruffly. 'Anything at all . . .' His voice seems to catch in his throat.

'Thank you,' says Vivienne.

'I mean it. Anything. Only have to ask.' Frank draws the starched white handkerchief from his breast pocket unfolds it blows his nose sharply. 'Still can't believe it,' he says. 'Old Jack. One of the best . . .'

'Yes.'

'Don't want to be the first to say it,' Frank says. 'But somebody's got to be the first. Sounds ridiculous but. He'd have wanted it that way. Old Jack.'

'Frank, *really*. I hardly think this is the moment . . .'

'I believe you're right,' says Vivienne.

'Never a man to outstay his welcome,' Frank says. 'More's the pity.'

Other people are still arriving. The Porters. The Wilsons. The Johnsons. The McBrides. A group of Texans from the oilfield who stand around awkwardly shuffling their feet until Vivienne says, Have a drink, why don't you?

Ted Johnson's eyes are red. 'That Jack,' he is saying. 'Helluva guy. They don't make 'em like that any more . . .'

One of the Texans has brought a wreath of white lilies which he goes to offer to Vivienne but Frank Riley intercepts him. *I say, old boy. Not quite the done thing, what?* The flowers are placed out of sight on a chair where Tony will find them next morning their fragile petals already turning brown.

There's a flatness to everything Tony thinks – a feeling of dullness. *Jesus H. Christ* Jack would say if he were to walk in now. *It's like a morgue in here. Did somebody die?* She can hear him say it; hear the sigh of relief as everyone looks round. *Here's Jack, at last. What took you so long, old boy?*

She can't quite believe it won't happen – that this isn't some crazy stunt he's pulled just to see the looks on their faces as he walks through the door.

Already she's finding it harder to remember what he looks like – although if she concentrates very hard she can summon up an image. But his voice – that's something she doesn't have to work at. Sometimes it sounds so real in her head it's as if he's there in the room with her. She'll turn around and there he'll be lighting up a cigarette and smiling at her. *Hey, girl, how's tricks?*

It seems to Tony watching from her corner that it has grown very dark although the sun is still shining as brightly as ever and the sky is still as blue. Maybe it's the suits the men are wearing the women's black dresses which make the room seem darker. Or maybe it's the haze of cigarette smoke which grows denser by the minute because everybody's smoking – *My God, I'm simply gasping for one* – having sat through the hour-long service without this relief.

If she closes her eyes she can make them all disappear. All that's left are their voices – their murmured regrets.

'Doesn't seem possible, does it? Only a week ago he was standing here as large as life and now . . .'

'I don't believe it. I just don't believe it . . .'

'Helluva guy . . .'

The Texans are in a huddle in the corner drinking whisky with silent determination. They have abrupt-sounding names like Hank and Bob and Joe. Names that sound like orders shouted into the wind. It's a lousy shame one says and another says, You can say that again. That's life I guess says the first and the other says, I'll drink to that.

The sun pours in through clouds of spiralling blue smoke and the sickly sweet smell of lilies is overpowering. Vivienne stands in the centre of the room pale as wax in her widow's weeds. From time to time she replies to something someone says to her but otherwise she is silent – smoking her cigarette and sipping her brandy and soda with the stylized grace of an actress performing these actions. After an hour she says to no one in particular I think I'll go and lie down for a little while.

As she is seen to leave a murmur of sympathy moves around the room like a sigh. There is a moment of silence and then someone says something and someone else replies and the mood lightens. With Vivienne gone they don't have to feel so bad about enjoying themselves Tony thinks.

Then after another few drinks people start to relax and someone tells a story about something Jack said or did and there's a ripple of laughter.

'Good old Jack. What a character . . .' Tony hears someone say and then someone else says, 'Remember that time when . . .' and starts to tell another story.

Listening to the stories and the laughter Tony knows this is the way Jack would have wanted things to be. Because the world doesn't stop just because some poor sucker checked out – isn't that what he always used to say? And looking around the room she sees that it's turned into quite a party after all.

She descends the steps and walks across the Tarmac. Heat rises shimmering from its melting surface. After the air-conditioned interior of the plane, the contrast is too sudden and she shivers as if she's running a fever. As she nears the airport building, she sees herself reflected in its plate-glass windows: a slight, insignificant figure in a crumpled suit.

Standing in line to get her passport checked, she is suddenly afraid: what if the whole thing turns out to be a terrible mistake? She has too much to lose, that's the trouble. She's invested far too much in what will almost certainly turn out to be a futile quest. For a moment she is almost tempted to turn back – but then the hard-eyed man behind the desk holds out his hand for her papers and she steps forward. In the end you don't have too much choice about these things.